THE KEY

by

Linda Sawley

Linric Publishing
England

Published in 2004 by LinRic Publishing
18 Victoria Lodge
READ, Lancs
BB12 7SZ

British Cataloguing in publication data
Sawley, Linda
The Key
I. Title
Classification: Historical Romantic Fiction

ISBN 0 – 9534329 – 4 - 7

Acknowledgements

Proof reading by Vicky Webster

Printed by Sherwood PF Ltd, Unit 5 Sherbrook Business Centre, Sherbrook Road, Daybrook, Nottingham NG5 6AT

Cover design by Nikki Moore of Design Department, Printing Services, University of Central Lancashire

Photograph on front cover by kind permission of and © to The National Trust Photographic Library/Andreas Von Einsiedel

Dedicated to Linda Mitchell

A very special lady in my life.

Also

A big Thank you to
Santa Montefiore

For help and encouragement.

By the same author

Everyone Else's Children (autobiography) 1998

A Ring in Time 2002

The Key
(Mitchell's Modes Saga Book 1) 2004
Changes
(Mitchell's Modes Saga Book 2) 2005
New Century: Changed Lives *(Kindle version only)*
*(*Mitchell's Modes Saga Book 3) 2014

The Survivor 2007

Anna 2010

Joshua and the Horrible History Project   2011
(recommended reading age 7 to 13 years, but enjoyed by 5 to 90 year olds!.)

Weaving Through the Years. 2012

Linda Sawley's Collection of Short Stories 2014 *(Kindle version only)*

The Rector's Pearl 2016 *(Kindle version only)*

Contents

Part One

The Workhouse

Chapter 1

Jenny Mitchell shivered on her hard straw pallet. The itchy, rough blanket that the Lancashire workhouse provided gave scant warmth. She pulled the thin blanket around her to try and get more warmth, with little effect.

Her thin little body had few clothes on to trap any warmth. Standard workhouse attire was a short shift to sleep in. Even though Jenny's body had started to develop, the same shift was given to her each night. It was now woefully inadequate.

She looked around the room at all the other, similar, girls. There were twenty girls on pallets like hers. It was still dark, so it was too early to get up yet. She wanted to go to the toilet, but it was more than her life was worth to get up before one of the warders banged the gong.

She heard a sniffle from the far end of the room. Jenny's heart went out to the little girl in the end bed. Her name was Marian and she had been admitted to the workhouse the day before. Both of her parents had died of cholera and poor Marian had looked after them. A parish visitor had found her alone in the house where her parents had been dead for several days.

There had been an argument regarding whether Marian should be admitted to the general ward of the workhouse, or into the hospital wing. Jenny had been an unwitting eavesdropper of the conversation. There had been nowhere else for Marian to go.

'Maybe she'll not catch cholera if she hasn't already developed it,' one voice argued. The chief warder of the workhouse suggested that the other inmates might also be at risk of cholera as well as Marian.

'That would be no bad thing,' another voice argued. 'It would be a relief on the rates if there were fewer paupers to feed.'

Jenny had turned sadly away when she heard this. She knew that their lives were not really valued in the workhouse, but to hear it actually spoken, cut her to the heart.

Jenny longed to go and comfort little Marian. She only looked about six years old and had not spoken since her arrival yesterday.

Jenny had tried to comfort her during the day, but Marian was too frightened to respond.

Her instinct was to call out to Marian, but she knew that this was unwise. If she was caught speaking whilst in bed, she would be on punishment tomorrow. Getting out of bed before gaining permission was an even greater crime, so that was also out of the question.

The punishments never fitted the crime and were always severe, for what to Jenny, seemed trivial offences. Jenny sighed, longing to go and comfort Marian, but knowing that she would have to wait until permission was given to get up. She did not have long to wait.

Even though it was still dark the gong sounded and all of the little girls instantly got up, turned their blanket down and stood to attention by their beds. Those unfortunate enough to have wet their beds were beaten by the warder on duty, then made to wrap their bedding up and take it downstairs to the laundry. Their names were recorded on a list and taken to the chief warder. Matron then read out the names at breakfast time.

The small girls were thoroughly demoralised and embarrassed. They would probably go to bed that night, so frightened of wetting the bed again, that their nervous state made them do the very thing that they were frightened of. It was a hopeless, vicious circle.

Suddenly, a bird started to sing outside in the trees. Its beautiful warbling voice cut through the weary examination of the beds and immediately lifted Jenny's spirits. She was woken from her reverie by the sharp sting of a birch twig swishing against her legs.

'Did yer 'ear me, girl?' an ugly voice shouted. It was Hargreaves, one of the worst warders on the female side of the workhouse. Jenny trembled. She had not heard her.

'I . . I . . er I'm sorry, I didn't 'ear yer,' stammered Jenny. Jenny felt another swish of the birch against her leg. She knew better than to cry out. This only seemed to make Hargreaves worse. Beating a pattern with the birch against her legs, each word heralded a harder swish.

'Yer lazy, good fer nuthin' whelp, I'll give yer yer never 'eard me.' The swishes were becoming unbearable and Jenny had to bite her lips to stop from crying out. 'I sed ter 'elp little brats ter tek th' wet clothes down ter t' boilers, dirty little tykes.' Jenny rushed to obey this cruel woman before she could administer any more swishes. She collected all of the piles of dirty linen together, and grabbing tightly hold of Marian's hand, dragged her along towards the door.

'Don't say nowt, she'll only go fer yer,' she warned Marian quietly. "Ere, 'old this corner of t' sheet then she'll think as 'ow yer 'olding yer stuff.' Marian needed no second telling.

'I didn't mean ter wet me bed, I never did at 'ome. I'm a big girl now,' Marian gasped.

'Shh, little un, they'll only get yer, and 'urt yer more fer cryin',' soothed the older and wiser Jenny. 'It's not so bad if yer do as yer told. Yer'll soon learn the rules. I'll 'elp yer when I can, but they don't like it when we speaks to each other.' Marian nodded and tried to control her sobs.

'Fanks,' she whispered to Jenny, after looking round to see that no one was watching. Jenny smiled back. The little one was learning fast. 'She would do,' thought Jenny, 'and I'll do all I can ter 'elp 'er.'

Jenny showed Marian where the back stairs of the workhouse were, and explained that she must never use the front steps, as they were for the warders, visitors and housekeepers only. She also explained that she must never speak unless she was spoken to and never after lights were out in the dormitory. Meals were also to be eaten in silence.

Marian asked why but Jenny had no answer, except that this was the way things were done in the workhouse. She also warned her about the birch and the liberal use that Hargreaves made of it.

Jenny could only hope that Hargreaves hadn't taken against Marian this morning for wetting the bed on the first night, as her life would be miserable forever. Jenny sighed. Her life was hard, but she was used to it now. She only vaguely remembered a soft loving kind person who used to cuddle her, and tell her that she was her own special princess.

Some princess she was now. More like a slave. But whenever her thoughts returned to that earlier time and that lady, Jenny could not remember anything else beyond the softness and a certain smell. Not even a face.

She knew from the warders that her mother was dead, but when she had asked about her, the warders had been nasty about her, and called her names. They reminded Jenny that she was lucky to be in the workhouse, getting well fed and looked after, not on the streets like some other children were.

Life on the streets sounded quite appealing to Jenny compared with her life in the workhouse. And as for the food, 'well fed' were not words that usually came to her mind when she was trying to eat the awful gruel and hard dried bread that formed the typical workhouse diet.

Sunday was supposed to be a treat, but even the meat was usually maggot-ridden. And on the bonus days when no maggots were visible, the meat was tough, stringy and very hard to chew, not to mention unappetising.

Sighing again, Jenny thought how hard it must be for Marian right now. She tried to talk to her about her parents, but Marian started to sob again, and as Hargreaves was hovering nearby, Jenny told Marian to shut up. Marian did shut up instantly, but was still shaking as she tried to control her sobs.

'Is that a face at winder, Miss?' Jenny shouted to Hargreaves, trying to divert her from the shaking Marian. Hargreaves turned towards the window and stalked across the room, looking right and left out of the small window.

'Who, girl, who did yer see at winder?' snarled Hargreaves.

'Dunno Miss, thought I saw a face,' replied Jenny.

'Well, I can't see anyone now. Were yer 'aving me on girl?' Hargreaves strode back to where Jenny and Marian were sat and gave Jenny a hard swish with the birch across her shoulders.

'I'll give it yer for wasting my time. Yer can do the toilets for that. And yer can take that snivelling thing sat next to yer an all. Some 'ard work should take 'er mind off snivelling. I'm not an 'eartless woman, and I was lenient to her yesterday as it was 'er first day, but she'll get no more sympathy from me. So get her taught 'ow ter do them toilets, and do 'em properly, or there'll be no supper fer either of yer tonight.'

The whole room had frozen in silence during this tirade. It was as if every child was holding its breath to see what would happen next. All eyes were fixed on Hargreaves.

'And the rest of yer 'ad better get yer porridge eaten or it'll be taken away and yer'll get nowt tonight either.' Suddenly all the frozen statues came to life, as if a fairy's wand had been waved over them and brought them back to life. But there were no fairy wands in the Clitheroe workhouse. Just a lot of young children who knew the rules and how to avoid getting singled out for punishment.

At a signal from Hargreaves, the inmates who were on kitchen duty went around the room collecting the dirty tin dishes and cups.

'Right table one, lead out,' roared Hargreaves. The children on the table nearest to the door jumped to their feet and scurried out of the door to take up their allotted tasks for the day.

Most children had set jobs or areas to work in, but this could vary at the whim of the warders. If any friendships seemed to be developing between the children, one child would be moved to another work area.

It seemed to be a constant attempt to keep the children from getting any consolation, even from friendship, whilst they were in this workhouse.

Table by table the children left the room, all forty of them. Jenny knew how many children there were as she often worked on kitchen duties and she had to know the number of places to set the places at table for their meals. She also knew that were eighty-seven women and sixty-four men.

Some of the children had parents in the other parts of the workhouse, but they were not allowed to live together. Only for one hour on a Sunday afternoon were the families allowed to mingle. The warders were present throughout this visiting period so that there was no chance of any physical contact between husband and wife, or between parents and children.

When admitted to the workhouse, the families were told that this would be the arrangement in order that they 'could not beget any more brats, who would be a charge on the parish rates.' For families who had only each other left for comfort, this was a hard blow, and the reason most families tried to keep out of the workhouse for as long as possible.

Jenny's friend Susy and her brother Jonny had come to the workhouse shortly before Jenny. Their mother was in the women's section, but their father was still 'outside' looking for work. Unfortunately, they had not heard from him in a long time, so they didn't expect to get released from the workhouse in the near future. Jonny was biding his time. He was fourteen next month and hoped to be allowed to look for work outside the workhouse.

Sometimes people came from the surrounding houses or businesses to get workpeople. But Jonny knew that there was only a slim chance of being taken on, as workhouse people had a bad reputation outside. They assumed that the inmates must be mad or lazy to have ended up living in the place.

Jenny had not actually spoken to Jonny herself as girls and boys were not allowed to mix. The dining room was divided, and although they ate at the same time, they were not allowed to converse. Susy, however, had pointed out Jonny to her. There had also been another brother, Martin, who was only a toddler when he came into the workhouse. The separation was just too much for a toddler. Martin stopped eating and eventually died of a broken heart.

Susy said that her mother seemed to go 'inside of herself' after that. She still loved all her bairns, but the light seemed to have gone out of her. There had been two other toddlers who had died before they came in the workhouse and Susy remembered how her mother had been quiet and distant for quite a time afterwards, swinging between forced gaiety with the surviving children and floods of tears when she thought that she was alone. Now, she was worse than ever and was a constant worry to Susy.

The warders had moved Susy's mother to work in the hospital wing after Martin's death. There, she would simply do as she was told and not ask questions or complain about the amount of work they gave to her. It broke Susy's heart to see her on Sundays. If only their dad could come back and rescue them, Susy often cried to Jenny, but they both knew that this was a hopeless idea.

Over the years, Jenny and Susy had built up a close friendship, carefully concealing it from the warders, in case they got separated again. They were both twelve years old, with only 10 days separating their individual birthdays. Not that those birthdays were ever mentioned in the workhouse, but it was a bond between them nevertheless.

In fact, these dates were probably not even their real birthdays, certainly in Jenny's case, but it was the only one she knew. During the eight years that they had been in the workhouse, Susy and Jenny had managed to give each other tiny presents on their birthdays, which made a little haven of pleasure for them in an otherwise intolerable existence.

Part of the pleasure was that they managed to keep it from the warders. Over the years, they had also managed to develop a kind of sign language with each other. With this they were able to communicate far more than any of the warders realised.

Susy and Jonny's last name was Marshall, which was not unlike Jenny's name of Mitchell. Jenny wasn't sure that Mitchell was her real name, as a former warder had told her that on the night she arrived, there was just a first name on the blanket in which she was wrapped. The only other information was that the mother wasn't married and had just died in childbirth, leaving no known relatives.

As the girls were leaving the dining room, Susy managed to whisper to Jenny that she was sorry about the toilet duties. Jenny replied that she was not bothered, as this would allow her to watch over little Marian.

'That's typical of yer, Jenny, always looking after th' little ones. Well be careful 'cos if 'argreaves finds out she'll be down on both o' yer.'

'I know,' Jenny mouthed back, 'I'll be careful.'

Chapter 2

The girls went their separate way, Susy going to the kitchens and Jenny leading Marian back up to the dormitories. They went through to the bathrooms and got out tin buckets and old clothes that were used solely for the cleaning. Jenny showed Marian how to clean the toilets thoroughly. There was a row of ten toilets, five on each side, with a bank of ten sinks. Only cold water was supplied to the sinks

By the end of the morning, Marian was much happier. Jenny had managed to explain a lot about the running of the workhouse. If they had been allocated another task, they would not have been allowed to talk whilst they were working, but they had relative peace in the bathrooms.

After finishing the arduous task, they were sent into the laundry. Here there was no chance to talk. The noise of the mangle and the wringer, combined with the hissing of the steam made a deafening roar. Marian seemed a little frightened of all the noise, but knew better than to say so. She hung on to Jenny's side and copied everything that Jenny did, or tried to.

They heaved the hot washing out of the vats and slopped it into the rinsing vats. They were soon both soaked to the skin. A bell rang and everything stopped. All of the inmates were marched into the dining rooms in silence.

They stood behind their chairs whilst Grace was said, before permission was given to sit down. An unappetising meal was offered, which they all ate hungrily, knowing that no other meal would be offered that day if they refused it. Working in the laundry was heavy, manual work and the body needed food to keep going.

'Will we be goin' back ter the laundry again after dinner?' asked Marian, but was only given a whack by Hargreaves for speaking out of turn.

'Silence, or yer'll get more,' she roared.

Marian dropped her head down, trying to hide the tears. Jenny squeezed her hand, after first checking that Hargreaves had moved away.

After leaving the hall, Jenny explained that they went to school in the afternoons. 'Yer'll be in the little 'uns class. Not wi' me,' she explained.

She showed her the way to the schoolroom and took Marian to the teacher and explained that she was the new girl.

'How old are you?' asked the teacher.

'Eight, Miss. Nearly nine.'

Jenny was shocked. She was only the size of a six year old, but then she had been ill before coming into the workhouse.

'Sit down there, girl. Can you read?'

'Yes Miss, and I can write an' all.'

'Good. We like all our children to be able to read and write whilst they are here, so that they can make their way in the world.'

'If we ever get out of here,' quipped one of the children, but was rewarded with a stony glare from the teacher.

'Get back to your own class now, Mitchell. Stop wasting time.'

'Yes, Miss.' Jenny scurried back to her own class, glad that Marian seemed as if she would be able to hold her own in the classroom, as many of the children could not read or write when they first arrived at the workhouse.

Slowly, Marian adjusted to the life in the workhouse, as all the other children had had to do. She looked upon Jenny as her mother, even though Jenny was only three years older than Marian, as she had no one else who could fulfil that role.

Marian eventually stopped crying for her mum, and derived as much pleasure as she could from living in the workhouse. With the others, she had to learn all the different workhouse tasks, so that she became skilled at any work that may be expected from her. Like Jenny, she hated the laundry. It was hot, heavy work which inevitably led to her own clothes becoming soaking wet.

Jenny had to introduce her to the boiling up of the women's monthly cloths. It was a job they all hated. Jenny remembered her own introduction to them. It had been far worse than Marian's. At least Jenny was able to explain things to Marian before she saw them, and the awful smell that accompanied the washing.

Not that the rest of the washing was pleasant – far from it - but the cloths had a horror of their own. At least on fine days, washing could be put out to dry. Then the girls could get a bit of fresh air as well as a change of environment. They didn't often get out of the buildings, so a visit to the washing lines was viewed as a treat.

Wet days were dreaded, as all of the washing still had to be dried. It was then festooned around the laundry on racks that were fastened to the roof. These were very heavy, and had to be winched down, then the newly wrung sheets were put on the racks, and winched up again, - this time much heavier than before.

On those days, the laundry took on a damp foisty smell of its own, as the washing dried. The vats of boiling water were another danger. It had been known for girls to fall into the vats and either drown, or die from the scalds which they received. But it didn't stop the overseers from telling the girls to lean over and drag out the washing.

Working in the kitchen held its own horrors, but also had its benefits. They would have to cook the poor quality food that the inmates got. But they also had to cook the much better food that the staff and visitors got, yet not be allowed to eat it.

Sometimes this had its benefits, as if you were quick, you could pinch a taste of whatever delicacy was on offer to the lucky people who were dining. Christmas and Governors dinners were especially good.

But woe betide you if you were caught. It would be bread and water for a day or two, not to mention a beating. Not that it stopped any of the youngsters who were usually hungry for most of their lives.

The piles of washing up were enormous too and the children were always relieved when they were on kitchen help rather than washing up.

Most of the time the children dreamed of being taken out of the workhouse. They talked incessantly about what they would do when they lived outside. They talked of family who were still outside and would come and rescue them.

Marian and Jenny had no outside relatives as Susy and her brother Jonny did (although no word had been heard from Susy and Jonny's dad for a long time.) But they dreamed of escaping anyway. If Susy, Marian and Jenny were feeling miserable, they would play at 'let's pretend'. They would invent rich relatives or handsome princes who would come and rescue them.

At least they were getting an elementary education, which was an improvement on the treatment of other children who had previously lived in the workhouse. The Matron had been forced to introduce schooling when a government act was brought into being.

She had argued against it, saying that it would give the children ideas above their station in life and anyway what did they need an education for? Sadly, that had been the opinion of many of the upper classes and was why the act of parliament was a long time in coming.

Susy, Jenny and Marian enjoyed school, even though by most standards it was basic and cruel. But it gave them a change of job for an hour or two. And they could sit down! Some of the brighter pupils in the class also thought that it might give them a chance in the outside world if they could read and write. If they could get outside.

The years slowly dragged on. Despite the awful food, young Marian started to grow. She came adept at avoiding trouble with Hargreaves just like the other children. But Hargreaves always had it in for Jenny, whatever she did or didn't do. The other children couldn't understand it. She was awful to all of them, but always picked on Jenny more viciously.

One morning, Jenny was busy scrubbing the table down after the breakfast had been cleared away. She was so busy at her task humming to herself, that she didn't hear Hargreaves come in. She just felt a painful swish of the birch against her leg. Jenny flinched and gritted her teeth, before turning towards the cruel woman.

'Sorry, I didn't 'ear yer, ma-am,' Jenny said 'I were so busy scrubbing.'

'Are yer giving cheek, girl, because if yer are, yer'll feel the birch again on those legs of yourn?'

'No, no, Ma-am, truly I didn't 'ear yer.'

'Well never mind now, get upstairs, Matron wants ter speak ter you.'

'Me, Ma-am, what does Matron want me fer?'

'Never you mind, yer'll find out soon enough. It won't be fer good behaviour, that's fer sure. Not wit' reports I've given in. Yer're far too cheeky and insolent fer that. Now get a clean pinny on, comb that thatch you call hair, and be back 'ere in two minutes. We don't want ter keep Matron waiting as well as whatever else yer in trouble fer.'

Jenny set off at a run to the bedroom dormitory and did as she was bid. Her heart was beating rapidly and her mind was churning over everything that she had done in the last few days, but she could think of nothing that was severe enough for her to be taken to see Matron.

In all of her time in the workhouse, she had never been sent for before. Jenny ran back downstairs and hurried towards Hargreaves.

'What kept you, girl? Come on now, apparently Matron has an important visitor and is not pleased that you have kept her waiting.' Hargreaves dug Jenny in the shoulder as she hurried past.

Jenny was taken up into the large room at the front of the building, on the first floor. She had not been in this office since the first day that she had arrived. But she could remember nothing of that. Hargreaves was knocking gently on the door.

'Come in,' shouted an imperious voice. Hargreaves opened the door, dragged Jenny through, and told her to curtsey to Matron and then stand in front of the big mahogany desk. Hargreaves stood at the back of the room.

'That will be all, Hargreaves. I will call you when I need you again.'

'Thank you Matron,' said Hargreaves, then after a glare at Jenny she quietly left the room. Jenny was glad that Hargreaves had been ordered out. Whatever punishment was coming her way, she did not want Hargreaves to be around watching her and gloating. Jenny remained with her head down, waiting for the sentence that was coming her way. She was ignored.

'This is the only girl that arrived on the 21st February back in '68. Do you think that this is the girl in question?'

'If this is the only one you had, then it must be the one I am looking for. Is the paperwork ready?'

'Yes sir. It is all in order,' replied Matron. 'Will you be taking her today?'

'Yes, those are my instructions.'

'I will get her belongings together. Jenny Mitchell, you are a very lucky girl. This gentleman has been appointed to take you to a house near Burnley, where you will work in the kitchen as a scullery maid. Now say 'Thank you' to the gentleman.' Jenny stared in amazement at Matron.

'Did you hear me, girl? Where are your manners? I did warn you that she is a heedless girl, Sir. Now you see what I mean. I hope that your employer has a harsh housekeeper who will be able to keep her under control.'

'I know nothing of the employer, Matron, I am purely working for a third party, as I explained before.'

'It is all very curious, I must say.'

During this conversation, Jenny dared to peek a look at her saviour. He was a small, rotund man with hardly any hair, yet he wasn't very old. She had not seen him before. She could hardly grasp that she was being rescued from the workhouse and taken away. Suddenly Matron rounded on her again.

'Well, what do you say, girl?'

'Er – er, Thank you Matron, Thank you Sir,' Jenny stuttered, curtsying slightly.

Matron gave a slight nod.

'That is more like it, girl. Now go and get your belongings from Hargreaves. She has been told to gather them. Then come back in here and be quick about it.' Jenny nodded and left the room. It wouldn't take Hargreaves very long to gather up her belongings, as she didn't possess much.

As she opened the door, Hargreaves nearly fell into the room. She had been eavesdropping! She stood to attention quickly when Jenny opened the door and tried to look away. She had a smile of triumph on her face, and as Jenny held out her hand for her bundle, Hargreaves sneered at her.

'Been thrown out of th' workhouse, have yer? Matron got fed up of yer too, I suppose? About time too.'

Jenny smiled back.

'That's right. I am leaving. I've got a post in a big 'ouse, and I never 'ave to live 'ere again and do what yer say.' Jenny quivered with fear. Years of obeying Hargreaves didn't leave her instantly and even though she was going, she still feared that she may have said too much to Hargreaves and would be prevented from leaving.

Besides, Hargreaves was quite capable of taking things out on her friends after she had gone. Jenny bowed her head, and opened the door back into Matron's office. Matron and the gentleman were working on some paperwork, when Jenny had a sudden thought.

'Please, Matron, if you please, if I am going on a journey, could I go to the dormitory before I go?'

'What for?'

'Er, er, the toilet, Matron,' Jenny looked embarrassed.

'Oh, of course, girl, now hurry up and be quick about it.'

Jenny fled the room and hurried not to the bathroom but to the laundry where Susy and Marian were working.

Susy, Marian,' she whispered, 'I'm leaving. I'm goin' ter live in a big 'ouse, near Burnley, wherever that is. I'll try ter write ter yer. I can't stop. I'm supposed ter be goin' ter t' toilet. Matron's waiting.'

Jenny hugged Susy and Marian then fled up to the bathroom. The excitement had made her need the bathroom after all, even though it had been a ruse to say goodbye to her friends. She hurried back to the Matron's office where she found that the gentleman was drawing on his coat and gloves.

'Here she is, Sir. And about time, too. Are you ready girl?'

'Yes, Matron, Thank you Matron.'

'And I don't want to hear that you are giving any trouble in your new place. I don't want you back here again.'

'No Matron, I'll do as I'm told, Matron, I promise.' There was no danger of her not doing as she was told. Not when she was being threatened with coming back here. Once she had left, she would make sure that she never, ever came back. Not as an inmate. Ever. She walked towards the door following the gentleman with her head held high and didn't look back at all.

Chapter 3

Jenny was helped into the carriage that was awaiting her, as if she was a lady. A blanket was opened on the seat and the groomsman placed it round her and asked if she was comfortable. Jenny nodded, her eyes brimming with tears. She had been shown more kindness in the three minutes since leaving the workhouse than she had received during the last ten years.

Her only sadness was in leaving her friends. They could be staying there forever, until someone could be found to be responsible for them in the outside world, like they had for Jenny. She vowed there and then that if ever she was in a position to help anyone to escape from the workhouse, then she would.

After the gentleman got into the coach, it set off and went towards the centre of Clitheroe. The horse slowed down as they climbed up the steep incline of the main street. Jenny looked around her with interest. She had never been this far into town before.

The streets looked lively, bustling with shoppers going in and out of the shops. Well-dressed ladies were passing the time of day with other ladies. Children, equally well-dressed, were playing by the roadside with marbles and spinning tops.

Horses and carriages intermingled with the shoppers, and a newsvendor shouted his wares. Gentlemen raised their hats to each other in greeting as they passed.

Jenny felt a keen interest in all that was going on in the town. How she would love to be a part of this town. It seemed so happy and friendly. The horse and carriage slowed down outside an office.

'Whoa, there,' shouted the groom to the horse. The horse waited behind another horse and carriage. Jenny was ushered out of one carriage and into the other by the gentleman. In this carriage sat a thin lady dressed all in black, staring out of the other window. Jenny paused on the doorstep of the carriage and looked at the lady, waiting for permission to get into the carriage.

'Get in girl,' said the lady sharply. Jenny's heart sunk. She sounded very much like Matron. Perhaps she was going from one prison to another. She scrambled into the carriage, and sat at the edge of her seat, back straight, hands clasped in her lap, and feet tucked under the seat, as Hargreaves had always demanded.

'Drive on, Wilks,' the lady commanded.

'Yes, missus,' a voice replied from the top of the carriage. Jenny leaned out of the window.

'Thank you, Sir, for all you have done.'

'It is nothing. Only following my client's instructions. Good day to you, Miss.'

The carriage pulled away slowly from the kerb and continued along the flat part of the main street before taking the steep decline of Moor Lane, then the open road towards the countryside. As she got to the outer part of Clitheroe, Jenny could see that here the people were less well-dressed going about their jobs, and she could see smoke bellowing from the mill chimneys.

She was glad that she was going into service in a big house. It couldn't be worse than the workhouse, however threatening this lady was, and surely it would be better than the mill. One of the inmates of the hospital had worked in the mill. She was a 'reacher in', whatever that job meant, and had nearly died when her hair got tangled in the machinery. She was only seven years old. Her death in the workhouse hospital through infection had been slow and agonising. Jenny had hardened her heart against the nurses ever since that day. They had been so callous.

'It's not right. Making me come all this way for a workhouse brat.' The voice suddenly penetrated through Jenny's brain.

'Er, er, sorry ma-am, did you speak to me?'

'Not really, I was just complaining. Heaven alone knows why the butler sent me to this God forsaken place to get you. Favour for a friend he says. Humph. I have my own ideas on that. But don't think that it will give you any grace or favour. You will be treated like all the other new girls. Workhouse brat or not. Favour or not.'

The lady wriggled in her seat as if to give extra force to her voice. Jenny sunk further into her seat and looked away out of the window. She assumed, rightly, that it would be unwise to say anything in reply.

The carriage was now travelling through lovely countryside and an enormous hill could be seen. Jenny wondered if it was a mountain. They had learnt about those in school once. The carriage drove around the side of the mountain and continued through open countryside. Jenny began to get a little tired, largely due to the rocking motion of the carriage. Her eyes started to droop.

Going over a bump in the road brought Jenny back to full consciousness. She looked around about her and noticed that the lady had fallen asleep as well. The bump must not have been strong enough to wake her up. Jenny took the opportunity to get a better look at her. She had been too frightened earlier.

The lady was all dressed in severe, black shiny material. The gown was of a thinner material, with neat white cuffs at the wrist and a small white collar. The cloak was of a thicker material, which Jenny thought looked very warm. Her hair was also black and was scraped back under her bonnet. Strands of grey hair were visible at the side of her hair.

Her mouth, in repose, had fallen apart and Jenny could see that several of her teeth were missing. Her brow was very wrinkled and she had quite a growth of hair on her top lip – just like a man. Jenny giggled at this, but soon took the smile off her face when the lady woke up.

'What's that, er, where are we?' she stuttered and blinked at the same time.

'I'm not sure Ma-am,' replied Jenny as politely as she could. 'I have never been out of the workhouse before, so I don't know where we are.'

'Oh, that is Gawthorpe Hall. We are more than half way home. That is the home of the Kay-Shuttleworths. A fine house they have. Very old. The Master sometimes visits them.' As if she realised that she had been too chatty, the lady stopped speaking, so Jenny looked tactfully the other way. The lady soon drifted off back to sleep and Jenny was able to watch the changing vistas from mill towns, to countryside, then back to mill towns.

The horse slowed down when it started going up a long, steep incline. After some time, at the top of the incline, the horse swung the carriage into a gateway. There was a man stood at the gateway holding the gate open. He tugged his cap as the carriage went through, then slowly closed the gate. Jenny saw the name of the house worked into the gatepost. Ormerod Hall.

Part 2

The Big House

Chapter 4

The house seemed to have been built right at the top of a hill. Further down the valley where they had come from, there was a sea of mill chimneys. It was almost as though a fog of smoke had settled over the town itself. Jenny wondered where all that smoke could have come from, never having seen so many mill chimneys before. 'Could be called Smoke Valley' she thought, as all she could see was smoke.

The drive of the house seemed to go on forever. Jenny was excited to get the first glimpse of her new home, even though she was apprehensive about this dour lady who was probably going to be her new mistress. The drive in front of them separated into two paths. The coachman took the left hand path and followed it through less dense foliage. Eventually a house appeared in front of them. The carriage stopped. Jenny was told to get out.

The house appeared to be fairly ordinary. Not even as glamorous as the workhouse. It was a little disappointing to Jenny. She had imagined 'the big house' to be far more grand.

'This is the entrance that you will always use. This is the servants and tradesmen's entrance. You must never go out of the front door, or go into the main part of the house without being summoned. The family do not wish to see the servants. Do you understand?'

'Yes, Ma-am,' answered Jenny respectfully.

'My name is Mrs Miller. You will use that name at all times.'

'Yes Ma-am, I mean Mrs Miller.'

'Come along and I will introduce you to the staff. Get your bundle.'

Jenny jumped down from the carriage and grasping her bundle, followed Mrs Miller through the doorway. The passage led into a maze of corridors and eventually ended up in an enormous kitchen, which was relatively quiet, but very hot.

'Cook, here is your new scullery maid. Her name is Mitchell. See to her. And send a tray up to my room. I'm exhausted after having to go all that way to get her.' With that, Mrs Miller left Jenny and walked out of the door. Jenny stayed rooted to the spot, not daring to move.

'Well, young lady. You're not very big. You could see through you if you stood sideways. Mind you, the workhouses are not known for getting their folks overweight.' The cook laughed to herself. 'I'll soon put some meat on those bones. But first we must get you sorted out. Mrs Miller should have done that, but she's fair put out about you coming. Likes to interview all her prospective staff before they come. Doesn't like being told that she had to have someone. I'll give you a word of advice, young Mitchell. Don't cross that one, or you have made an enemy for life. Now, what's your given name? We only call ourselves by our last name when the family or Mrs Miller are around. Oh and Mr Fothergill. He's the butler and thinks he's above us in every way. Mind you, every one calls me cook all the time,' Cook laughed again to herself. 'Now what shall we call you?'

'My name is Jenny, Ma-am.'

'Here, none of that Ma-am stuff with me. Cook I am, and Cook you can call me. Jenny. Mmm, that is a nice name. We've never had a Jenny before. Now I bet you could do with a nice cup of tea. We usually have one before we start the evening meal. Just sit there.' Cook pointed towards a stool. Jenny sat down gratefully.

'Martha,' yelled Cook unceremoniously, 'get your body in here, now. Agnes, get a tray taken up to Mrs Miller's room, and I mean NOW.' Jenny was taken aback by the force of Cook's voice. A scurrying of feet from another room soon resulted in a hot and dishevelled girl appearing through the doorway. She was about Jenny's age and had a large white mobcap covering her hair. She wore a dark grey gown and with a starched white pinny to match her mobcap.

'Martha, this is Jenny. She'll be sleeping in the room next to you. You can take her up there when you have both had a cup of tea and show her the ropes. Miller says that she will be helping you for now.'

Eyeing Jenny up, Martha sat down on a stool and leant her arms on the long trestle table.

'Where you from, then?'

'I'm from the workhouse at Clitheroe.'

'What about before then?'

'I don't know. I can't remember.'

'Well, I can. I comed from down Burnley. Mi mam had eleven of us. She couldn't feed us proper, so I comed 'ere.'

'Martha, what have I told you about speaking better. You came here, not comed here.' Cook shook her head, laughing at Martha. But didn't seem angry. This was a new experience for Jenny. She was used to people being angry with her, but not laughing at the same time. In fact, laughter was not something that was a frequent event at the workhouse. At least, not whilst the warders were around.

She still couldn't believe her luck. However hard this job may be, it couldn't be worse than the workhouse. She was so grateful for being given a chance that she would do all in her power to work hard here. If the other staff were like Cook she would be happy. Martha seemed friendly as well, so Jenny felt that life could only improve.

Cook placed large mugs of hot sweet tea firmly on the table.

'Here, get this down you both, then the real hard work will start.'

Jenny sipped the lovely sweet tea as if it was ambrosia. She had never had sugar in her tea before and found it very much to her taste. She could also taste the tea, instead of it being very weak and diluted, not to mention the very poor quality like it had been in the workhouse. Not that she had known that it had been poor quality until now. Now she knew what real tea tasted like she decided that she could get a liking for this life.

The door suddenly opened and a severe looking man came in wearing a look of disgust on his face.

'Cook, what is going on? I turn my back for one minute and it turns into a tea party. Why isn't Clegg working, and who is this?' He pointed a finger at Jenny. Martha dropped her mug and ran back into the scullery.

'Now, Mr Fothergill, don't upset yourself, this is the new girl, Jenny Mitchell. She has just arrived after a long journey, and I made her and Clegg a cup of tea, then Clegg was to show her where her room is.'

'Right Mitchell,' said Mr Fothergill frostily, 'don't think that you will be spending your time supping tea all day here. Your job is to work, and by God, you will work hard, my girl. Or I will want to know the reason why? Understand?'

Jenny nodded and stood quickly upright to show respect. Mr Fothergill nodded back and then ignored Jenny.

'Right Cook, I have just come down to tell you that the young Master is coming home from university tomorrow.'

'Tomorrow? That's early. He's not due until next week.'

'Mind your own business, Cook. He's coming tomorrow, and all you need to know is that he will need his special favourites making, her Ladyship says.' With that, Fothergill swept out of the kitchen with the same authority and suddenness with which he had arrived.

'Huh,' said Cook, 'I wonder what mischief that young 'un has been up to now? I would love to know. Sit down, Jenny. He's gone now. Just show him the respect that you did then. He likes to think people are respecting him. Likes to think he's the bloody Lord of the Manor half the time. Eh, sorry about my language, I don't use bad language normally, but that man drives me to it. As you will find out before long, young Jenny. Now get supped up, then Martha'll take you upstairs.'

Jenny gratefully drank the rest of the tea, then took the cup over to the sink and washed it out, looking round for a cloth to dry it. Finding none, she spoke to Cook.

'Beggin' yer pardon, Cook, but where's pot cloth?'

'Eh, God Bless you, young Jenny, leave it there on the draining board. We'll sort it out later. Well, I am impressed with you. Most young 'uns haven't any gumption at all. What were your job in the workhouse?'

'I did most jobs. We got moved round all th' time. I liked th' kitchen best, although sometimes I 'elped out in th' hospital, an' I liked that an all.'

'Well, there may be some of that here as well. Her Ladyship is not well. I'm glad the young Master is coming home. That will perk her up.'

'What is wrong with her Ladyship?'

'Never been right since she had the last child. Took to her bed when it died. Nearly killed her being born, it did. She's bled a lot since then. You know what I mean, Jenny, I suppose you are old enough to know by now?' Jenny nodded, remembering her introduction to the monthly rags in the laundry.

'His Lordship were demented. Especially as the child was a boy. They always want the boys. Need an heir and a spare, they always say. Need to pass the title on. Not that they didn't get plenty of girls. Here, listen to me rambling on when there's work to do. Martha,' Cook screeched in her raucous voice, 'get in here and sort Jenny out.'

Martha scurried in from one of the other rooms in the kitchen and stood next to Jenny.

'This way then Jenny. I'll 'elp yer wi' yer bundle.'

'Help, not 'elp,' boomed Cook.

'Sorry Cook, I meant help.' Martha exaggerated the 'H' making Cook open her mouth to say something, but Martha grabbed Jenny's hand and dragged her out of the kitchen. They hurried along a long, dark passage until they reached a steep staircase.

'These are the staircases that we have to use. We never have to go down the main staircase, unless told to. Come on.' With that, Martha hurried up the staircase behind Jenny. At the top, they turned on to another staircase, then another, until Jenny was panting for breath.

Martha laughed. 'You'll get used to all the stairs. That's all we do all day. Up and down stairs. That is, when we are promoted out of the kitchen.'

'Yer talk nice, Martha. Like th' gentry.'

'Got to,' replied Martha. 'They make you talk nice here. Best if you learn to do it too.' At last they seemed to have stopped climbing stairs. Jenny got her breath back.

The corridors were plainer up here on the top floor, the walls were darker and the ceilings lower. Martha opened a door and led Jenny into a small room. It had an iron bed, a chest of drawers and a hard looking stand chair. A small window was facing the door with neat but plain curtains.

'This is your room. It's next to mine.' Jenny stared around her in awe.

'My room, yer mean only me'll sleep in 'ere?' she asked incredulously.

'Yes, most of us have our own rooms. What did you expect?'

'I've never slept on mi own before. I've always 'ad about twenty other girls sharing. It'll feel queer, like.'

'I know what you mean. We slept five to a bed at our house, with only one blanket between us, except when it was in the shop.'

'Oh, yer 'ad a shop?'

Martha stared at Jenny, not quite believing her.

'No, I meant the pop shop.'

'Pop shop?' asked a confused Jenny.

'Where we took our things to get money, when me dad were laid off work from the mill. Don't tell me you never went to the pop shop at home?'

'I don't remember a home,' said Jenny sadly, 'I was put in the workhouse when I was about three.'

'Eh, I'm sorry Jenny. I didn't realise. Well, look, if you feel lonely at night, come in my room. We could talk a bit before we get to sleep. Mind you, most nights, we'll be too tired to talk,' Martha warned grimly. 'Come and look at our room.'

'Ours?' asked Jenny curiously, 'do you share?

'Yes, our Effie is here with me, so they let us share. She's sixteen and has been promoted to being upstairs. Oh, the tales she tells us about what goes on upstairs.' Martha opened the door to the next room and Jenny noticed the two iron beds that were in this room, although it was only slightly bigger that her own. There was a small mirror on the wall and Jenny went to admire it.

'We bought that with our wages. We got it on Burnley Fair last year. Saved up for ages, we did,' said Martha proudly. 'Most of our money goes to our mam, but she lets us keep a bit. Makes it more homely, doesn't it? And look at this too.' Jenny looked at the threadbare rug that was proudly displayed between the two beds.

She had never possessed anything in her life and was impressed that these two young women could own anything that they had bought themselves. Suddenly a word came back into her mind.

'Did yer say wages?'

'Course, we saved up ours to buy stuff.'

'I've never 'ad a wage. Will I be able ter keep it fer mysel'?'

'Course. They only pay four times a year, though. Not every week like in the mill. You have to go up to the estate office and get it from the steward.' Jenny became silent again, unable to take in the wealth that would be hers. Not only her own room and good food, but wages as well. She began to cry.

'Here, don't take on, what's the matter?' asked a worried Martha.

'I'm just so 'appy to 'ave cum 'ere,' cried Jenny.

'Wait 'til your back aches and your legs and feet feel like fire. You'll not be so happy then,' warned Martha. Footsteps on the corridor made both girls turn round. A smartly dressed parlour maid came into the room.

'Effie, come and meet Jenny. She's come from the workhouse to live with us. She's going to work in the kitchen with me. She's got the room next door.'

'Hello Jenny, I'm glad Martha's going to have a friend her own age. Cook says to tell you that you have to hurry up and get downstairs now. There's work to be done.' The two girls scurried downstairs and went into the kitchen.

Chapter 5

'Now Jenny, let's see what you're made of. Go into the back kitchen and wash all those pots. They've been soaking since lunchtime, so should come clean now.' Jenny went in the direction Cook was pointing. Her heart sunk when she saw the pile of pots in the sink. It was like when the Governors of the workhouse had been for one of their special dinners.

Jenny drained the water out of the large stone sink and dragging the kettle over, put the hot water in, after the cold from the bucket. She worked hard for an hour and slowly the pile of clean pots were stacked on the side of the sink.

Adding some more hot water to the sink, Jenny attacked the pans that were the final part of the washing up. This was a much better method than she had been accustomed to at the workhouse, as they were made to wash up without soaking, which meant that it was hard scrubbing most of the time. When she had finished, Jenny went into the kitchen to ask Cook what to do next. Martha was peeling potatoes in a corner by the fire.

'Martha, show her how to dry them and where to put them away. Don't put the pans away though, I'll need them for tea.'

Martha showed Jenny the routine after the washing up was completed. Jenny was tired. It had been a strange day with so many new things to take in. The kitchen was busy now as Cook and Martha prepared the evening meal. After the family had eaten their meal, (five courses to Jenny's astonishment) the servants all gathered around the kitchen table to eat.

Fothergill came in as all the servants were gathering and said a mumbled Grace about being grateful for what was provided and happy with their station in life. Jenny thought that it was a strange Grace, but said a respectful 'Amen' with the rest of the staff. After Grace, Fothergill left the room followed by Martha who took two trays of food out of the kitchen and returned empty handed a short time later.

'Fothergill and Miller eat upstairs. Too posh to eat with the likes of us common folk,' explained Martha, only to be rewarded with a clip round the ear from Cook for giving cheek and being disrespectful to her superiors.

The kitchen was now full, with probably about twenty people sat round the long wooden table. Jenny had never seen so much food. It was just like the Governor's dinners. The other strange occurrence was the noise. Everybody seemed to be talking all at once. And eating as well.

Jenny open-mouthed with amazement. She was so used to having to eat in silence that she simply stared at all that was going on around her, trying to catch some snippets of conversation, but hardly catching any due to the noise.

'Come on Jenny, tuck in. It'll get cold if you don't. I don't like food going to waste in this house,' said Cook, 'I'll tell you who everyone is later.'

Jenny tried to eat some of the food that was in front of her, but the portions were so large that they over faced her, and she didn't feel like eating at all. But the little food that she ate was the best food that she had ever tasted in her life. The meat in the steak and kidney pie melted in her mouth; the vegetables were crisp and tasty instead of being boiled to a mush; and the mashed potato was light and fluffy.

The servants all seemed to eat enormous amounts of food very quickly, with a lot of hilarity and joking going on at the same time. Jenny thought that she would never get used to it.

Cook introduced Jenny to all of the staff, who in turn told Jenny who they were. Jenny knew that it would take her a long time to get to know everybody. She already knew Martha and Effie, but there was Rosie, the other kitchen girl, too. Effie was one of four 'upstairs' maids, the others being called Elsie, Alice and Mary. The senior maid, who stood in if Mrs Miller was away was Joan. The laundry maid was Sally, the dairymaid was Mollie; and then there were the outdoors staff.

Jem, John and Jake worked in the stables and were usually called the three 'J's for ease. The head gardener was called Hector, and his two assistants were Enoch and Willie. There was also a boy called young Willie who lived in the house and seemed to be at everybody's beck and call. As Jenny was to learn later, he was usually in trouble with Fothergill most of the time. It didn't seem to bother him though; he just philosophically nodded and carried on with what he was doing.

When the meal had finished, Cook sprang into life. 'Come on Jenny, let's get this lot washed up, then we can go to bed.' Jenny, Martha and Rosie quickly cleared the table and washed up again.

By now, Jenny was exhausted. It had been a long day, with many new and strange things to get used to. She was falling asleep on her feet. Cook sent her up to bed with a candle. Once there, Jenny got quickly into bed, so tired that even the newness of her situation didn't prevent her falling deeply asleep.

She was woken suddenly by Martha calling to her. Jenny felt that she had only just gone to sleep. It was still dark. Jenny jumped quickly out of bed and replied to Martha. She went outside the room to find Martha and found some hot water in a bowl outside her room, with a pile of clothes beside it. Martha opened her door, saying good morning to Jenny.

'Who 'as left this water and clothes?'

'That'll be young Willie, it's his first job of the morning. They must have found some clothes for you, too. Let's see if they fit. Mine were miles too big when I first come. They are very good here, we get new clothes every year and we don't even have to pay for them,' Martha enthused. Jenny tried the clothes on, but they were all on the big side.

'I reckon I'll soon grow inter 'em, when Cook puts some meat on mi bones,' Jenny quipped.

'Well, Miller might not like how you look, and may get you some new ones. She does that sometimes. These aren't bad, at least there are no holes in them.'

'After what I 'ad ter wear int' workhouse, they're dresses fit fer a princess.'

'Come on, have you had a wash? If we're not down soon, we'll be in trouble.' Jenny and Martha clattered down the back stairs into the kitchen area, only to run headlong into Miller, who roundly shouted at them, threatening all kinds of dire consequences if they ever did that again. Jenny and Martha both shrunk back against the corridor wall, Jenny by this time visibly shaking.

'This doesn't bode well for you girl, if this is how the workhouse have trained you, you can go straight back.' The tears came into Jenny's eyes, but she had long years of training not to let them fall.

'Sorry Mrs Miller,' she mumbled.

'I'll be watching you very sharply, Mitchell, so you had better be very careful or you will be back to Clitheroe before teatime.' With that, Miller stalked off up the stairs, leaving Jenny sobbing against the wall.

'Don't let her upset you, Jenny, I'll help you, just stay out of her way.' Hearing sounds on the stairs, Jenny and Martha scuttled into the kitchen, but it was only Cook coming down.

'What? No water on yet, Martha? What are you playing at?'

'I were helping Jenny wi' 'er uniform and then we ran in ter Miller and she 'ad a go at us. Told Jenny she were goin' back ter th' workhouse,' Martha stuttered out, her speech reverting to her natural rhythms in her distress.

'Well, you should know better than to cross that one by now. Get the kettle on, I'm fair parched for a cup of tea.'

'Young Willie's put it on already,' Martha replied, calming down a little.

'Well, I'm glad someone's got their head on this morning. Come on girls, it's going to be a busy day. Like all of them in this household,' she remarked grimly to no one in particular. Jenny and Martha scurried round putting tea into the large teapot and setting the mugs out.

Martha showed Jenny how to set up the tray for Miller and Fothergill. Jenny had never seen trays so finely laid out, and this was only for the upper servants. She couldn't imagine what the family used. Martha took Jenny up the back stairs and then up another flight to Miller's room, and then knocking gently on the door, announced that her tea was ready.

Miller came out of the room, and took the tray from Martha and glared at Jenny.

'What has she come for, to hold your hand?' Miller said sarcastically.

'Cook said I was to show her the ropes, Mrs Miller.'

'Well, you don't need to show her how to do my trays; I don't want her in here. That is your job Clegg.'

'But, what about when I go . .'

'Be silent, when I want you to speak, I will say so. Now, get downstairs the both of you and don't trouble me again today.' The two girls slunk quietly downstairs again, not speaking. As they got near to the kitchen, Martha said quietly, 'She seems to have taken against you, Jenny, you're going to have to watch her. She can be right evil when she wants to be.'

Jenny nodded grimly. So much for thinking she had landed in Heaven. She had just swapped Hargreaves for Miller.

On entering the kitchen, Cook fired orders at both of them, leaving Jenny no time to think about her circumstances. First, the family all had to have a tray of tea, then their breakfasts, and then all the servants had to have their breakfasts.

Next it was a mammoth washing up session, followed by fetching and carrying for Cook whilst she and Martha did the baking and made lunch. They had managed a quick cup of tea between finishing breakfast and starting luncheon, but then there was all the special baking to do for the 'young Master', Master Jeremy.

By half past two o'clock, there was a little lull in the kitchen, so Jenny, Martha and Rosie, had 'five minutes', with a sit down by the fire and another cup of tea. Cook gave them all a large piece of fruitcake that she had made for Master Jeremy, having made an extra few cakes for all the staff. Suddenly, there was a commotion outside the kitchen.

'Master Jeremy, you should not be down here in the kitchens,' shrieked Miller. But he was obviously taking no notice, as he burst into the kitchen as large as life.

'Well Cook, I'm home again. Couldn't stand the food up at Cambridge. It's too bad that Mama wouldn't let you come with me. Perhaps then I could have stayed a little longer.' He laughed raucously.

'Get away with you, Master Jeremy, what would I be doing up at Cambridge, with all those young toffs? And get your hands off my fruitcake. You are not too big to put over my knee for a spanking yet.' He laughed raucously again.

'Cook! How could you speak like that to Master Jeremy? Any more and I will give you notice,' said Miller in a cold voice.

'Over my dead body,' replied Master Jeremy, 'if she goes, I go, Miller. And you as well if I have anything to do with it.' Miller looked shocked, but said nothing. Master Jeremy leaned over and took a large piece of fruitcake and winking at Cook, started to leave the room, until he saw Jenny.

'And who is this skinny little thing? Just got her from the workhouse, or somewhere equally dreadful?'

'This is Mitchell. And yes, she is from the workhouse,' Miller replied coldly. Master Jeremy looked Jenny over very carefully, making Jenny feel unclean and naked. She was very uncomfortable, but kept her head down and averted her eyes. The whole room seemed to be frozen, with people holding their breath. After what seemed a long time, Master Jeremy looked away and left the kitchen. The whole roomful of people suddenly started breathing again and went about their business.

'Watch that one,' warned Cook, 'he's a danger to decent young girls. Remember Janie. ' But she didn't explain any further to anyone. It was obvious from her voice that she didn't really like the young master, even though she had been friendly enough with him, when he was in the room. Probably knew what side her bread was buttered on. Be polite to the future Lord, but think her own thoughts when he wasn't there.

The day carried on similarly to the previous one. Jenny couldn't believe how much food was needed for one family, or even how many servants were needed to look after one small family. Once, when Effie came down to the kitchen for the family's food, she told them all about the row that had been going on upstairs, just before the evening meal had begun.

'Oh, Effie, you shouldn't be listening in at doorways, you'll get caught,' said Martha.

'I wasn't, I was cleaning the drawing room next to the library. You could hear it all over the upstairs of the house. Lord Ormerod and Master Jeremy were going at it like hammer and tongs. Words like 'sent down', and 'guttersnipe', and 'not fit to be of a noble family'. Oh, he were right mad were Lord Ormerod. I wouldn't like to be in Master Jeremy's shoes. I think he has gone too far this time. Mind you, he's been too far a few times, and still got away with it, hasn't he?'

'That is enough, Effie. I don't approve of young Master Jeremy, but you shouldn't be discussing the family like this in the kitchen, with everyone listening.'

'You don't object when there's nobody else around, though Cook, do you? Different story then,' replied Effie cheekily.

'That's enough, I said. I don't think you would want Miller to know about this, would you?' Effie shrugged her shoulders and went back upstairs. All this time, Jenny had been carefully cleaning the kitchen and not looking at anyone in particular.

Chapter 6

When the girls went to bed that night, Jenny asked Martha about the girl, Janie, that Cook had mentioned. Martha told her how Janie had been with child, and she was adamant that Master Jeremy had given it to her. The family threw her out without a character, and she ended up in the new workhouse, Primrose Bank that had been built on the other side of Burnley going out towards Colne.

'What 'appened to 'er?'

'She is still there, with her little girl.' Jenny remained silent. She had met other girls who had been 'forced' by the young man of the house to do things against their will, and there had always been a baby afterwards.

Jenny wasn't too sure what went on in the making of babies, but she assumed from the stories of the young girls, that it wasn't pleasant. She would have to make sure that Master Jeremy didn't 'force' her and decided that she would avoid him.

The next morning, however, she was to meet him again. Immediately after breakfast, Miller came down to the kitchen and told Jenny to put a clean pinny on and follow her.

Her heart quaking, Jenny did as she was told and followed Miller, worrying that she was going to be sent back to the workhouse. They went up the back stairs, and then through a door that Jenny had been told she must never go through.

As they went through the door, Jenny noticed the thick carpet on the floor. There were coloured walls, in the palest of pastel shades, small, highly polished tables with bowls of flowers on them, and big paintings of rich looking people on the walls. There were tall ceilings with ornate mouldings and light, airy windows; and beautiful, shiny chandeliers twinkled with candlelight.

Jenny walked slowly behind Miller, gazing intently at all the things she could see.

'Hurry up, girl. I can't abide dawdlers.' Jenny needed no second bidding, as the dread fear of where she was going returned. Perhaps she was going to be sacked already. She dearly hoped not. She would love to stay here forever.

Miller ran up the flight of stairs and stopped at the end of the long corridor. She gently tapped on the door and a frail voice said 'Come in.' Miller opened the door and motioned Jenny to follow her. Jenny went into what seemed to be a large 'L' shaped bedroom, which had a kind of sitting room in one side of the 'L'. Jenny stared round at the opulent furniture, until Miller pushed her forward.

'Your ladyship, this is the new girl. Mitchell.' A thin frail looking woman lifted herself a few inches from the bed and stared at Jenny.

'Not much of her, is there, Miller? I hope she is strong enough for all the work.' A deep laugh appeared to come from the curtains at the large window.

'Exactly what I said yesterday, Mama, we'll have to fatten her up.' Jenny looked to see Master Jeremy sat on the window seat, where he had been hidden by the lush velvet drapes. Jenny blushed. She wasn't used to people talking about her like this, as if she wasn't there.

'Be quiet, darling, the servants are my responsibility, not yours. Now where did you find this one Miller? Somebody's sister?'

'No your Ladyship, workhouse.'

'They certainly don't overfeed them there, do they?' the Lady laughed. 'Do you love God and know your place in life, Mitchell?' Jenny nodded, too frightened to speak to a real Lady. She felt a clout in the back from Miller.

'Say 'yes your Ladyship' and curtsy,' roared Miller.

'That will do, Miller, she won't have picked everything up so soon. Now, do you like your room?'

'Oh yes your Ladyship! It's beautiful, Thank you your Ladyship,' as she bobbed up and down constantly. Her Ladyship laughed.

'See, Miller, she is learning already. I think she will do well. You may go.' With that, her Ladyship waved her hand vaguely towards the door upon which Miller half dragged Jenny out of the room and into the corridor. Jenny was hurried back downstairs as quickly as possible and Miller warned her what would happen to her if she misbehaved.

She especially told her that she was not to go anywhere near Master Jeremy, or to lead him on. Jenny hadn't a clue what Miller meant by 'leading him on', but she nodded politely to Miller and scurried back to the kitchen as quickly as she could. She decided that she would ask Martha, but she didn't get chance until bedtime. Martha laughed at Jenny's questions.

'Do yer know nought? It's what men and women do, yer know, ter make babbies.'

'Er, no, I don't know, tell me.'

'Well, you know, the bed thing, did yer never see yer mam and dad at it, or hear them?

'No, I don't remember my mum or dad. I've been in th' workhouse since I wer little.'

'Well, men shove their thing inter the women, then the women has a babby nine months later.'

'Oh,' said Jenny, still totally confused.

'And men are always wanting to be doing it, so you'd better watch out. 'Specially that Master Jeremy. He's a rum 'un with the girls.' At that point Effie entered the room, so Jenny went back to her own room, little wiser than before, but able to put some of the tales that she had heard from the workhouse women, together with what Martha had told her.

It was all very strange. She wondered if this was what being 'forced' meant. She would make certain that no one forced her, it all sounded awful.

Jenny nearly found out what it was all about quite soon afterwards. Master Jeremy caught her on the back stairs, coming down from her bedroom. He should not even have been in that part of the house.

'Ah, the new maid, Mitchell, wasn't it? I always remember a pretty maid's name. Now what is your given name? The one before Mitchell?'

'Er, Jenny, sir,' replied Jenny bobbing a curtsey. He caught her hand as she got up from the curtsey, and pulled her close to him. 'Mm, very nice curves you have got Jenny,' he said as he ran his hands all over her body. Jenny didn't like what he was doing and pulled away, trying to push his body away from her. That only seemed to excite him more; he pawed her harder, beginning to hurt her. He pressed her against the wall, pushing his hand up her skirt, tearing at her underclothes, when suddenly Miller walked up the stairs.

'Mitchell, get out of here, now.' The imperious voice startled Master Jeremy and he jumped away from Jenny. She straightened her dress as quickly as she could, her face blushing furiously. Master Jeremy laughed at her discomfiture, and at Miller.

'Trust you to spoil my fun, Miller. Were you jealous? How long had you been watching?' He gave a sneering laugh and then sauntered slowly along the corridor, laughing as he went along, shouting 'I'll get you next time, Mitchell.' Miller waited until he had gone and then rounded sharply on Jenny.

'What did I tell you about leading him on? You slut. I should have known, bringing you from the workhouse. You are probably the daughter of a slut, too.'

Jenny gasped. 'But I never . . .'

'Silence, slut. I saw what was happening. It won't give you any favours in this house by trying to entice the young master. Now get back to the kitchen where you belong.'

Jenny ran down to the kitchen and burst into tears when she arrived. Slowly, the whole story was sobbed out to Cook, who made her a nice cup of sweet tea. Effie came in during the story, and told Cook that she would let her Ladyship know what had happened, but Jenny pleaded with her not to say anything. She was too embarrassed. But Effie decided in her own mind that she would tell her Ladyship quietly anyway.

'Did he get inside you Jenny? You know what I mean?'

'N-no, but he was tearing at my drawers.'

'Thank God for that anyway. Oh, it's not right. Girls should be safe in a house. He wants stringing up. And not by his neck,' added Cook meaningfully. Jenny had never seen Cook so vindictive or angry. She felt pleased that Cook protected her and believed her story, unlike Miller.

Over the following weeks, Jenny made sure that she didn't go anywhere near Master Jeremy, or go up the back stairs without telling someone where she was going. She felt nervous for a long time, and jumped at the slightest noise behind her. Master Jeremy was then sent to a friend's house, the atmosphere in the home became lighter and Jenny felt more at ease

The routine continued in the kitchen, with extra work being necessary because of Master Jeremy, when he returned some weeks later. It amazed Jenny how one young man could make so much work.

There was also talk of Master Jeremy getting married to a young girl called Hortense from Derby, the daughter of an earl. They were to live in the house to begin with, whilst a new house was built for them, and were to be married in the Spring.

Miller had talks with Cook, and agreed that they needed more help in the kitchen. She asked Martha if they had any more sisters at home ready for coming into service. Martha had shook her head and said that all the little ones under her were boys, and the next girl was only five. Jenny remembered Marian.

'Do you think that Miller would have my friend Marian from the workhouse to work here? She is so unhappy there, and it is so good to work here.'

'Is that the young lass you go and visit each month on your day off?' asked Cook gently.

'Yes, she would be no trouble. Would she Martha? You've met her. She would love to come and stay here.'

'She's a nice girl, Cook, and she is a lovely sewer, too. That work she were doing when you took me were right lovely.'

'That might help if she can sew, we've no maids that are any good at sewing, so all the work has to be sent out to the town dressmaker. Especially as the wedding is coming up. Yes, I think Miller would accept her as a sewer, even though she is your friend. I'll tell her about that first, before I tell her where she lives. How old is she?'

'She's just thirteen, Cook'.

'Well, that should be all right. I'll speak to Miller.'

Jenny waited in anticipation for a few days until Cook gave her the good news that Miller had agreed to give Marian a month's trial. Jenny was overjoyed.

What Cook didn't tell Jenny was that Miller had argued against having anyone that Jenny suggested, or anyone from the workhouse, but the ability to sew overcame her objections. Eventually! She was to be brought over from Clitheroe next week. Jenny could hardly wait.

'Could she go in my room, do you think, Cook?'

'Yes, I'm sure that will be all right, but you will have to check with Miller first.'

Jenny's heart sunk, but she asked Miller anyway.

'Certainly not,' was the lady's reply. 'She is coming here to work, not to have a life of luxury with you. The audacity of you asking is beyond me. Now get about your work.'

Jenny slunk out of the room, wishing she hadn't asked, as now Miller would probably take against Marian as well. Jenny couldn't win. Whatever she suggested seemed to upset this woman or be wrong in some way.

Eventually Marian arrived, looking every bit as frail as Jenny had when she had arrived herself. Jenny was able to take her up to the small bedroom, further down the corridor from her own room and give her the dress that she was to wear.

It was far too big, but Marian made alterations to her own dress the first night that she had arrived and it looked far better than Jenny's had done.

Marian was taken up to her Ladyship's room as Jenny had been. She came back full of praise for her Ladyship.

'She 'as given me somat ter alter fer her, and I'm ter go up an' check it on 'er termorrer. A real lady, Jenny, I can't believe it. She talked ter me.' Jenny smiled to see little Marian's face all aglow. She had not seen her so happy in all the years they had known each other.

Chapter 7

Next morning the kitchen was buzzing. There was to be a dinner party on Sunday. It was a rare event as her Ladyship was not keen to either entertain or go out to dinner parties. Going to dinner parties brought obligations, as one had to return the favour. Anyway her Ladyship was reluctant to be seen in her present fragile condition. But this was a special event; Lady Hortense and her family were coming to stay.

They were all arriving on Saturday morning, and the whole house had to be scrubbed from top to bottom, even though it was already immaculately clean. Miller saw to that all year round.

It was a baptism by fire for Marian. If she hadn't known the routine at the beginning of the week, she certainly knew it by the weekend. Even Jenny went in rooms that she never knew existed. The guest bedrooms had to be prepared for all of the visitors, as well as bedrooms for all of their staff.

Jenny found it to be the hardest week of her life in the house. Marian knew no different, but was relieved to know that this intense introduction to the house was not a normal week. The staff all fell into their beds and were asleep before their heads hit the pillows.

Tempers were frayed frequently. Jenny found it hard to believe that Miller could be any worse than usual. But she was. Shouting and screaming at the staff for anything or nothing. Even Cook was inclined to be bad tempered, telling Rosie off for dawdling and Marian for dropping and breaking a plate.

In the middle of the week, some of the Ormerod's family arrived as well, as if they hadn't enough to do. Extra guests just brought extra work, mumbled Rosie, to no one in particular.

Saturday dawned, and at long last everything was ready. There couldn't have been more effort made if it was Royalty themselves coming to stay, Jenny thought. Her thoughts were disturbed by Miller's voice screeching at her.

'Mitchell, go and get everyone from the kitchen and get them upstairs into the hall. The family is here, and we have to welcome them.'

Jenny needed no further prompting. She ran hurriedly down to the kitchen and passed the message on. Cook became all flustered, Rosie started wailing that she didn't want to meet the family and general chaos reigned, as they straightened mob caps and put clean pinnies on.

Jenny grabbed Marian's hand as they ran up the stairs and into the hall. 'Stay by me, I'll tell you what to do,' advised Jenny to Marian, who was a little overcome by everything that was going on.

In the hall, everyone was gathering, resembling a shoving, jostling crowd. Fothergill was trying to get everyone to line up neatly. There didn't appear to be any sign of the family – either their own or the visitors.

Eventually, they were all in line, Miller ordered them to stand to attention. Just in time, as young Willie came running round the corner to say that he had sighted the carriages at the entrance to the drive.

In the distance, the sounds of horses could be heard. The servants stood silently, waiting until the first carriages appeared around the corner. They watched carefully as the horses drew to a halt.

Lord Ormerod and the whole family excepting her Ladyship came out onto the front steps. Young Master Jeremy leading the way, standing at the front, a proud, formidable figure.

The grooms jumped down from the carriages and opened the doors for the people seated inside.

Slowly the carriages emptied.

'Miss Hortense, welcome to my home. Come and meet my family,' said Master Jeremy.

Goodness, thought Jenny, what a difference. If only she knew what she was letting herself in for. She wouldn't mind talking to this girl and telling her a few home truths. Jenny looked at the young girl. She was only sixteen. A dainty slim girl, with bouncing, shiny ringlets framing her delicate face, which displayed prominent cheekbones and a pointed chin.

'My father you have already met. I will take you inside to meet my mother.'

Lord Ormerod inclined his head graciously.

'Welcome, Miss Hortense. It gives us all great pleasure to receive you and your family here,' said Lord Ormerod. 'Ah, James, so glad that our families are going to be united. A long time since we were at Eton together, what?' he continued, having turned to speak to a tall grossly overweight man.

'And this must be your good lady wife.' Lord Ormerod took the lady's hand and bowed over it, brushing his lips against her hand.

'Pleased to meet you, I'm sure,' replied the lady.

Jenny could see whom Miss Hortense looked like. Her mother was a carbon copy, but older version of her daughter. They both shared the lovely, soft looking skin and tiny figure. It was in their clothes that they differed.

As ever, Jenny portrayed a keen interest in the clothes that they were wearing. The daughter was adorned in frills and flounces, whereas her mother was more sedately dressed, albeit in a sunny, yellow shade.

'I don't think that I would have chosen that colour for the mother,' thought Jenny to herself. 'It makes her look very sallow. She would have looked better in a warmer colour. And fancy Miss Hortense travelling in a white gown. That's asking for trouble,' muttered Jenny in her head, 'but then the gentry can afford to wear what they want, with no thought for how impractical it is. They just give it to the servants and it returns nicely laundered, with no thought of how it got like that, or how much work went into it.' Jenny sighed to herself, she was getting bitter in her old age, she decided. The sigh earned her a glare from Miller. 'Oh dear,' thought Jenny, 'more telling off when I get in.'

The introductions were continuing. Lord Ormerod's daughter Morag and husband Montague Martin, were now being introduced to the Marple family. Jenny thought that it was rather a silly idea. Why couldn't all these introductions take place indoors? Then they could all get about their own work, instead of standing here, in the chilly wind.

Eventually when everyone seemed to have been introduced, Lord Ormerod turned to the line of servants. He introduced Fothergill, who in turn, introduced Miller. She, with an imperious wave of her hand towards all of the servants said, 'And the rest of the staff.' At this command, all of the servants bowed or curtseyed, depending on gender, to the newcomers.

'I'm sure that our guests would like to be shown to their rooms, Miller,' suggested Lady Morag.

'Ha,' thought Jenny, 'somebody with a bit of sense at long last.' Suddenly, everybody was moving and ushering the guests inside. Miller was detailing all the female servants to escort the ladies and gentlemen up to their rooms.

The male servants were quickly carrying numerous boxes of luggage into the house and up to the guest bedrooms.

Jenny liked Lady Morag. She wasn't stuffy like a lot of the gentry were. She had first met her two days ago, when they arrived in advance for this weekends gathering.

Jenny had been assigned to be a ladies maid for Lady Morag. This was a sort of promotion for Jenny and she strove to do her best for Lady Morag.

She had some beautiful clothes, and although not physically beautiful, knew how to make the best of herself. She seemed to have a knack of knowing what would suit her and show her off to an advantage.

Lady Morag was very pleased with Jenny. She said that Jenny was the only one who had ever been able to do her hair properly. She had fine, wispy, mousy coloured hair. It was probably the fact that it was not unlike her own hair, which meant that Jenny could work with Lady Morag's hair.

Lord Martin and Lady Morag lived in a little village called Gisburn, which was not far from Clitheroe. Even so, they were not regular visitors to Ormerod Hall, as they had rather a large family and a large estate to maintain.

They had several working farms on their land as well. Lord Montague Martin liked to keep abreast of all the latest developments in farming and was very involved in the day-to-day running of the estate and farms. He preferred to work alongside his estate manager, rather than being an absent landlord.

He knew all of the local families by name, many of whom had been estate tenants for many generations. In fact, his manservant told them all in the kitchen, that some of the tenants called him Farmer Giles behind his back.

The kitchen was on full alert. All the guests needed a refreshing drink after their long tiresome journey, not to mention their servants as well.

And there was dinner to get ready for. They were to have a small cold collation at lunchtime, but even this was like feeding an army, with all of the extra people involved.

Cook was just pleased that Lady Morag hadn't brought her servants as well. They seldom did as they usually came without their numerous children. The poor servants were all left behind to cope with the children.

As soon as the food was prepared for luncheon, the evening dinner had to be commenced. All seven courses of it. How anybody could eat so much at one meal escaped Jenny, but she didn't really complain, as the servants got many of the leftovers to sample.

The weekend was a tremendous success. Her Ladyship sent word down to the kitchen to thank everyone for the hard work that they had done. The wedding date had been set, and all the parties were happy. Her Ladyship was very pleased that the wedding was taking place locally.

'It will be a lot more work with the wedding,' said Cook darkly, when the message of thanks was given. 'Oh well, that is what we're used to. Now I suppose we had better get on with today's food.'

After the workhouse food, Marian couldn't believe the amount of food that was given to her. At first, her stomach couldn't take all the rich food and she had to build up the amounts that she ate gradually. Slowly, Marian thrived on the good food, absence of beatings and poor lifestyle.

Her body started developing and her lovely auburn hair shone like burnished gold, although it was kept hidden by her mobcap for most of the time.

Eventually, Marian was a regular visitor to her Ladyship's room. The first piece of work had been soundly approved and increasingly harder work had been given to her. Marian was often to be found in her Ladyship's boudoir, as she said that it helped pass the time away to watch Marian sewing.

Marian enjoyed making the frilly garments that her Ladyship required, even though she was an invalid. Although the clothes for her Ladyship for the wedding were coming from London, Marian was given the task of making all of the new clothes for the staff prior to Miss Hortense coming to take up residence at Ormerod Hall.

As her ladyship was too weak for the journey to Derbyshire Miss Hortense had agreed to hold the wedding at Burnley Parish Church and the wedding breakfast at Ormerod Hall.

The staff all liked Miss Hortense. She was a lovely gentle young girl, and all the staff wondered how she would cope with Master Jeremy. He was an irregular visitor to Ormerod Hall now, as he spent more and more time at Marple Hall in Derbyshire, Hortense's family home.

The date of the wedding quickly arrived. Extra staff and servants were taken on by Miller to cope with the extra work. The preparations included three weeks of scrubbing and cleaning, with no days off for any of the staff during this time.

On the day of the wedding, there was great excitement. The staff had been given permission to watch the wedding at the Church. Donning their new uniforms, they were all taken down in advance by carriages and told to sit at the back of the church. Jenny and Marian looked around the beautiful parish church of St Peter's, with its high ceilings and elaborate chandeliers.

Miss Hortense looked beautiful. Her gown was made of silk satin and damask trimmed with lace. The overskirt was made of patterned damask, and was deeply pleated over a small bustle. The long train was made of pleated organdie; and the bottom of the front of the gown had small box pleats, with a satin rose in each gathering of the overskirt.

The bodice was loosely fitted, with the same lace trim as the train. The dress had a 'V' shaped neckline, adorned by a heavy diamond pendant, given to Miss Hortense by her father as a bridal present.

The sleeves had tiny box pleats at the shoulder to match those on the skirt of the dress, which finished in a point just below the elbow.

Elbow length lace gloves completed the outfit, apart from the long Honiton lace veil, that was one of the Ormerod family heirlooms.

Following the sumptuous feasts, the bridal pair changed into their going away outfits. They were to have a year long Grand Tour around Europe, before settling in to married life. As Ormerod Hall was so large, it had been decided not to build another house, but to give them the East Wing for their use. As soon as they went away, work started on completely refurbishing this suite of rooms to their taste.

Sadly, they did not stay away for a full year.

About four months after the wedding, Lord Ormerod had a seizure and died three weeks later. Letters had been sent to Venice, where they thought that the young couple were, to tell them to return home immediately.

Unfortunately, they were too late. Lord Ormerod was dead and buried before they got home. Lord Jeremy and Lady Hortense went to pay their respects at the graveside in the parish church, but did not stay long.

Life with the new Lord Ormerod, or Lord Jeremy as people referred to him, was not easy. His wife was expecting their first baby, and was feeling unwell. It should have been a glorious time in their lives, but it seemed to make Lord Jeremy angry.

Lady Hortense was often heard crying, and everyone was glad that Lord Jeremy often took himself off to a friend's house, leaving Lady Hortense at home.

The house took on a happier atmosphere when he was away, and all of the staff felt very sorry for Lady Hortense. She seemed, though, to be very friendly with the old Lady Ormerod and they spent many happy hours together, reported Marian, who was often in the room with them.

When Lord Jeremy came back, there was an unholy row one night. The staff were fearful for Lady Hortense's safety. Eventually, Lord Jeremy roared down to the kitchen and asked for some help with his wife.

Lady Hortense's personal maid, Annie, went up to help and took Jenny with her. She soon sent Jenny back to get help. Lady Hortense was losing the baby. The doctor was called for, but he said that it was too late, and the baby was too young to survive. It was a girl.

Both Lady Ormerod's were distraught about the news. Lord Jeremy was indifferent. He stood there with the doctor, and when he was told that the baby had died, he simply asked what sex it had been, showing no emotion. When told that it was a girl, he said 'Oh, well, might be a boy next time.' He did not ask how his wife was. Hearing this, Jenny could not believe the callousness of this young man.

The doctor then went on to ask how Lady Hortense had acquired the bruises on her body. Lord Jeremy shouted at the doctor to get out of the house, if he was going to ask stupid questions like that. He also said that the doctor was only present for the confinement, and wouldn't be invited there again.

The doctor looked at Jenny and Annie, but said nothing. They quietly followed him out of the room, and managed to tell the doctor that they would watch over Lady Ormerod. But they knew that they couldn't watch over her all the time.

Soon after the baby died, Lord Jeremy went on a hunting trip with some friends and peace descended on the house again. But it didn't last for long. When he was home, Lady Hortense found out she was expecting another baby. The staff thought that he would be delighted, but again he went about like a caged tiger.

When he was at home, he made his presence felt. As she was going to bed one night, Jenny thought she heard somebody crying further along the corridor. She followed the noise and found that it was Marian. She was curled up on her side on the bed, with her back towards Jenny. Jenny rushed to her side and touched her gently. Marian jumped in alarm, naked fear showing on her face.

'Marian, it's me, what is the matter?'

'Oh, I thought it was him.'

'Him?'

'That Lord Jeremy.'

Jenny's heart pounded.

'Why? Are you frightened of Lord Jeremy?'

'He followed me up here and dragged me on the bed and hurt me.' Marian rolled over in the bed and Jenny saw then that all her clothes were torn round her neck. Her skirt was in disarray, and there was blood between her thighs. Jenny held Marian close and rocked her until the sobs subsided.

She helped her to clean herself up, and then when Marian had fallen into a fitful sleep, Jenny went down to the kitchen and told Cook all that had happened. Cook shook her head and said that she had hoped that the young Lord would calm down after this baby was born.

Next day, a subdued Marian went quietly about her work, far from the happy girl she had been when she had first escaped from the workhouse to Ormerod Hall. Eventually, her mood lightened and she began to smile again, but there was often a haunted look about her as she walked around the house.

It was Effie that first suggested that all was not well with Marian.

'Is Marian with child?' she asked the stunned audience in the kitchen.

'Why do you ask?' said Cook.

'Heard her being sick a few mornings. Always the same with my mam. Sick in the mornings, then her belly would swell.'

'I hope not. But I'll ask her,' Cook replied, looking wearily at Effie. After some quiet questions about her monthly cloths, the news was confirmed to Cook. She advised Marian to say nothing until the baby started to show.

Inevitably, Miller found out and treated Marian like a woman of the streets. When Marian tried to say that Master Jeremy had forced her, it seemed to make Miller even angrier. She told Marian that 'she got what she asked for,' a statement that Marian didn't understand at all. Slowly, Marian withdrew into herself, and became morose.

As soon as she started showing, Miller dismissed her from her post and sent her back to the workhouse. She clung to Jenny sobbing, when Nat came to pick her up to take her back to Clitheroe. Jenny promised her that she would start visiting her again as soon as she could.

As Marian was almost forcibly dragged out of Jenny's arms and taken into the waiting carriage, Jenny wished she had never brought Marian here to the house. She thought that it would have improved her life, but now it had made her life far worse, and it was all Jenny's fault. A sadder but wiser Jenny cried herself to sleep that night.

Chapter 8

Although Jenny had been used to hard work at the workhouse, she was still very tired at the end of her working day. Her life however, had taken on a pleasant routine. She had good food, was well dressed, and had some money saved up, as she had nowhere to spend it.

Once a month, on her day off, she would go and visit Marian in the workhouse. Marian never really got back to her happy self. She just got unhappier as the birth got nearer.

Eventually Marian had the baby. A little boy. She named him George, after her father. The first time Jenny saw him, she fell instantly in love with him.

'Oh Marian, he is a beautiful baby. You're so lucky.' Marian gave her a strange look.

'Lucky? It's not my idea of luck,' she said morosely.

'No, but he is so lovely. I love him already,' enthused Jenny. 'I will bring him a present next time I come. What would you like?'

'Anything you like. But what's the point? Will they let me keep it?'

'Well, I've brought you some food today from Cook. I'm sure that you'll enjoy that.' Marian grabbed the food, and shoved it in her pocket, whilst looking round quickly to see that the warders weren't looking.

Jenny sighed. She was so lucky herself. If only . . . still, it was no good saying if only. It had already happened.

'How do you feel about the baby, Marian?'

'Oh, I love him. Don't misunderstand me, I do really love him. I didn't think that I would, because of, you know, the way I got him. But you are right, he is beautiful, and I love him dearly.'

'Well, next time I will bring something for him. I will make it a surprise for you.'

'Thank you Jenny. I really appreciate your visits. It gives me the strength to carry on.'

'I'll have to go now. The carter will be going back soon, and I daren't miss him, or Miller will cancel my next day off. I'll see you next month.'

Marian nodded quietly and went slowly back to the dormitory after dropping George off at the baby ward.

Meanwhile, back at Ormerod Hall, Lady Hortense had another girl, which lived this time. But before long, she was pregnant again. Cook muttered about Lord Jeremy never leaving her alone, and how was a body to get well if she was pregnant all the time. Lady Hortense looked old before her time. Her haggard looks and haunted expression made it difficult to believe that she was only eighteen years of age.

Most of the time Jenny was now promoted to looking after the old Lady Ormerod, or Dowager as she had become, even though she was only in her early fifties. She had been the relief maid for years whilst Effie and the other maid were on their days off, but now the other maid had got married, Jenny took on most of the work with Effie. They got on very well together and the Lady liked how Jenny worked

The Dowager Lady Ormerod took up a lot of time, but Jenny still liked to go down to the kitchens when she could and see all of the other staff. It was whilst she was in the kitchen one day that she heard Fothergill shouting for her.

'Mitchell,' shouted Fothergill, 'you're to go upstairs immediately. Mrs Miller wants to see you. She didn't look pleased at all.' Jenny's heart sunk.

What now? She really seemed to upset this woman without even trying, Jenny mused to herself, whilst checking the cleanliness of her apron. She knocked on Mrs Miller's door gently and waited.

'Come in.'

'You wanted to see me, Mrs Miller.'

'Yes, you have a letter. This is very unusual. We are not used to staff getting letters,' said Mrs Miller disapprovingly.

Huh, wasn't my fault, I didn't send it, thought Jenny mutinously to herself, but standing silently, polite and respectful all the time. She waited until Mrs Miller passed it over to her, then thanked her, pushed the envelope into her pocket and turned to leave the room.

'Aren't you going to open it, girl?'

'Oh no, Mrs Miller, I wouldn't dream of doing that, not in the day time, I'll save it for tonight when I'm free.'

'Are you being insolent?'

'Of course not.'

'Well, I give you permission to open it now.'

'Thank you, but I must get back to my duties. I'll save it for tonight.'

Mrs Miller looked furious, but couldn't force her to open it. Jenny knew that she was avid to know what was in the letter, as Jenny was herself. But she wasn't going to let Mrs Miller know that. It was obvious that the letter was an official one, as the envelope was on good quality paper, like Lord Jeremy used.

As soon as Jenny left the room, she ran up to her room and tore open the letter. It was from a firm of solicitors in Clitheroe, dated the 6th November, 1883, requesting the pleasure of her attendance, at her earliest convenience, whereby she would hear something to her advantage.

Jenny laughed. It was like something that Martha read in her 'Penny Dreadful' novels. What on earth could it be? She couldn't think what could be to her advantage from anyone she knew. It was very intriguing. Well, the only way she could find out was by going there to find out.

She hurried back down to the kitchen and found Martha icing some biscuits for the mid-morning snack for upstairs.

'Martha, Martha, you'll never guess what old Miller wanted. I've got a letter from a solicitor asking me to attend on him. What do you think about that?' Jenny passed the letter over to Martha.

'Probably a bill that you haven't paid,' Martha teased. 'Seriously though, I hope it is good news, and not bad.'

'Bad news? Whatever bad news could it be?' Jenny looked worried.

'No, it's just that I've never had a letter from a solicitor before, so I don't know what it can be. But it does say 'advantage', so I suppose it will be good news,' Martha tried to soothe.

'Well I won't know 'til I go and find out, will I? Oh dear, I'll have to ask Miller for a day off. That won't please her.'

'But you didn't have any days off for ages when you came here at first, and even now you only go and visit Marian and little George.'

'Well, I've nowhere else to go, have I? Yours is the only house I've been in besides here and the workhouse. Anyway, I must get off. I'll let you know as soon as I can what it's all about.'

Jenny put the letter back in her pocket and hurried back to her duties, her mind constantly on her letter throughout the day. That evening, she asked Miller if she could have a day off the next day. Miller was difficult, but when Jenny said that she had to attend a solicitor, her mood changed.

'Well, I suppose you can go, but this will be instead of your Sunday off next month.'

'Yes, I quite understand that, Mrs Miller, Thank you so much.'

She would have to try and get to see Marian and George tomorrow as well. She couldn't bear not to see them for another month. Jenny took a long time to get to sleep that night, her mind working overtime trying to guess what the future might hold, but the letter had been so vague, she became even more frustrated as the night lengthened.

Her final thoughts, as she drifted into sleep were that perhaps some member of the visiting gentry that she had served had left her a small token of jewellery in her will. Whatever it was, she would honour and treasure whatever was 'to her advantage'.

Chapter 9

Jenny got off the cart that had taken her to Clitheroe. The carter had dropped her off near the top of Moor Lane. She looked again at the letter, wondering how it was going to change her life, if at all. She walked up to the address on the envelope, took a deep breath and walked inside.

It was a gloomy room, with two men sat on high seats working furiously, their quill pens scratching as they worked by the light of the flickering gas lamps. After a few moments, one of them looked up, and stared at Jenny.

'Yes, Miss?' he enquired without interest.

'I have been asked to call on Mr Shoesmith at his earliest convenience. I have a letter here,' replied Jenny in her most perfect accent. As soon as she spoke, the clerk jumped up and gave her more respect. The clothes had suggested a servant, but her speech and a letter from his boss was a different matter.

'Please do sit down, Miss - er - Miss?'

'Mitchell. Miss Jenny Mitchell. Thank you.' Jenny perched carefully on the proffered chair. The clerk scurried out of the door and left Jenny looking round at the dismal room. Shortly the clerk returned and begged that Miss Mitchell would follow him. Jenny inclined her head and followed him, trying not to smile. Miss Mitchell, indeed.

The clerk led her upstairs into a larger more pleasant room, announcing her arrival to Mr Shoesmith as if she were a lady.

'Ah thank you, Jennings, and please do bring Miss Mitchell a cup of tea.' Jenny gulped and sat in the chair that Mr Shoesmith was drawing out for her. My, if only Martha and Marian could see her now! She looked at Mr Shoesmith as he shuffled his papers on the desk, and asked her about her journey to Clitheroe, as if she was an equal.

He was an elderly man with long straggly grey hair. He was tall and portly, with an expensive looking watch and chain stretching over his large corporation. When Jennings returned with the tea tray, Mr Shoesmith poured the tea into a dainty china cup and handed it to Jenny. Jenny accepted it with a smile as if this was a normal occurrence for her, to spend her days taking tea with friends.

'Well, my dear, I have good news for you.' Jenny's heart pounded. 'You have been left a legacy by a benefactor, but it is a very curious one. I can tell you details of your inheritance, but not where it has come from.'

'Inheritance?' thought Jenny to herself, 'that's the sort of words used by the rich, not the likes of me.' She tried to contain her wild thoughts.

'You have been bequeathed a shop and a small amount of money.'

Jenny gasped. 'A shop? Where? What sort of shop?'

Mr Shoesmith smiled.

'A gown shop, here in Clitheroe. The terms of your bequest are that you are not to know who your benefactor is for three years. If the shop is making a profit in three years, then you will be able to know the full story. Also, the top floor of the shop is sealed. If you should attempt to open the top floor of the shop, or fail to make a profit the will is revoked. Do you accept these terms?'

Jenny nodded, her mind too full to take in what he was saying.

'Now then, my dear, let us go and take a look at your shop. There has been a manager there for the last fifteen years, who is answerable to me on behalf of my client. I am sure that she will be very helpful to you. You are rather young for all this responsibility.'

Mr Shoesmith led Jenny out of his office and down the stairs into the front office. They went out into the bright winter sunlight and walked down the hill for a few yards. They stopped outside a large, four storied, double-fronted, gown shop, which was obviously designed for the rich.

As they entered the shop, a thin, middle-aged woman stood to attention by the mahogany counter. Her face showed obvious distaste, but as she spoke to Mr Shoesmith, her manner was respectful, rather than resentful.

'Good morning, Mr Shoesmith. You are a little early this month. It is not time for your usual visit. I am afraid the month end figures are not available. Please do sit down, I'll get some Madeira wine and a biscuit for you.' She had totally ignored Jenny up to now, but went behind a curtained area and shouted 'Sarah, bring Mr Shoesmith some wine,' in a less than pleasant voice.

'My dear Bruce, I have not come to inspect the books. I have come to introduce you to the new owner of the shop. This is Miss Jenny Mitchell.' Jenny smiled and nodded her head at Bruce, then noticed that Bruce had gone an ashen colour.

'New owner?' she stuttered, looking like she had seen a ghost.

'Yes, you always knew that you were only in charge here until the real owner was revealed. That was made very clear to you,' replied Mr Shoesmith.

'But . . .but. . I thought, er . .that there would be more time.'

'What does it matter? You have been a faithful servant and have been well rewarded for your labours. Now you can hand over to Miss Mitchell and explain the running of the shop. She will not be taking over immediately as she has to settle her affairs in the first instance.'

Jenny tried not to giggle at this, as it was her notice as a servant that she needed to sort out. The woman appeared to recover a little and turned to Jenny.

'Welcome, Miss Mitchell, I am sure that you will find everything in order. I will bring the books up to date whilst you are 'sorting your affairs out' and before you settle in. Shall I show you round now?'

Mr Shoesmith cut in.

'I don't think that will be necessary today. Suffice it to say that you have a shop with four floors. The first floor consists of the shop room, the second floor is the sewing rooms and the store-rooms, the third is living accommodation; and the fourth is, as you know, out of bounds.'

At this point a rough looking man appeared at the back of the shop. He had been going to walk into the room until he saw Mr Shoesmith.

Jenny observed that the woman gave him an urgent nod, telling him to leave, which he promptly did. Jenny got the impression that he was used to the run of the shop, but Bruce was explaining to Mr Shoesmith that he was just an errand man.

Mr Shoesmith quickly gave his respects to Bruce, and gently drew Jenny out of the shop.

'I'm sorry, Miss Mitchell, but that lady does not command my respect. I have found that the shop does not make much profit, and yet it should, as it is the premier gown shop in Clitheroe. I must be honest and say that I am worried for you. I only hope that you can make a living out of this business. Do come to me if you need any help. I'm sure that you are not used to dealing with a business.'

'Indeed not, Mr Shoesmith. I am only a servant. A good one, but nevertheless a servant. The news today has completely amazed me.

But if a business requires good, honest, hard work, then I shall achieve. I have never been afraid of that.'

There was a deep silence. Jenny turned to look at Mr Shoesmith, who appeared to be lost for words and blushing. Eventually he spoke.

'I am sorry that I may have offended you, Miss Mitchell. It was not my intention. But I do not want to give you the impression that you will have an easy passage.'

'I am sorry too, Mr Shoesmith. I know how important you will be in my life. I know that I will have to rely on you for all business matters in the first instance.'

'I will ask Mr Briggs to advise you. He is my junior partner and will be responsible for the day to day running of your business, and checking that you have fulfilled the terms of the will.'

By this time, they had arrived back at the office. Mr Shoesmith opened the door for her and led her inside. In the office was another slightly younger gentleman, slim and dark where Mr Shoesmith was portly and grey.

'And here he is, right on cue. Mr Briggs, may I introduce our mystery young lady who has just inherited the gown shop nearby. Miss Jenny Mitchell.' Mr Briggs looked appreciatively at Jenny before bowing graciously to her. 'Goodness', thought Jenny, 'what a difference an inheritance makes. Being treated like a lady.' But she just inclined her head as graciously as he had done.

'I believe that you are to help me with my shop.'

'It will give me the greatest pleasure. I will check that the books are in order before you take up residence. When will that be, do you suppose?' Jenny had no idea. She 'supposed' that she would have to give a months notice at the Hall, but had no idea really. With a confidence that she didn't feel, Jenny said that it would be a month.

'Well, Miss Mitchell, we will make you an appointment for one months time and look forward to meeting you again. Would you like to partake of further refreshment?'

'No Thank you, I have to make a visit in the town before I go back to Ormerod Hall.'

'Perhaps my carriage could be at your service? Then we could call at the bank and introduce you to Mr Humphries at the same time. Goodness, that reminds me. I failed to mention the money that you have been left. The sum of one thousand pounds is deposited in your name in Humphries Bank. It is down the street, where the road divides.' Jenny gasped.

A thousand pounds. Jenny had never heard of anyone having a thousand pounds. It was suddenly all too much for her. She sat down in the office and wept.

The two solicitors were nonplussed, neither having any idea how to deal with her. Mr Shoesmith gave her his large handkerchief, whilst Mr Briggs ran round like an old woman, telling the clerk to prepare some tea, and if there were any, some smelling salts. Just in case. Eventually, Jenny regained her composure.

'Perhaps I will have that drink after all. And perhaps I will take up the offer of your carriage as well. I might as well tell you. I am going to the workhouse. My young friend is in there. She was sent there when it was found that she was with child. A child that was forced upon her, if you understand my meaning.' Jenny blushed at having to use such words in the presence of these gentlemen.

'Of course, my dear,' said the kindly Mr Shoesmith. 'I will send Briggs with you, to ensure that no harm comes to you. In the meantime, I will give you five guineas on account from your money, as I am sure you will need to purchase some things prior to taking over your shop.'

Mr Shoesmith handed over a small velvet purse, the chink of money making a satisfactory thud in her hand. She had never had so much money in her hand before. It was more than her quarterly year's wages. And yet, she had far more than this waiting in the bank.

She could hardly believe it all. Any minute now, she would surely awake from this dream and she would be transported back to her little room in the top of the Hall. Jenny looked up at the two gentlemen and gave a slow smile.

'Before I go to the workhouse, I would like to buy something for my friend and her baby. Would you just give me a few minutes? Then I will be ready to go, if it is not too much trouble?'

Jenny left the office and crossed to Crabtree's bakery where they made lovely home-made steak pies. She bought a large one for Marian. Next she went to a baby clothes shop and bought a warm blanket for George.

She knew that eventually, the blanket would be stolen from George, or washed in too hot water, but he could have the pleasure of it for however long it lasted. She knew that she was spending rashly, but she wouldn't make a habit of it. Besides, Marian deserved it.

'I am ready now. I have got my purchases.'

'Well, Miss Mitchell, it has been a pleasure to meet you. I look forward to doing business with you.' Mr Shoesmith held the door open for her himself, whilst Mr Briggs took the bag from her and helped her into the waiting carriage. They were like two elderly uncles, not sure how to treat this young person in their midst.

Jenny tried hard not to smile, and was glad when the carriage set off down the street, past the bank, and out towards Chatburn, where the workhouse was.

'I have a favour to ask you, Mr Briggs.'

'How can I help, Miss Mitchell?'

'Would you come into the workhouse and wait for me. They are never very happy when I come to visit, and I am sure that your presence would ease my passage.'

'With pleasure, then I can escort you back to Clitheroe town. What time is your carriage returning for you?' Jenny giggled. Nat's cart was not exactly a carriage. She couldn't pretend.

'I came in on the carriers cart. I persuaded him to give me a lift on his way to market.'

'Then perhaps I can give you a lift home again? It would give me great pleasure.'

'Oh, no, I couldn't ask you to. No, I'll be fine with Nat. Besides, what would they think at the Hall if I arrive with you in tow? No, I'll go home the way I came.'

Mr Briggs looked a little disappointed, but said that he understood.

'There is something else, Mr Briggs.'

'Yes, Miss Mitchell?'

'Will I have enough money to give Marian a home with me? In the shop I mean. She hates it in the workhouse. She has really lost her personality. You'll see what I mean when you see her.'

'Yes, if you are careful, you should be able to care for your friend. Has she a trade?'

'Oh yes, she is the most exquisite sewer and embroiderer. In fact, she could be instrumental in my shop becoming a success,' said Jenny, warming to her idea.

'Then I am sure that you can offer her a home, as well as a job, if that is what you wish.'

'Oh, it is, with all my heart. I want to help all my friends if I can.'

'Well that is very philanthropic of you, but you had better make some money before you announce to all and sundry that you are going to help them,' advised Mr Briggs cautiously. Jenny wasn't sure what 'philanthropic' was, but she wasn't daft. As soon as she had money, she would help all her friends.

They walked through the entrance of the workhouse and Jenny held her breath momentarily.

'I still feel peculiar coming in here. I am always frightened that I will end up back in here. Like Marian did. Well hopefully not for the same reason,' said Jenny blushing, 'but you know what I mean.'

At that point, Hargreaves answered the doorbell, giving Jenny a less than welcoming look, until she saw Mr Briggs.

'Humph, got a protector, have you? Can't say I'm surprised,' said Hargreaves in an aggrieved tone. Jenny stared at her, but fortunately Mr Briggs answered for her.

'No, I have accompanied Miss Mitchell here from our offices, where she had business with Mr Shoesmith. I find your tone very insulting, woman. What is your name? I happen to be a governor on the Pauper's board.' Hargreaves demeanour changed instantly, and became fawning and obsequious.

'Be silent,' he roared, 'and get Miss Mitchell's friend here instantly.'

Hargreaves hurried off, and returned with Marian.

'Where is George?'

'He's in the nursery. I'm only allowed to see him on Sundays. That's why you usually see him. Why are you here today? It's only Tuesday,' said Marian dully, not even commenting on the man that was with Jenny.

'I got a letter from a solicitor saying that I had an inheritance. Marian, you will not believe it. I have inherited a gown shop in Clitheroe. And I am going to take you and George out of here to live with me. You can sew in the shop and you will never have to live here again. What do you think of that, Marian?'

Mr Briggs watched as the young woman slowly smiled at Jenny.

'Leave here? Honestly?'

'Honestly. I'll have to go back and give my notice, but I should be back in a month or two. Then I'll come and arrange for you to live with me in Clitheroe.' Marian began to cry.

'Don't cry Marian. It will be good. And George will be able to live a proper life, with good food and fresh air. I need to go now, but I will be back for you both. I'll see Matron now about the papers, whilst Mr Briggs is with me. He is one of the solicitors that I got the letter from. He will help me get you out of here, won't you Mr Briggs?' He nodded his assent.

Hargreaves came back into the room.

'Time up now. Please leave,' she said curtly.

'First I would like to see matron, if you please,' Mr Briggs demanded. Hargreaves quailed, as if she thought that he was going to make a complaint about her to matron. Hargreaves scurried away, a frightened look on her face.

Matron appeared shortly and Mr Briggs explained all the circumstances of the case. There was no problem. The papers would be in order one month from today, at Mr Briggs convenience. Still dazed, Marian left the room, and Jenny left with Mr Briggs. He took her back to the market where she had arranged to meet Nat.

Jenny said a polite goodbye to Mr Briggs, and then hurried to a pie stall. She had not eaten all day, and suddenly she was hungry. She sat on the pavement at the side of the market going over the day's events.

She still could not believe it, but someone had believed in her, so she would make sure that she didn't let that person down, whoever they were. She would work hard and make sure that her business was a success. Although she hadn't really liked Bruce, she would work hard with her, so that she could learn how to run the business.

Chapter 10

Nat looked cheerily at Jenny as he drew up with his cart.

'Well then lass, 'ave yer 'ad a good day, then?'

'Very good, Nat. And you look like you have had a good day too, Nat.' Had rather a few drinks as well, thought Jenny. But she trusted Nat, even with a few drinks inside him.

'Well let's be gettin' off 'ome, then. It looks like rain.' Jenny climbed on to the cart and sat down gratefully. Nat seemed in a mood for talking, but all Jenny wanted to do was to think about what had happened today.

It wasn't to be. Nat kept up a steady flow of conversation most of the way home. He liked having company, as it made his trips more interesting.

Jenny was glad to get back to Ormerod Hall. She went straight up to her room and took off her coat and hat before going back downstairs to the kitchen. The kitchen was quiet. Martha and Cook were dozing in front of the fire. Jenny put the kettle on to the fire and got the small teapot out, carefully measuring the scoop of tea into the pot, after warming it. As she poured the tea out, Cook woke up.

'Eh Jenny, lass, when did you get back?'

'Just this minute. I knew you would wake up when you heard the tea being brewed.'

'We'll have less of your cheek, young woman. Just pour me a cuppa and I'll say no more.' At this, Martha woke as well, expecting her cup of tea.

'Just a scivvy for you two, that's all I am,' Jenny teased, 'but not for much longer.' Jenny left the sentence in the air, willing one of them to ask her further, but they didn't.

'Did you hear me? Not for much longer.'

'Why, you got a new job or something. You look like the cat that got the cream,' said Cook.

'Er, yes, I suppose I have got a new job. In a shop.'

'A shop, are you sure that's a good idea?' said Cook. 'They will work you just as hard as here, and you may not get as much food as you do here. What's made you go for shop work? What if you don't like the owner? Oh, I'd think very hard Jenny. I didn't know that you were unhappy here. You should have said.'

'I'm not unhappy here. And I think I will like shop work. And I think I will like the owner, 'cos it's me,' Jenny burst out. There was a long silence in the kitchen, and then Martha laughed out loud.

'Eh, you got me going then, Jenny, what will you say next. Oh, you are a wag. A shop owner.'

'It's true, Martha, I wouldn't lie to you. That is why I had to go to Clitheroe. You know that I got a letter saying that I would learn something to my advantage? Well, I have inherited a shop and I haven't any idea from who, or why, so don't ask me.' There was another long silence.

'Well, I had better go and see Miller and give her my notice. Oh, I'll enjoy that. She has always looked down her nose at me. I'll see you both later.'

Jenny hurried up the stairs and knocked on Miller's door. There was no reply at first, so Jenny knocked again. At this second knock, an aggrieved voice ordered her to come in.

'Oh, it's you. I might have known. A body can't even have a moment's peace in this house, without somebody pestering her. Now, what is it, girl?'

'If you please, Mrs Miller, I would like to give notice.' Jenny was pleased to see that Miller was stunned into silence. Jenny too stayed silent, whilst her news sank in. eventually Miller spoke.

'Give notice? Why? What will you do? You don't know when you are well off, girl. You won't find as easy a position as this house is. And you won't receive a reference if you decide to leave. Where are you going to?'

'Clitheroe, Mrs Miller. To a shop.'

'What do you know about shop work? What has got into you, girl?'

'I'm going to work in a gown shop in Clitheroe, and nothing you say will make me change my mind.'

'Well, it is very inconvenient. You will have to work three months notice, so that I can find someone else. It is most inconvenient at this time of year. It will soon be Christmas. Yes, You will have to work three months notice to see us over the Christmas period.'

'But the last maid didn't give three months notice,' Jenny argued, her heart sinking when she remembered the promise that she had made to Marian.

'Never you mind the last maid. This is up to me. I shall recommend to her Ladyship that you serve three months notice. You may go.'

Heartbroken, Jenny slowly walked out of the room. What was she going to do? As soon as she could, she would write to Marian and warn her that it would be a little longer before she could rescue her from the workhouse.

As she went back down the stairs to the kitchen, Jenny remembered Mr Briggs. Surely he could help her sort out whether or not she needed to give three months notice or not. Considerably brightened by this, Jenny opened the kitchen door.

'Well, what did old Miller say about you inheriting a shop?'

'Oh Cook, she was awful. But I didn't tell her that I had inherited the shop. I just told her that I was going to work in Clitheroe. She didn't ask where or what I would be doing.'

'Serves her right. I wouldn't tell her if I was you.' At this point, Effie interrupted them and told Jenny that she had to go up and see her Ladyship immediately,

'Why, what does she want me for?' asked a bewildered Jenny.

'Dunno,' replied Effie, 'but you had better go. You know that she doesn't like being kept waiting.'

Jenny took off her pinny and hurried up the back stairs, then went through the door, into the main part of the house. She knocked gently on the door and was told to come in.

'You wanted to see me, your Ladyship?' asked Jenny curtseying as she entered the room.

'Mrs Miller tells me that you are leaving. May I ask why? You seemed so happy here. I have come to rely on you when Effie is on her days off. Has something happened to upset you?' Her Ladyship had always been uneasy since the episode with Marian.

'No one has upset me, your Ladyship. It is just that I have come into an unexpected inheritance and wish to leave to take up my inheritance.' Her Ladyship looked shocked at Jenny's news.

'Inheritance? What do you mean, Mitchell?'

'I've inherited a shop in Clitheroe. I've not been told who from. But I would like to go and start running it as soon as possible, your Ladyship. That is, as soon as you can possibly spare me.'

'Mitchell, what a surprise! I am pleased for you. What kind of shop is it?'

'A gown shop, your Ladyship.'

'Well, you should do well. You always have had good dress sense. Perhaps I could come and visit you sometime?'

'That would be lovely, your Ladyship,' Jenny replied politely, not looking her in the eye. They both knew that she wouldn't be visiting her. She was too frail to go out now, and was not long for this world. Just hanging on for the birth of her next grandchild. But both of them played along with the little story.

'Thank you your Ladyship for everything. I have been very happy here.'

'If you will stay until the end of the month, I think that will be satisfactory. I am sure one of the maids will have a little sister who needs a place. Yes, you may go at the end of the month.'

'Why, thank you your Ladyship. That is most gracious of you.' Jenny curtseyed and flew out of the room before her Ladyship could change her mind. Twenty-three days. That was all she had left to work here. She danced her way down to the kitchen and dragging Martha off the chair, swung her round the room.

'Only twenty-three days to work. Her Ladyship says that I can leave at the end of the month.'

'Jenny, put me down, you're making me feel giddy. That's better. You are so lucky. I wish someone would leave me a shop. Are you sure you haven't got an admirer?'

'When would I have a chance to get an admirer? Besides, if I had, you would already know about it. I tell you everything. Martha. I've just had a good idea. You could come and work for me later, when I get myself sorted out. Would you like that? I have to sort Marian out first, you understand that, don't you?'

'Eh, I don't know, Jenny. It's kind of you to ask, but I would miss my mam. And besides, our Effie is here as well. I couldn't leave her.'

'I think Effie will be leaving you before long,' Jenny teased mischievously, 'I've seen the way she and Ernest look at each other when he delivers the groceries.'

'She still says they are just friends.'

'Oh, they all say that, Martha. Well, anyway, think about the offer. If I can help you sometime, let me know.'

'I will. Oh Jenny, I'm so pleased for you. And Marian will be so pleased too. You deserve it. You have had such a hard life up 'til now.'

'Who hasn't? We all have hard lives, except them upstairs,' replied Jenny. They were interrupted by Miller coming into the room, and she did not look pleased.

'Mitchell, what have you been saying to her Ladyship?'

'Nothing,' quaked Jenny, the power of this woman still hanging over her.

'Nothing? Well how come she says you can leave at the end of the month, not in three months time as I said?'

'Well,' stammered Jenny, 'when I told her about the inheritance, she said . . .'

'What inheritance?' screamed Miller.

'Th . . the shop. The shop I inherited. That is where I am going to work,' stuttered Jenny.

'And whom did you 'inherit' this shop from?' roared Miller. Before Jenny could reply, Fothergill came storming into the room.

'Mrs Miller, what is going on in here? I can hear you up in the house. Whatever will his Lordship think?'

'This young chit has been behind my back to her Ladyship. Well good riddance to you, and all I can say is that I hope your shop fails to make good.' With that, Miller stormed out of the room. A long silence ensued. Nobody moved. Eventually Fothergill moved.

'Come along. This is time wasting. There is work to be done.' Slowly, everyone carried on what they had been doing before the outbursts.

'Eh, she's an evil bitch, that Miller. Can't even be glad for you,' stormed Cook after Fothergill had gone. 'Never mind lass, I'm sure your shop will do very well. She's just jealous.'

'Her ladyship said that she will come and visit me,' Jenny said mournfully.

'No,' said Cook incredulously, 'she never would.'

'No, I think we both knew that. But it was kind of her to say it. At least she wished me well. More than can be said for Miller.'

A commotion on the stairs heralded Effie rushing into the kitchen.

'Quick, get lots of hot water. Lady Hortense's waters have just gone, and her only seven months as well.' The whole kitchen was galvanised into action, as everybody ran round, getting in each other's way. As fast as one jug of hot water went upstairs, another one was being prepared. Young Willie was sent to get Doctor Phillips first, and then to go for the nurse who had been appointed for the birth months.

The whole house seemed a hive of industry, well into the night. At a little after four of the clock, the sad news came down to the kitchen that the baby had been born dead. It was a boy.

Cook sat rocking in the chair, crying.

'That poor girl. I bet she had it early 'cos of him. He never leaves her alone. Always going on at her, Annie says. This won't help her Ladyship either. She was hanging on for this one. Oh, what will become of us? It's a bad business.'

'Come on Cook, everyone will be wanting a cup of tea. Let's get the kettles back on the fire,' said Jenny. Martha jumped up, glad of having something to do.

The atmosphere in the house remained gloomy for the rest of the month, and Jenny was not sorry to be leaving it. But it had made her final days tinged with sadness.

As she left Ormerod Hall for the final time, hardly anyone gathered to say goodbye. With mixed feelings, Jenny left the home that had saved her from the workhouse and given her hope for the future.

But she looked forward to that future, determined that she would make use of the opportunity that she had been given and fulfil the trust that someone must have had in her.

Part Three

The Shop

Chapter 11

Jenny was dropped off by Nat in the same place where he had left
her less than one month earlier. As he helped her down
from the cart, Jenny thanked him for his help, promising
that any time he came to market, he could call at her shop
for a cup of tea and a bite to eat.
Nat visibly cheered, grateful of the promised refreshments. He
handed her down the two bags that she had brought with
her. Most of her stuff she had left with Martha. Waving
Nat off, she called into the offices of Mr Shoesmith and
announced her name to the clerk. She was taken instantly
upstairs.
'Miss Mitchell, how good to see you. Do sit down, whilst I get a
cup of tea for you.' Mr Shoesmith hurried out of the room, without
even looking her in the eye. Jenny thought this was odd, but
dismissed it. He shortly returned, bringing Mr Briggs with him.
'Now my dear, I am afraid that I have some news that will not
please you.' Jenny's heart sunk. What could it be? Had someone
taken her inheritance away from her? Was Marian unable to come?
Had something happened to George? Her mind raced.
'Pray tell me, what has happened?'
'It is about the shop,' replied Mr Shoesmith.
'What about it?' Jenny's heart was still pounding.
'Bruce has disappeared. Today. She was still there last evening and
said that she would have the books ready for Briggs to sign today
before the handing over of the business to you. This morning, the
shop was empty and young Sarah didn't know where Bruce was. We
must let Sarah know who you are. She is obviously very fearful.'
'Why do you think that Bruce has gone?' asked Jenny.
'I suspect that she has been dishonest and didn't want you to find
out. Her and that brother of hers. I don't think they ever believed that
the rightful owner would turn up so soon. It has been a worry to
Briggs for some months that the shop was failing to make any profit,
and increasingly so. He felt that he must have been missing
something when he checked the accounts, but he could never detect

any erroneous entries in the accounts book. I am sorry my dear, this makes things so much harder for you, especially since the terms of the will say that you must make a profit.' Jenny sat in silence, unable to take in what Mr Shoesmith was saying.

Eventually, Mr Briggs broke the silence. 'We will do everything in our power to help you get the business back in a more viable position.' This seemed to wake Jenny from her reverie.

'Yes, the business. I had better go there and get started. I will never make a profit if I sit here like a goose all day.' Jenny stood up, squared her shoulders, picked her bag up and walked towards the door. Mr Shoesmith and Mr Briggs both gazed proudly at her, admiring the determination to succeed that was evident within her.

As Jenny got to the door, they both jumped up and rushed towards her, vying to be the first one there to open the door for her. Jenny smiled to herself to see these two grown men falling all over her, a mere servant. No, she corrected herself. She was now a shop owner, not a servant, even though her shop was a failure.

'Briggs will take you up to the shop and show you the accounts, such as they are. Perhaps you will allow me to take you to the Swan Inn for luncheon. It has a respectable room at the back where ladies may dine privately.'

'I am sorry, luncheon will have to wait. I will be too busy today,' replied Jenny.

'Then if you will permit me, I will send up a light repast from Crabtree's bakery. The food that they supply is of the highest standard.'

'Thank you, that will be very kind of you,' replied Jenny again. Jenny and Mr Briggs went down the stairs and out into the street. As they got to the shop, Jenny took a deep breath and walked through the door. Sat in the corner by the counter was a small girl of about twelve, who looked emaciated.

The girl jumped to her feet and was visibly quaking when Jenny came near her. Jenny moved nearer to her and the girl flinched. Jenny recognised that. People only reacted like that when they were used to being beaten. She stepped back again, to keep a distance between them.

'Hello, I am Jenny. Are you Sarah?'

The little girl nodded.

'I am the new owner. Did Mrs Bruce tell you that I was coming today?'

Again the little girl nodded, more strongly this time.

'What did Mrs Bruce tell you about me?'

'That you'd beat me more than she did,' came a little voice.

'I won't beat you, and I won't let anyone else beat you either. Did Mrs Bruce beat you?'

'Yes Miss, is she coming back?'

'No, I don't think that she will be back.'

'That would not be advisable in the circumstances, Miss Mitchell. We will have the Constable on to her if she sets foot within a furlong of this town,' Mr Briggs cut in.

'I suspect that she won't be back. But never mind her. Sarah, can you show me round the shop?'

'Yes Miss, come this way.'

Briggs said that he would stay downstairs and look for the daily accounts book, so that he could show Jenny the system of book keeping.

Sarah set off into the back part of the shop. Here there were three fitting rooms, a store cupboard and an empty room. A further tiny room appeared to be a small kitchen where drinks were prepared for the visiting clients. Sarah then led Jenny up the stairs.

The first room was a large storeroom, covering most of the upstairs floor. There were many empty racks to hold clothing in readiness for the shop downstairs, but little evidence of any stock. The next room was a small sewing room, where all the repairs or alterations were carried out.

Finally, Sarah led Jenny into a tiny room, which simply had a small canvas bed and a chair in it.

'Who sleeps here?' asked Jenny.

'This is my room,' replied Sarah, 'and I pays out of my wages for it.' Jenny just nodded, unable to believe the sparseness of the room, or the fact that Sarah was being charged for it.

'Take me up to the next floor then, Sarah.' The two went up the stairs again. There were more storerooms on this floor with a further kitchen, larger than the one on the ground floor. Sarah passed the next door, but Jenny stopped her.

'What is this door?'

'I'm not allowed in this room,' replied Sarah.

'Well I am,' replied Jenny forcibly, and opened the door. It was a large sitting room, which was very comfortably furnished. Another door led into a large bedroom, with a toilet room through another door off the bedroom. Further down the corridor was another bedroom, rather smaller than the first one, but still quite well appointed. Young Sarah stared all about her, and it was obvious that she had never seen these rooms before.

'Must be where Mrs Bruce and her brother stayed. Coo, it aint half nice. Better than my room anyway,' sniffed Sarah.

'Did her brother live her as well?'

Sarah looked guilty, as if she had said the wrong thing, and didn't answer.

'It's all right to say. She's not coming back,' encouraged Jenny.

'Yes Miss. But I wasn't to say if anyone asked me. Are you sure that she's not coming back?' Jenny nodded.

Sarah smiled an enormous smile, which melted Jenny's heart. What sort of life had poor Sarah had living here with Mrs Bruce and her brother. She dared not imagine.

'You can stay here with me,' Jenny found herself saying, and then remembered Marian. Well, she would just have to make sure that she earned enough to keep all of them. As they passed the end of the passage, Jenny noticed a door that was boarded up. This then, was the top floor – the floor that she was forbidden to enter. Well, never mind, she had enough to be going on with, without worrying about what was up on the top floor.

'Go and put the kettle on. I think we all need a cup of tea, don't you Sarah?'

'Yes Miss. I'll go right now,'

'And Mr Briggs will want one as well.'

'Is 'e yer gentleman, Miss, begging yer pardon?'

Jenny laughed. 'No, Sarah, he is not. I have no 'gentleman'. And if I am to make a success of this shop I will have no time for any gentlemen either. It is going to be very hard at the beginning, and I will need all the help I can get. I am going to rely on you a great deal, as I have no knowledge of running a shop. Will you help me?'

Sarah visibly swelled. 'Yes, Miss, I'll 'elp yer. I'll go now an' put kettle on.' With that, Sarah hurried off to the kitchen. Jenny went back downstairs and found Briggs in the storeroom.

'I have had a quick look round Miss Mitchell, and there appears to be hardly any stock. I suspect that Bruce has taken it all with her. There is no sign of any books, either.'

'What will I do, then?'

'In some ways, it could be advantageous. You will have a new start and only sell gowns that you wish to. On the other hand, it will mean drawing on your savings to establish a stock.'

'Where will I get any stock at such short notice? Do you know of anywhere?'

Mr Briggs smiled. 'I'm afraid not, Miss Mitchell. It is not quite my line. Perhaps one of the other shops in the town would help you in this matter.'

Jenny sat down heavily in the chair, trying to work out what to do. She suddenly thought of Marian. 'Is there a material shop in the town?'

'I am sure there will be. There may be one on the market, too.'

'I need to get Marian out of the workhouse. Today.'

'With all due respects Miss Mitchell, would it not be better to leave her be for another day or two until you are more settled?'

'No, that is the point. Marian is an excellent seamstress. She will be able to make some dresses quickly, and then at least I will have something to sell.'

'I hope that you do not think that I am being too bold, but as I understand things, this shop catered mainly for the gentry. Are they going to want to buy some home-made garment?'

'They won't look home-made when Marian makes them. She really does have a gift. Besides they will be unique. That would surely be a strong selling point?'

'Hmm, you could be right. It's worth a try. Better to have something on the shelves rather than nothing. Shall I go to the workhouse and get Marian out for you?'

'No Thank you. I will take great delight in doing that myself. But first you must give me a lesson in book keeping.' Jenny and Mr Briggs sat down by the table and he explained the rudiments of incomings and outgoings. Mr Briggs then left and Jenny went to find Sarah. She was sat, a little disconcertedly, on the tall stool by the side of the glass fronted counter, which housed the gloves and scarves. Sarah jumped to attention when Jenny entered the shop.

'Don't look so scared, Sarah. I am not going to eat you. Talking of eating, have you had anything to eat today, apart from the food from Crabtree's?'

'No Miss.'

'Well, I think that we will shut the shop and go out for something to eat. There must be somewhere in the town.'

'Yes, Miss, there is a shop on t' market that sells tripe and black peas.' Jenny pulled a face. She had got used to better fare at Ormerod Hall.

'Well, let's go and see what there is. Come on Sarah.' They both got their cloaks out and wrapping them round themselves, set out into town. On the way down King Street, Jenny noticed a printers and sign writers shop. She called inside. 'Do you have a piece of large card?'

'Certainly Miss. How big were you wanting?' the young assistant replied courteously.

'Large enough to put a sign in my shop window,' replied Jenny. At this, an older gentleman came into the shop from the back room.

'Good afternoon, madam. May I help you? Which shop would yours be? I don't think that I have had the pleasure of your acquaintance. Canning's the name. Hector Canning at your service.'

Jenny bowed her head slightly, just as she had seen Lady Ormerod do. 'Mitchell. Miss Jenny Mitchell. And this is my young assistant, Sarah. I have just taken over the gown shop on Castle Street. I have decided to close the shop for a few days until I reorganise the stock and would like to place a notice to this effect in the window. What size would you advise?'

'I could make you a notice here, Miss Mitchell. Just give me your requirements and I will get someone on to it straight away.'

Jenny panicked. How much would he charge? Could she afford it? He must have seen some of her panic, as he said 'Of course, it will be a free will gesture to you, in honour of you being the new owner.' Jenny visibly relaxed and accepted gratefully. She explained what she would like on the sign and prepared to leave, thanking Mr Canning most profusely. Sarah and Jenny went on to the market and found a pie and pea stall. Eating ravenously, they bought some pies for later, then returned to the shop.

They had not been back at the shop very long when a young man arrived with the sign. He offered to put the sign in the window for her and Jenny accepted, sending Sarah off to make the man a cup of tea to help him in his work. The sign duly fixed, Jenny told Sarah to make an inventory. Sarah looked blank until Jenny explained what she meant.

'Whilst you are doing that, I am going to the workhouse to get my friend Marian and her son George. Will you be alright whilst I am

gone?' Sarah's face dropped, and she nodded glumly at Jenny.
'What's the matter now?'
'Will I have to go when your friend comes?'
'Go where?'
'Home. Have I lost my position?'
'Certainly not. I will need both you and Marian to help me in the shop.' Visibly cheered, Sarah thanked Jenny and offered to make them all some tea for when they got back.

Chapter 12

Jenny set off to the workhouse in a hansom cab and knocked on the front door, asking the cab driver to wait. Oh, how she enjoyed coming to the front door. After years of only being allowed through the inmate's back door, it felt good. She was ushered in to Matron's office and offered a cup of tea. She refused. She didn't want to waste any time on pleasantries, but wanted to get Marian and George out of here as quick as possible.

Matron was obviously ill at ease during the procedures, but all the paper work was ready, so Mr Briggs must have made an impression on her. Jenny signed the requisite papers and then asked for Marian. After a short while, Susy arrived carrying a small bag, with Marian and George following her.

'Susy! How nice to see you. How are you? How is your mum?' Susy looked uncomfortably at Matron and replied 'I'm well, Thank you.' Jenny would have talked further with her, but Matron ordered her back to her work. Feeling a little uneasy, Jenny got hold of George and hurried out to the hansom cab, bundling Marian inside.

'Poor Susy. She didn't look very happy.'

'No, her mum is worse. She hardly knows anyone now.'

'I wish that I could help her, but I am not in as comfortable a position as I thought I was. I will have to be careful for some time, but eventually, I will try and get Susy out of there, too.'

'Do you want to leave me here, then?' asked a woe begotten Marian quietly.

'No Marian, I do not. You are an important part of my plans. I have virtually no stock left. The manager of the shop took everything. I have closed the shop and want you to make some clothes to get me started. We will go to the market now before it closes and you can buy some material and such like.'

'What about George? I won't be able to do much work and still look after George.'

'Don't worry about George. He is used to being cared for by others. I have a young girl helping in the shop. She can look after George whilst you sew.'

The two friends dropped George off at the shop, introduced him to Sarah and then set off to the market. There they bought lots of gaily-coloured material in silks and satins, but also some more serviceable material in darker and more practical colours. They also bought trimmings, lace and buttons to decorate the garments. Jenny quailed at the amount that she had spent, but knew that she had to get some stock before she could open the shop again.

Whilst walking home, Marian became rather quiet.

'What's the matter, Marian? You've gone very quiet.'

'I was just thinking. It's going to be very hard making all these gowns by hand. I was wishing I had Lady Ormerod's sewing machine. It was such a help, and if I had one, it would make a big difference to how many gowns that I could get ready before the opening.' Jenny thought for a while.

'Yes, what you are saying makes sense. I will ask around and see if I can get you one. Happy now?'

'Oh yes, very happy. I'll pay you back when I can, then I don't have to be beholden to you.'

'You will do no such thing. It will belong to the shop; therefore there is no need for you to pay for it. Come on, let's get back home.'

Home. What a lovely word, reflected Jenny. For the first time in her life, she actually had a home and even owned it herself. Smiling to herself, Jenny hurried Marian up the street back to the shop.

On their return, they found Sarah and George laughing uproariously in the back room, rolling about on the floor. Sarah jumped up quickly when Jenny entered and apologised to her.

'Don't apologise, Sarah. I have never seen George so happy in his short little life. That gives me an idea. Would you like to look after George regularly whilst his mother is sewing for me?'

'Oh yes, Miss. I'd love that. I miss the bairns at 'ome, but Mrs Bruce wouldn't let me go 'ome to see 'em. Said they were common.' Saddened by this response, Jenny waited a while before she spoke.

'Do you live in Clitheroe, Sarah?'

'No, in a village called Waddington a few miles away. Me dad's a farm labourer, but there were that many of us, I 'ad ter gerra job. I was ever so grateful ter get this job.'

'Do you not go home, then?'

'No Miss.'

'What about Sunday when the shop is closed?'

'No Miss.'

'Do stop calling me Miss. My name is Jenny. Why did you not get to go home on Sundays.'

'She med me clean t' shop on Sundays, Miss. Er, I mean Jenny, Miss.'

'Well you can go home every Sunday from now on, Sarah. Starting with this Sunday,' replied Jenny laughing. George started to grizzle, now that he wasn't the centre of Sarah's attention. She stooped quickly to pick him up and hugged him to her. George was instantly all smiles again.

'You seem to have a way with him, Sarah. I think you'll do well. You can look after him in that small back room, so that it will be convenient for me if I need to ask you anything about the business. And now we must make a start on some gowns. Can you sew at all, Sarah?'

'Yes, but Mrs Bruce said I were no good at it. But I did try.'

'Well you can help Marian and me. Marian will do all the intricate work, and you and I can do the plain sewing. Come on Marian, I'll show you to your room, and then you can find the sewing room. I think that you'll spend most of the next few days in there,' Jenny laughed.

'That sounds like heaven to me. I've not been able to do any decent sewing since I went back to the workhouse. I've really missed it.'

'You'll get plenty of sewing now, Marian, believe me. Come and look at the stock that's left.' The two friends set off into the stock room and discussed the type of gowns that Marian should concentrate on to begin with.

Sarah announced that tea was ready and they all went upstairs to the small dining room. Whilst they were sat drinking their tea after the meal, Marian asked what the shop was called.

'Do you know, I haven't even thought of a name. What shall I call it? If we are going to have a new beginning, we would be better with a new name. What about Miss Jenny's gown shop?'

'Mmm, no, I don't think that sounds right. It needs to be something more stylish, more modish,' replied Marian. They were all silent for a moment.

'What about Clitheroe Gowns?' suggested Sarah.

'No, I don't think that is right, either,' replied Jenny. Marian nodded her agreement. A longer silence reigned.

'Mitchell's Modes. What about that?' said Marian suddenly. Jenny sat for a while, trying the words on her tongue.

'Yes, I like that. Mitchell's Modes – bespoke gownmakers. We could have a new sign, and perhaps send some letters out to local people about the re-opening. I could ask Mr Canning about those in the morning. I will make a list of all the things that I need. But I think that it's time for you to get George into bed. He looks very tired. You'll have to make do and mend tonight. We can sort out the bedrooms tomorrow.'

Sarah and Marian went upstairs with George, leaving Jenny downstairs making plans for the next day. Although she had spent a lot of money on material and trimmings, she knew that she could make quite a bit of profit from having her own dressmaker. Time would tell.

But it had all been worth it when she had seen Marian and George going up to bed, a radiant smile on Marian's face for the first time in many months.

The following morning, Marian started sewing, whilst Sarah looked after George. Jenny decided that she would have the main downstairs room of the shop decorated whilst the shop was shut.

'What colour do you think you'll have?' asked Marian.

'Um, not sure,' replied Jenny. 'Any ideas?'

'Not really, but a pale colour, so that the gowns and other things will stand out.'

'Yes, that sounds a sensible idea. What about a neutral cream?'

Marian thought for a moment. 'Yes, but it may be too pale. What about a second colour, so that there's some contrast?'

'What about cream and light brown?'

'Yes, that would be nice. It's the shades in vogue this year. Look at all the choice of material available in those colours on the market. We could wear brown and cream clothes as well. And we could have brown and cream curtains, and cover the chairs in brown and cream, and we . . .

'Just a minute, young woman,' cut in Jenny, 'you're very good at spending my money. I think that you're getting carried away.' The conversation was interrupted by the door opening. Jenny was about to say that they were not open for business, when she saw that it was Mr Briggs.

'Good morning, ladies. Just called in to see how you are fairing?'

'And very welcome you are too, Mr Briggs,' said Jenny, an enormous smile on her face. 'Marian was just spending all my money. Her and her big ideas,' Jenny laughed, whilst Marian blushed.

'Come Miss Marian, what were your big ideas?'

'Well, I thought that it would be good to have everything matching, and paint this room, if we are going to be shut for a few days.'

'Sound like good business sense to me,' replied Mr Briggs, 'but I wouldn't take too long over it all. It is nearly the Christmas season and it would be advantageous to have your shop open by then. If people call in for a small purchase for a yuletide gift, they may like what they see, and return. Or even better, inform their friends. That is how you will rebuild your custom. Now what did you have in mind, Miss Marian?'

'Er, well, I thought that we could have everything in the same colours, say brown and cream.' Marian continued to describe how everything would look if all the colours were matching.

'This sounds excellent, Miss Marian. Miss Mitchell, I would strongly recommend that you follow your friend's advice. But I would urge you to make haste.'

'Could you recommend someone who could paint the shop?' asked Jenny.

'Yes, I'll send our man Aggett over to you. He is very thorough, and will work quickly. He even worked through the night for one of our customers.'

'Oh, that would be excellent. We could be working on the stock during the day, whilst he painted at night. Please ask him to come here as soon as he can.'

'I will send out a messenger right away. Well, I am glad to see that you are getting ideas. I will go now, and let you carry on. Good morning.'

All three young women said goodbye, and sat silently for a few moments. Suddenly Sarah spoke.

'Please Miss, er I mean Jenny, it's second day of December today.'

'Yes,' replied Jenny, wondering what the significance of the date was.

'Well, a traveller comes at beginning of every month with stuff, er, I think it was called stock, or someat like that.'

Jenny and Marian grinned at each other.

'That is excellent news, Marian. Now you go and check up on George, and why not make us a cup of tea. All this thinking is thirsty work, isn't it?' Sarah grinned, and went out of the room.

'Marian, if we could buy in some stock, you could adapt some of it, so that it all looks like original items.'

'Yes, and we could get some small items suitable for gifts, being the season of the year.'

Jenny got out her notepad, and she and Marian spent quite a while making lists of suitable items that they would need, whilst Sarah took George out for a walk.

Shortly after lunch, two visitors arrived together. A small stocky man and a tall slim one. They both removed their hats. One asked for Miss Mitchell, the other for Mrs Bruce.

'I am Miss Mitchell. How can I help?' Jenny said in her most imperious manner.

They both started introducing themselves together. Jenny laughed.

'One at a time, I think.'

'I am Aggett, Miss,' the shorter, older man said. Mr Briggs asked me to call at your convenience. As I see you have another visitor, perhaps you would like me to return at a later time or date?'

'Certainly not, I need you most urgently Mr Aggett. May I ask who you are, Sir?' said Jenny turning to the taller younger man.

'I am Williams. A traveller in ladies goods. I make a call here each month, to see Mrs Bruce.'

'Mrs Bruce has left; I am the new proprietor of the shop. My name is Miss Mitchell. Jenny Mitchell. If you would be so kind as to wait whilst I talk to Mr Aggett, I will look at your stock. Whilst you are waiting, I will get my dressmaker to look at your wares. Marian . .'

Jenny looked at Marian, who jumped suddenly and turned to look at Jenny. Marian had been staring at Mr Williams, and blushed when Jenny spoke to her.

Jenny tried not to smile. It was the first time that she had ever seen Marian look properly at a man. Perhaps there could be healing here for Marian, through this man. She would have to wait and see.

Mr Williams opened his suitcases and started to show his stock to Marian, whilst Jenny outlined the ideas that they had for the shop. In the end, Jenny decided to have the outside painted as well, in the same colours.

After Aggett had left, Jenny turned to look at what Williams had to offer. Marian had made a provisional list of several items. Jenny increased the order, adding lots of gloves, scarves, bonnets, lace collars, brooches and other fripperies, so dear to the heart of women. Jenny started to look at the ready-made gowns; she found a plain brown serviceable gown, with long sleeves and a high neck.

'Do you have this gown in several sizes?' asked Jenny.

'Yes, Miss Mitchell, and also in other colours.'

'I would be interested in purchasing six of these gowns, but must have them immediately. Could you deliver them before the end of the week?'

'Certainly.'

'And I'll have a selection of these gowns in black and grey, in all sizes.'

'Certainly Miss Mitchell. Thank you for your order, Miss Mitchell. It is gratifying that you have increased the order quite substantially. There is just the matter of the outstanding payment, which is due. Mrs Bruce always paid on my monthly visit, but as I am sure that she informed you, she did not pay for the last two months. Here is your account brought up to date,' said Mr Williams as he handed over a piece of paper.

Jenny quailed as she opened the bill. It was for £66 17 shillings and 6 pence. How much stock had this woman had, and where was it now, Jenny wondered? Probably starting Bruce up in another shop somewhere.

Jenny fumed inwardly at the evil this woman had done to her. Pulling herself together, Jenny quietly told Mr Williams that she had no available cash that day, but when he brought the goods, he would be paid in full. With that, Mr Williams left the shop, leaving a despondent pair behind him.

'Well, should we have cancelled the order, do you think, Jenny?' said Marian.

'Certainly not. How would we be able to open the shop if we have no stock, or nothing to wear? We will just have to be very careful at first, until we can start getting some money back. Come on; let's have a cup of tea. I'm sure that it will all turn out alright.'

Whilst they were talking, Sarah suddenly interrupted. 'I saw some brown and cream chairs in the furniture shop down King Street when I was out with George. They would look lovely in here, after the painting is done. It said special offer,' Sarah enthused.

'I'm not sure that we can afford anything else just now, Sarah, but thanks anyway,' replied Jenny. 'I'll have a look at them later when I'm in town. It's time that we all started work again, if we're ever going to get this shop open.' The girls got to their feet and started sorting out the existing stock, George playing with the tassels of the dark green chenille curtains by the back of the shop.

Chapter 13

Early next morning, Jenny went back to Mr Canning's shop. On arriving at the shop, Jenny asked to speak to Mr Canning. He came instantly and asked Jenny to come through to his office. A lady was in the office, filing some papers, whom Mr Canning introduced as his wife. She was despatched to make a drink for them all.

'How can I be of service, Miss Mitchell?'

'I am wondering if you could give me an estimate for some work that I would like doing.'

'Certainly, what had you in mind?'

'I would like a new sign with the name of my shop on. Also, I would like some small leaflets saying when I will be reopening the shop. And could you suggest where I could purchase some bags and hatboxes to wrap my goods in when they have been purchased. I would like each item given a separate price.'

'I can do all those things for you Miss Mitchell. I can also make the bags and hatboxes to your requirements.'

At this point, Mrs Canning came in with a tray of tea. She poured them each a cup of tea, carefully passing the delicate china cup and saucer to Jenny. Jenny thanked her, openly admiring the china. Mrs Canning looked visibly pleased and murmured her thanks. She then sat back down at the desk to resume her filing.

'Is there a special reason why you would like the items priced separately?'

Jenny blushed and stammered over her answer. 'Well, er, I am, er not sure. . . .

'If it is a question of money, do not hesitate to place an order with me. I send my bills out at least a month after the work is done. Isn't that correct, Mrs Canning?'

'Yes, dear, there would be no pressure from us. We understand how businesses need to get started.'

Jenny smiled, and thanked them. It didn't make good business sense to leave bills for a long time, but if this was how they would help her, then she was very grateful.

'Thank you Mr Canning, Mrs Canning. That was a concern of mine. Unfortunately there is hardly any stock left in the shop and I have to make a large inroad into my money to replenish the stock. I would be grateful if you didn't tell anyone else about this problem. I don't want my business being discussed around the town.'

'Certainly not. It is nobody's business except yours,' replied Mr Canning, whilst Mrs Canning nodded. 'In fact, I was going to tell Mrs Canning to go and order a new gown for herself as a Christmas gift. Perhaps we could come to some arrangement that my bill is paid in gowns?' Mr Canning laughed jovially as he said this.

'That would be very acceptable. If Mrs Canning would call in as soon as we are open, we can discuss her requirements,' replied Jenny, beaming at Mrs Canning.

'Now, let us talk about your requirements. What you would like, not what you think you can afford!'

Jenny outlined the idea that everything was to be in cream and brown, so that there was a theme to all the refurbishment, along with the packages that the ladies or their servants carried away.

Mrs Canning complimented her on her ideas, saying that it would bring the shop back to the standard it used to be before Mrs Bruce became the manageress. Jenny thought about that, but decided that she would ask Mrs Canning about the previous owner at a later stage. Her curiosity would have to wait.

After the order was placed, Jenny went back up King Street and couldn't help but notice the brown and cream chairs that Sarah had mentioned.

They were perfect. Sarah was right. They had curved tops with Queen Anne legs and were made in brown and cream brocade. They looked very elegant and very expensive. Jenny went cautiously into the shop. An elderly gentleman came forward, gently asking if he could help her.

'I am interested in those chairs in the window. The brown and cream ones.'

'Ah, it is not just chairs. They form part of a suite. If you would care to come to the other side of the shop, Miss . . .er . . Miss?'

'Mitchell. Miss Mitchell. I am the new owner of the gown shop on Castle Street, and wish to purchase some chairs. These are exactly the colour, which I would require, but I had only thought about chairs.' Jenny was following the man through the shop whilst they were talking.

She stopped suddenly. There, at the back of the shop, were two long low settees to match the chairs. They were perfect. Jenny could see them placed around the large room in her shop. For the first time in her life, she desperately wanted something. She knew that if she was to make a success of this shop, then the shop had to look right. She cleared her throat nervously.

'And how much would they cost for the whole set?'

Jenny paled when the man named his price, but cautiously said that she would think about it.

'Of course,' the man continued, 'there would be the usual discount because you are a fellow tradesman, or should I say, tradeswoman. 20% overall, Miss. And I would expect the same off any goods that I purchased at your establishment.'

'Gladly, Sir, I am sure that that can be arranged. Yes, I'll have the suite. Please could you await delivery until the refurbishing is completed?'

This is good, thought Jenny. I dress all the local wives and get cheap goods or services for my shop. She wondered if this was how normal trade relationships were conducted, or were they just a friendly group of people in Clitheroe? She had certainly met with kindness in Clitheroe up until now. Well, since she left the workhouse, that is, she reminded herself grimly.

Jenny walked back to her shop, extremely pleased with the morning's plans. As she got back to the shop, she stood on the other side of the street, and looked at the shop for a long time. She imagined it with the brown and cream paint and the new sign. The double fronted aspect made it the widest shop in the street. The two shops on either side were as tall as Jenny's, but much narrower, being only single fronted.

The shop to her left was a bookshop, and she had yet to meet the owner. Its windows were dark and the piles of books looked cluttered and untidy.

To her right, there was a food store, which supplied everything that could possibly be needed in a well-stocked kitchen. On the second floor, there was a small tearoom, where ladies met to gossip and keep up to date with local issues. Jenny decided that once the shop was established, she would go in there on a regular basis, to try and meet some of the townsfolk. But for now she was far too busy!

The next week was the busiest of Jenny and Marian's lives. By day, the girls cut out, sewed, trimmed and generally built up their stock, with the addition of the goods brought by Mr Williams.

Mr Aggett had transformed the shop during the nights, whilst the girls and George slept. As he finished the decorating, the furniture was delivered.

Sarah had polished all of the display cases until they shone like burnished bronze, taking advantage of the times that George was asleep, or having some time with his mother.

She had arranged all of the small items in these drawers, making a neat and attractive display. Leather gloves to the right, and cotton gloves to the left. Evening gloves in the middle. Scarves, scarf rings, dainty handkerchiefs, small handbags, delicate lacy shawls, warmer practical shawls, hoods, warm hats, all neatly arranged.

In a small box on the top of the counter, was a small display of costume jewellery to complement the outfits. A large container held parasols of every different hue, all of which matched the colours and shades of the gloves exactly.

Mr Canning arranged for a young boy to go out delivering leaflets to all of the big houses in the town and surrounding areas. The leaflet advertised the grand reopening of the shop and offered all who came on the opening day, a cup of tea or wine with biscuits.

At last, the shop was ready. Jenny couldn't believe the transformation that had been achieved in such a short time. Many garments were already made, so that they would have something to show the ladies when they opened, but most of their work would be by personal order.

A few days before the shop opened, Mrs Canning came in to be measured for her Christmas gown. Marian looked at her lovely auburn hair similar to her own, and cautiously suggested the fashionable shades of brown and cream, but Mrs Canning would have none of it.

'I've worn those shades so much, I want to be a little more daring this year. The Clitheroe annual ball is quite the fashion event of the year. What is worn is talked about by the ladies for months to come.'

Marian stood with her head on one side for a while.

'Emerald. That's the answer. Emerald satin, with just a small bustle at the back, and puffy sleeves trimmed with black lace. It would so compliment your colouring. What do you think, Mrs Canning?'

'That sounds delightful. Are you sure that I would suit emerald with my colouring?'

'Oh yes, I'll just get you a sample of the material.' Marian disappeared upstairs and soon came down with a bolt of shimmering, rich, emerald green satin. She held it against Mrs Canning, and led her to the mirror.

Mrs Canning gasped.

'Yes, I see what you mean. The colour does become me. How clever of you. I can't wait to see the finished gown.'

'And I can make you a small headdress to match if you like. A little cap of satin, trimmed with black lace, which will fall below your hairline. I'll start on it right away.' Marian hurried off to her sewing room, taking the bolt of material with her.

After the fitting was complete. Jenny talked to Mrs Canning about how she had no idea how to price the garments. Mrs Canning advised her to treble the cost of each item, so that she made a profit and was able to pay all her overheads and wages.

Jenny was amazed at this formula, but priced her goods accordingly. She was worried at the prices of some items, but not as worried as she was by the huge hole that had been made in her £1000 to refurbish the shop. She would have to charge such prices to give herself enough money to keep replenishing her stock.

The last thing that Marian did was to dress the dummies to put in the window. After seeing the cluttered state of the bookshop window next door, Jenny had decided that the windows would be very sparse, with only one dummy in each of the two windows.

On looking at the windows, she decided that this had been a good idea, as they looked uncluttered and elegant. Jenny sent everyone to bed early on the night before the reopening.

She stood quietly on her own, admiring the shop, sitting on the furniture. Touching the brown velvet curtains with brown and cream velvet swags and tails. Checking the neatness of the drawers, even though she knew that Sarah had left them in immaculate order.

Even the mirrors were in brown and cream. The brown and cream bags and hatboxes were ready and waiting to receive the purchases. The name 'Mitchell's Modes' spelt out neatly on the sides.

Jenny took a deep intake of breath and let it out very slowly. This was it then. She had less than three years to make this venture work. She turned off the gaslights, picked up her candle and went slowly up to bed.

Just as she was about to get into bed; she noticed her new work gown hung up on the clothes chest. A large cream collar made of lace had been added. It made the very plain work gown rather stylish. She had certainly not asked Marian to trim the gowns, so it must have been her own idea. She went across to Marian's bedroom, knocking gently on the door, so as not to wake George. Marian called to her to come in.

'Marian, the trimming on my gown is lovely. Have you trimmed yours and Sarah's gowns as well?'

'Yes, see, mine is there, over by the wash bowl.'

Jenny looked. Marian's gown had a small discreet collar in plain cream material.

'Why, your collar is far plainer than mine. Why is that?'

'Because it is your shop. You are the proprietor. You have to look different.'

'So what is Sarah's gown like?'

'The same as mine, but Sarah's gown has sleeves that can be buttoned up for when she is with George, or making meals.'

'Thank you Marian,' said Jenny in a small voice. 'I am so fortunate to have you as a friend. You are so thoughtful.'

'It is I who is fortunate. You have made my life so much happier. I can never thank you enough. Ever. Even if I work for you for the rest of my life for nothing.' Jenny felt a lump in her throat, and swallowed quickly, hoping that she would not break down in tears. She smiled tightly, wished Marian good night and hurried back to her own bedroom.

Chapter 14

It was still dark when Jenny, Sarah and Marian came downstairs the following morning, resplendent in their brown and cream gowns. For the time being, they left George in bed, so that they could get on with preparing the shop for its first customers. They had not long to wait. A plump bustling middle-aged lady stalked into the shop just after they had opened.

'Carter, Miss Carter's the name. I have the shop next door,' she shouted. 'What is all this about offering drinks and biscuits to your new customers? I am trying to run a tearoom, and you open up in direct competition to me. Did you not think to ask if I minded? Why, you are no more than a slip of a girl. The cheek of it all.'

Jenny stood in silence for a few seconds, before recovering her thoughts.

'I'm sorry, I had no intention of spoiling your trade, it was just a special offer, Miss Carter, in celebration of the reopening of the shop. Believe me, I had no wish to offend.'

Slightly calmer, Miss Carter replied, 'Well, that's all right then. As long as you know where you stand and where I stand.'

'Certainly, Miss Carter. I thought perhaps that when ladies come to my shop, they might come next door to you to have refreshments afterwards and the opposite way round as well. When they come to you for refreshments, their curiosity would make them come into my shop and look at the new gowns.' Miss Carter seemed to visibly warm to the idea and could see that the advantages might be mutually convenient. The business side of her call over, Miss Carter started to look around the shop.

'Well, I must say young lady, you have certainly improved the look of the shop, although you don't seem to have many gowns on show.'

'That is the whole idea, Miss Carter. And by the way, my name is Mitchell. Miss Jenny Mitchell. We aim to make gowns specially suited to each customers requirements, as well as having a small supply of gowns available.'

'Well Miss Jenny Mitchell, I wish you well. May I look at that pale blue parasol over there?'

'Certainly. Here it is. I will let you open it, so that you can see that it is of the finest quality.' Miss Carter started handling the parasol.

'And we also have some delicate little gloves in exactly the same shade. Don't they look just perfect together?'

'Yes, you are right. They do go well together. I really haven't had time to get my sister anything for Christmas. These would be perfect, as she has bought a dark blue gown, which is trimmed in pale blue for the Christmas ball. How much would they cost together?'

Jenny remembered the lesson that she had learnt from Mr Canning. 'The prices are on the ticket, but of course, there would be 20% discount, because you also have a local business.'

'Why, that is very kind of you. I will take the gloves and parasol. But I had better get back to my own shop. Could you send the purchases round later, please?'

'Certainly. I will bring them round personally this evening. And thank you for coming in Miss Carter. I hope that we will be friends. I am new to the running of a shop and would be grateful for any advice that you can give me.'

'My family have run the shop for many years, so I can help you. After poor papa passed away, my sister and I had to look to the running of the shop, or we would have ended up in the workhouse. That threat alone was enough to make us work hard to succeed.'

Jenny shivered. The power of the workhouse still loomed over her. Until she was making profit, this venture was a great risk.

'What ever is the matter, my dear, you have gone visibly pale. Did I say something wrong?'

'No, no,' stuttered Jenny. 'It is just that I was in the workhouse for many years of my childhood. It was not a nice place.'

'I do apologise. That was thoughtless of me. Now I really must go.' Jenny could tell by the look on Miss Carter's face that she had reassessed Jenny and was wondering how she had come to own a shop if she had lived in a workhouse. But good breeding had taken over and she had merely left the shop. Jenny knew that Miss Carter would be curious until she heard the full story. Well, as much of the story as Jenny herself knew.

Jenny sat down in the chair, a little overcome at the way things had turned out.

For the next two hours, nobody came into the shop. Jenny was despairing. What would happen if the shop were a failure? The words about the workhouse were all too close for comfort. Sarah made them a sandwich for lunch, and they laughed at little George's antics, as he tried to feed himself with some of Sarah's sandwich.

'Don't expect the gentry to come shopping so early in the day. They don't get up 'til eleven of the clock,' teased Sarah.

'That's true,' laughed Jenny. 'They're not known for early rising. Unless it's for a ride on horseback or hunting.' At that point, the little bell tinkled on the shop door.

'I'll go,' said Jenny, as she jumped up. She went into the shop and saw a lady looking at the gloves. 'Good morning, madam,' said Jenny, 'may I help you, or would you wish to browse unattended?'

'I will browse, thank you,' was the reply from a very cultured voice.

'May I get you some refreshments whilst you browse?'

'Yes, thank you.'

'Some wine, or a cup of tea?'

'Oh tea please, it is a little too early for wine', she laughed. Jenny left the lady browsing and asked Sarah to prepare her a tray of tea. Carrying the tray through to the lady, Jenny placed it on a small table and stood over on the other side of the shop. Unobtrusive, but ready to help the lady if she needed it.

Jenny watched the lady approvingly assess the tray, looking at the china cups, the small matching teapot and sugar bowl, the delicate tray cloth. She was glad that she had bought good quality articles for her customers; it was obviously making an impression.

'Those cream gloves, may I look closer at them?'

'Of course, I'll just get them out for you.' Jenny brought them over to the lady and showed her the delicate pearl buttons that went from wrist to elbow on the satin gloves. As she approached the lady, Marian came into the shop and waited at the back of the display cabinet.

'Lovely. I'll have four pairs.' Jenny couldn't help but look surprised at an order for four pairs. 'Four daughters, two sets of twins,' drawled the lady. 'They cost a small fortune to dress. And now that they are all out, they only like to be seen in white or cream. I can't buy for one without the other, so four pairs it will be. They are all wearing cream dresses for the Clitheroe ball, so these will be perfect.'

'Have you seen these small bags? They are made of the same satin and have a pearl button trim as well? They would be perfect to place their handkerchiefs and other little items in,' said Jenny.

'Yes, you are right. Perfect. I will have four of those as well. And a white bag and gloves as well. I am wearing a dove grey gown and I always think that white and dove grey compliment each other'. Jenny was agreeing with her, when Marian cut in.

'If you will excuse me Madam, have you thought about wearing pale pink with dove grey?'

The lady turned round sharply, looked at Marian and then said to Jenny, 'Who is this?'

'This is Miss Marian, my dressmaker.' Jenny had frozen, worried that perhaps Marian had gone too far with her opinions.

'Why did you suggest pink, Miss?'

'Well, er, er, Madam, grey and white is so obvious, pink is er, different. And the pink would compliment your skin colour. May I show you?' The lady nodded. Marian disappeared into the back of the shop, and came back with a bolt of grey cloth. She wrapped this round the lady's shoulders, and then placed the pink gloves and bag along with a pink shawl on her shoulders. Next she led the lady towards the mirror. 'Can you see what I mean?' asked a worried Marian.

The lady preened in front of the mirror. 'Yes, I do. I do see what you mean. You have a way with colours, young lady. Thank you, I'll take the pink gloves and bag. And I will take the pink shawl as well. Please send them round.'

Jenny blanched. Send them round? How was she going to do that? She had no form of transport. But she recovered quickly. 'Certainly Madam, if I could just have your name and address?'

'Lady Jolley, Holme Manor, Waddington. Thank you, good day.' With that she swept out of the shop, leaving Jenny and Marian staring after her.

Jenny was the first to recover. 'Well, our first Lady! And what an order. Four pairs of gloves and bags, and then the pink set. And four daughters. I hope that she comes back for more!' chuckled Jenny. 'I thought that you had gone too far Marian, but she accepted your advice. I think that perhaps I should have you in the shop all day, giving advice like that.'

'No, I would never get the sewing done if I was in here all day,' replied Marian.

'Marian, how am I going to get them delivered? We have no transport.'

'When Sarah takes George out for a walk, she can ask one of the carriers to deliver them for us.'

'Good idea, I will ask her now. She will probably know where this Holme Manor is, coming from Waddington herself. Oh, that's an idea, she could go with the carrier, and visit her parents. I'm sure she would like that.'

'Yes, I'm sure that she would, but how will we look after George between us and the shop?'

'Don't worry, we'll manage. I'll go and ask her now.'

Whilst Jenny was out of the shop, Marian wrote the last purchases into the ledger for Jenny, and then tidied up the gloves section of the display cabinet. At this rate, they would be running out of gloves before Christmas, she mused.

As Jenny returned with Sarah, Marian suggested that they might run out of gloves before Christmas, and the next visit of the wholesaler.

'Oh yes, are you suggesting that I should contact Mr Williams then, Marian?' Jenny asked with a twinkle in her eye.

Marian blushed. 'No, I was just meaning . . .'

'It's all right Marian, I'm only teasing. And yes, you are right. You are going to have to contact him to bring some more stock. Would you like to write him a note, and then Sarah can post it whilst she is out? After all, you are responsible for stock are you not Marian?' Only slightly mollified, Marian left the room, set on writing to Mr Williams.

'Jenny?' asked Sarah tentatively, 'do you think Marian would let me take little George with me to Waddington? My mum would fair like to see him. She loves bairns.'

'I'm not sure, Sarah, you'd better ask her yourself. She is very precious about him.'

'I'll go and ask her now.' Only seconds later, a beaming Sarah was back in the room, saying that Marian had said 'yes'. Good, thought Jenny, that solves our problem as well. Sarah and George set out for their walk, taking the letter to the post for Marian.

Sarah arrived back to tell Jenny that the carrier was going over to Waddington the following afternoon, then he had to go to a farm way over Waddington Fell which would take about two hours, so he couldn't bring her back until the late evening. Sarah was flushed and joyful about the forthcoming trip, looking forward to seeing her family, as well as having a trip out.

At that point, the doorbell rang again, so Jenny shooed the excited Sarah out of the shop. It was a young gentleman.

'Good afternoon Sir, how may I help you?'

'Ah, good afternoon,' said a cultured voice. 'I would like a small gift for a young lady. Nothing too personal, but we are quite well acquainted and I have been asked to her birthday party. I don't want to give the wrong impression by giving too personal a gift.'

'As you don't want to get too personal, is that it?' suggested Jenny inquiringly.

'Oh, on the contrary, I would like to get more personal, but it is too early in the acquaintance, if you know what I mean. I think that by being invited to the party, they are showing signs that I might be suitable, but I don't want to spoil my chances.' He laughed and then said, 'Young lady, I seem to be telling you my life story, I do apologise.'

'Not at all,' replied Jenny laughing, 'I only wanted to be sure before I made any suggestions for a gift. Now would you like to see what we have?' Jenny showed him the display cabinets, but he didn't seem to know what to choose.

'Do you think those handkerchiefs would be suitable, Miss?'

'They would, but they are hardly likely to set a girl's heart a flutter, if that is what you want to achieve.'

The young man laughed heartily. 'Well what would you suggest?'

'You could buy handkerchiefs, but have them personally embroidered with your young lady's name on. That would be eminently suitable, and yet be very special to her.'

'That is a lovely idea, but the party is on Thursday. Would you be able to complete them by Thursday?'

'Of course. Now you pick the handkerchiefs that you require, we will embroider them and trim them with a little lace, wrap them and deliver them to your young lady on Thursday. Would that be to your satisfaction?'

'Oh yes, that would be excellent. Her name is Miss Bethany Duxbury and she lives at Irving Hall, Low Moor, Clitheroe.'

'And your name and address Sir, for the receipt?'

'Lord Hastings. Hastings Manor, West Bradford.'

'Thank you, Sir. I'll attend to that immediately. Thank you for your custom.' The young man left and Jenny pondered. She knew that the mill owner of Low Moor Mill owned Irving Hall. Now what would one of the gentry be doing going courting down there? Money of course, the Duxbury's was trade and wanted respectability.

The Hastings were probably poor gentry, who needed a wealthy bride. Well, it was nothing to do with her. She only hoped that the bride was happy. At least he seemed quite a decent sort of chap, for the gentry.

Jenny decided that she would never marry for convenience, only for love. That is, if she was ever out of debt long enough to risk getting married. Well, she mused, thinking these thoughts wouldn't earn her any money. She had better get this order to Marian, or there would be no beautifully embroidered handkerchiefs being sent to Irving Hall at all.

After the shop was closed, Jenny, Marian and Sarah reviewed the day's proceedings. They had met the lady from next door, sold six pairs of gloves, five handbags, a shawl, a parasol and an order for handkerchiefs. The till looked healthy enough, but they hadn't sold one gown, or even had an inquiry about a gown. 'Never mind,' Jenny said reassuringly, 'we have made quite a bit of money anyway. I am sure business will improve as word gets about.'

She smiled confidently at both of her employees, hoping that she wasn't giving them false hopes. But if it took hard work, there would be not a shortage of that. They would all work as hard as they could to make a success of the venture.

Chapter 15

Jenny was the first one up the following morning. She wondered what the day would bring, but her first customer was a long time coming. It was a young woman, in service, who wanted a gift for a friend. She decided on some handkerchiefs and was delighted when Jenny wrapped the gift up carefully in the brown and cream paper.

The long morning dragged on. Jenny's only customer was a young mother who wanted a pair of gloves. They were for the Clitheroe Ball. At least some of her gloves and parasols would be going, even if she couldn't go. It seemed to be the highlight of the local social scene, where everybody went.

Perhaps one day she would be able to go herself, but perhaps she was only dreaming. Just as she was closing the shop, an elderly gentleman came into the shop.

'Good evening, Miss. I am your next-door neighbour. From the bookshop.'

'Oh good evening. How kind of you to call. I'm Miss Mitchell, Jenny Mitchell.'

'Forbes. Gerard Forbes Esquire, at your service,' he bowed low over her hand. Jenny noted that his cuffs were frayed, and his linen crumpled. His hair needed a good trim, and his shoes weren't polished, but despite this, he had a sense of old world courtliness about him. Jenny warmed to him straight away. He was rather overweight and wheezed a little when he spoke.

'I need a gift for my lovely young goddaughter. She has just started putting her hair up and feels very grown up, my sister tells me. That's her mother, my sister, so she is my niece as well as my goddaughter. And I need it quickly because I will have to post it. They live in Bury St Edmunds.'

'What about a lovely shawl? That would appear very grown up and yet cost little in postage, without any danger of getting damaged in the post.'

'Excellent. An ideal choice. I will have the green one, which is her favourite colour. Matches her eyes. Could you wrap it for me so that I can post it tomorrow?'

'If you could write a card for me, I could send Sarah to post it for you tomorrow. To save you leaving your shop. And of course, there will be the usual trade discount.'

'Thank you Miss Mitchell. That would be very convenient. It is hard to leave the shop sometimes, to attend to errands. Living alone doesn't help either. I have no one to help with these things. You have made an old man very grateful.'

The rest of the day was quiet again but Jenny was determined not to be despondent. She realised that by offering a personal service such as delivering or gift-wrapping, the customers were grateful and hopefully would come back.

On the next day, Saturday, the town was busier; consequently a few people came into the shop. But again, they were only shopping for small gifts. Nobody seemed to want dresses. As the skies darkened, a middle-aged lady dressed as a servant came rushing into the shop.

'Oh, I am so glad that you are still open. His Lordship has just died, and they all want mourning clothes. Servants as well. Have you got anything?'

'Do come in and sit down. You look all in,' said Jenny. 'I'll get you a drink. I'm sure you could do with a cup of tea.' She went to the back of the shop and asked Sarah to make a cup of tea. 'I know what it's like when this happens.'

'Do you?' asked the servant, looking at Jenny in a new light.

'Yes, up until two weeks ago, I was a servant over at Burnley. Our Lord died, so I know how you feel. Who is your employer, by the way?'

'He is, or should I say, was, Lord Carroll. We live out Langho way.' Jenny didn't know the name or the area.

'I'll just get my seamstress to come in and help us. I won't be a moment.' Jenny left the room and returned with Marian. For quite a while, they discussed the requirements. The servant's clothes were easily dealt with, as Jenny had bought a lot of black gowns from Mr Williams. The family were more difficult. In the end, Jenny suggested that she and Marian went to the house with the servant, to deal directly with the family. The servant, Mrs Wharton, looked mightily relieved at this.

'Do you have transport?'

'No,' replied Jenny, 'how did you get here?'

'I came in the carriage. Could you both come with us now?'

'Yes,' said Jenny. 'Marian will just see to her little boy and then she'll be with us.' Mrs Wharton looked shocked that a girl as young as Marian had a baby, but said nothing. Whilst Marian was out of the room, Jenny told Mrs Wharton what had happened to Marian. Mrs Wharton nodded sympathetically, remembering how it had happened to a friend of hers in another house where she had lived.

After satisfying herself that little George and Sarah were all right, Marian returned carrying coats, warm scarves and gloves to guard against the cold. They quickly put them on and followed Mrs Wharton outside.

The three women got into the carriage. They took the servants ready-made dresses with them, to save delivering them later. Jenny was glad now that she had chosen a dark colour for their shop clothes, as it looked respectful when visiting the bereaved.

On arriving at the house, the women were escorted to a room, which was obviously a dressing room. One by one, the female members of the family came in to be measured. Jenny gave her commiserations to each person and wrote the orders and measurements down for Marian. Black neckerchiefs and armbands were also ordered for all the men folk of the house, including servants.

The widow of the Lord asked how soon the clothes could be ready. Jenny promised to get them to the house by Monday evening. For the first time, a small smile appeared on the widow's face.

'Thank you so much. It is a great relief to know that I can forget about mourning clothes now. Especially at this time of year,' she said gracefully, and left the room silently. Jenny and Marian looked at each other, quite overcome by the raw emotion that they had witnessed.

After a large supper in the servant's hall, the pair were bundled back into the carriage and driven home, freezing cold and feeling jostled by the coach by the time that they arrived.

George and Sarah were sleeping peacefully when they peeped in to the bedroom. They quietly went to their own rooms, deciding that they would have enough to do tomorrow and would benefit from an early night.

Most of Sunday was spent upstairs, Jenny helping cut out, whilst Marian sewed the gowns on the Singer sewing machine. Sarah turned hems up and sewed black armbands.

At first, Jenny was worried about working on the Sabbath, but Sarah pointed out that it was only the same as being a servant. You always had to work on the Sabbath in service. Jenny felt happier about that afterwards.

'Besides,' said Sarah, 'you are helping the bereaved. Isn't that a holy thing to do?' Jenny smiled at Sarah's logic, quite relieved at the practical turn of mind that Sarah often showed. The bulk of the sewing was finished by Sunday evening, so Jenny promised them that next Sunday, they would all go out together to make up for Sarah missing going home, and them all having to work on their day off.

'I saw my mum anyway this week, when we delivered those things to Lady Jolley. She was very impressed when I turned up in a carriage, and had just been to Lady Jolley's. The carter let me carry the things into the kitchen. It was very grand.'

Marian and Jenny laughed at the look on Sarah's face. Her eyes were wide open as she told her tale of splendour. Sleep came easily to all three girls that night, each dreaming of a better future than they had had previously, but in different ways.

Monday was fairly quiet, but Mrs Canning had told Jenny that Mondays were often quiet in the town, as people tended to wait for Tuesday, so that they could also visit the market.

Tuesday morning brought the busiest trade that they had experienced so far. Their first visitor was Mrs Canning.

'Oh Miss Mitchell. Thank you so much. I was almost the belle of the ball. At my age! So many people came up to me and complimented me on my gown and asked me where I had purchased it. Mr Canning was fair puffed up with pride. Said it took years off me. Now where is Miss Marian? I want to tell her as well.'

Jenny called upstairs for Marian to come down as a customer wished to speak to her. Marian came down a little nervously as Jenny had kept a harsh tone in her voice. She was very relieved when she heard the story of the ball and how much her gown had been admired.

'So many people complimented me on the shade, and said how perfect it was for my colouring. Thank you so much. In fact, Mr Canning suggested that I might have another gown to wear on Christmas Day. He was so impressed. He has never made such a fuss before. I was very thrilled by all the attention.'

Marian smiled. 'Perhaps you would like to come up to my sewing room and chose some material for the next gown?' The pair went upstairs, whilst Jenny marvelled at this potential change in fortune. Perhaps at last, they would start to sell gowns. She was not wrong in her surmising.

The doorbell tinkled and two ladies entered. 'Good morning to you both,' said Jenny respectfully. 'Welcome to my establishment. May I get you some refreshments?'

'No Thank you,' said the older lady, 'we have just had a cup of tea at Miss Carter's. She was telling us about Mrs Canning's gown at the ball. We were not able to go due to a prior engagement. My daughter has a ball to go to on Christmas Evening. Could you manage to make her a gown by then? She already has plenty, but now she wants another,' she said apologetically.

'Certainly Madam, I will just ask my dressmaker to attend you.' As if she had heard, Marian came through the door, with Mrs Canning.

'Good morning Mrs Canning.'

'Good morning Mrs Bradbury, Miss Bradbury. I trust that you are both well.'

'Indeed we are, Mrs Canning. We have been hearing about the ball. We were sorry to miss it.'

'Oh yes, it was quite spectacular. I had a lovely time, but I must leave you. I have a lot of messages to do this morning. Goodbye to you both.'

'Goodbye,' replied the two ladies together, staring after Mrs Canning.

'Marian, Miss Bradbury would like a ball gown for Christmas Evening. Can you accommodate her?'

'Of course, what style and colour were you thinking of, Miss Bradbury?'

'She would like white,' replied Mrs Bradbury.

'Mama, I always wear white. I would like a change.'

'But Helena, darling, you should wear white at your age. Once you are married, you will be able to wear other colours.' Miss Bradbury was looking thunderously at her mother.

'What about a white dress with different coloured trimmings?' asked Marian. 'Then you would both be happy.' Both mother and daughter turned to stare at Marian.

'What exactly do you mean?' asked Miss Bradbury.

'Well, you could have a basic gown of white satin, with an overskirt of another colour, and then this second colour would be picked out in the trims and flowers.'

'Mmm, that sounds quite unusual. What colour would you suggest?'

'What ever colour you had in your mind when you said that you didn't want a white one.'

'Pink. A pale pink.'

'That would look lovely. The bodice could be tight fitting, with a modestly low cut front, in respect of your age. The bottom of the bodice could come down to a point, with a pink rosebud at the point.

From the waist, the overdress of pink voile would be gathered into the side of the gown, with a small bustle at the back. There could be trails of ribbons down the overskirt, drawing the material up into loops, with a rosebud at the end of each ribbon. Round the hem, there could be a ruched frill, with pink rosebuds at certain points along the hem. How does this look?' Marian had been drawing her ideas whilst she had been talking.

'Oh yes, I like that,' Miss Bradbury enthused. 'And yet, Mama, it is still a white gown. Oh please say that you like it and that I may have it?'

'Helena, of course you may have it. I have never seen you so enthusiastic about a gown before.'

'Well I don't like going to Miss Sharples' shop. She has such old-fashioned ideas. This is perfect. Just exactly what I want.'

'Are you sure that it can be ready by Christmas Evening?'

'Oh yes, if you will call in for a fitting five days before then, to make sure that it is to your satisfaction,' replied Jenny. 'If you would go into the dressing room with Miss Marian she will take your measurements now.'

'Oh Mama, I have just had a thought. Do you remember those new white satin slippers that you bought me in Blackburn? Wouldn't they look the dearest if Miss Marian sewed a pink rosebud on the front, to match the gown?'

'Why yes, you are right. Could that be done? Do you trim slippers?'

'Anything that will enhance the gown, Mrs Bradbury,' replied Marian respectfully. 'I could also make a little bag in the white satin with rosebuds on as well. A short time later, an excited mother and daughter went out of the shop, happy with their order.

Jenny and Marian looked at each other. Apart from Mrs Canning and the bereavement clothes, this was their first order. It augured well for the future.

Chapter 16

Throughout the day, Jenny, Marian and Sarah were rushed off their feet. Many ladies came into the shop, either mentioning Mrs Canning's gown, or saying that Miss Carter from next door had recommended them. Several gowns were ordered for Christmas delivery and many fripperies were bought, with the result that they almost ran out of gloves and parasols by Christmas, despite Mr Williams' reinforcements.

Five days before Christmas, Mrs and Miss Bradbury arrived for the fitting. Jenny kept Mrs Bradbury with her, whilst Marian took Miss Bradbury into the fitting room. A few minutes later, Miss Bradbury emerged at the back of the shop. She slowly walked towards her mother, a look of radiant delight on her face.

The gown was perfect. It fitted beautifully and the pink rosebud theme made it look extra special. Miss Bradbury came to the front of the shop and turned round slowly for her mother to get the total effect of the full skirt, and the ruched effect made by the ribbons over the bustle.

'My word, that is lovely, my dear. I am so pleased with the finished garment,' beamed her mother. Miss Bradbury looked up as the door opened and a young gentleman walked in. He stared at Miss Bradbury, unable to take his eyes off her. Jenny excused herself from Mrs Bradbury, and asked the gentleman if she could assist him.

'Er, well, er' he stuttered, 'I would . . er would like er. May I say Miss, how ravishing you look in that gown? It has quite taken my mind off my errand. I am sorry madam, if I have been too forward,' he said to Mrs Bradbury

'Why thank you kind Sir,' cut in Miss Bradbury giving a small curtsey, and behaving quite coquettishly. Mrs Bradbury looked on in amazement.

'Perhaps you would like to remove the gown now, so that it doesn't get creased before the ball?' asked Marian. Looking quite reluctant, Miss Bradbury and her mother followed Marian into the fitting room. Jenny then attended to the young gentleman.

'What was it that you were looking for? A gift for a mother, sister, or perhaps sweetheart?'

'For my mother, I have no sweetheart,' he said in rather a loud voice. Jenny chuckled silently to herself as she turned away to re-arrange a display. Perhaps she could become a matchmaker at the shop, as well as everything else. Cupid had certainly smitten this young man.

'Do you know which ball she will be wearing the gown to?'

'I am afraid not. Now what did you have in mind? A present for your mother was it?'

'No, not a present, she has need of a new pair of cream lace gloves. The parlour maid has just scorched one of them. She wants them to go up to the elbow.'

'I am afraid that we have sold a lot gloves this week. I have only one pair to show you. Here they are. Are these what your mother would normally wear?' The young man gave a cursory glance at the gloves.

'Oh yes, they'll be fine. Thank you.' Jenny wrapped them up in the distinctive paper, received his money, and was making ready to say goodbye. The young man seemed in no hurry to go. He looked at other things in the display cabinet, whilst keeping one eye on the back of the shop.

'Would there be anything else, Sir?'

'No, I will just look round, if you don't mind.'

'Certainly Sir. May I get you a little refreshment? Or do you intend to visit Miss Carter's tearooms afterwards. Many of my ladies go in there after making purchases.'

'Miss Carter's tearooms?' he repeated. Jenny nodded. 'Yes, that is a good idea. I will go to Miss Carter's tearooms now,' he shouted in a loud voice, near the back of the shop. He picked up his purchase and walked slowly out of the shop, giving a last glance to the back of the shop as he closed the door. Jenny watched as he walked straight next door to the tearooms.

Only a few seconds later, Marian and Mrs and Miss Bradbury came out of the fitting room. Miss Bradbury came out first and looked round the shop eagerly. 'Oh, has the young man gone?'

Jenny laughed. 'Yes, very reluctantly. I suggested that he might take refreshments in Miss Carter's tearooms. I think that he has gone there now.'

'That is just where we were going next, wasn't it Mama?'

'Were we?' asked her mother with a wry look on her face. 'Well, all right. I think that would be a good idea, as we will miss luncheon today.'

'Do enjoy the ball, Miss Bradbury,' said Marian.

'Yes, do,' agreed Jenny, 'and thank you for your custom.'

'We will be back for more, I hope, Miss Marian. You seem to know just what suits me. Thank you and goodbye.'

The two ladies left the shop, and headed straight for Miss Carter's. Jenny and Marian both burst out laughing together.

'I hope that they come here for the bridal gown,' quipped Jenny.

'So do I,' replied Marian. 'I would love to make a bridal gown. Do you remember Lady Hortense's? That was beautiful wasn't it?' All of a sudden, a cloud came over Marian's smiling face.

'Don't Marian. Don't torture yourself. Forget Ormerod Hall and all that happened.'

'I do forget most of the time, but it does return to my thoughts sometimes. But I must think of good things. I have George because I went to Ormerod Hall.' Marian turned and walked quietly away to the back of the shop towards the fitting room. Jenny sighed, and wished that she hadn't said anything. But then, it was Marian that first mentioned Ormerod Hall.

The tinkling of the doorbell wakened her from her thoughts. It was the postman.

'Good morning Miss Mitchell.'

'Good morning Jack. Thank you for these,' she said as she took the pile of letters from his hands. She looked at the letters and saw one with a crest on. 'This looks interesting,' she said, showing Jack the letter.

'Yes, that's from Langho, it's Lord Carroll's crest. Or should I say, young Mr Matthew's now. Sad business, that. Only a young man was Lord Carroll. Well, must be getting on my way. I'll say good day to you, Miss Mitchell.'

'Good day,' replied Jenny, and turned to open the letter.

Dear Miss Mitchell

I am instructed by her Ladyship to thank you for your prompt attention to the supplying of clothes during her recent bereavement. She was especially touched that you had included a jet-mourning brooch as a token of your respect.

Thank you once again

Yours sincerely

Mary Wharton
Housekeeper

Jenny sat down on the settee, with the letter in her hand. That had been a good idea of hers, to include the brooch. It wasn't an expensive one, but had obviously touched Lady Carroll. She would remember that another time when dealing with the bereaved.

Jenny looked again in the envelope. There was nothing else. No money or bankers cheque. Still, she supposed, they would hardly be likely to send money through the post. But she had sent a bill to them.

Never mind, paying bills would be the last thing on their minds at present, but it was a substantial amount outstanding. She would leave it until after the Christmas season.

As she was shutting the shop, Mr Forbes from the bookshop entered the shop.

'Miss Mitchell, I have just received the most lovely letter from my goddaughter. She was delighted with the shawl. Thank you so much for arranging to post it. It was greatly appreciated.'

'It was a pleasure. I am so glad that she liked it. Mr Forbes, you said that you weren't going down to Bury St Edmunds for the Christmas season. Where are you going?'

'Why, nowhere. I will stay at home as usual.' Jenny thought of the dusty shop, and wondered what sort of Christmas he would have.

'Would you like to share it with us, here?'

'Oh, I couldn't possibly intrude on you.'

'It would be no intrusion. We would welcome you.'

'Well if you are sure, I would be delighted. What time shall I come?'

'Oh, I'm not sure. Do you go to church, Mr Forbes?'

'Why yes, my dear, don't you?'

Jenny blushed. 'Well I want to do, but I've never got round to it since the shop opened. We've had to work most Sundays to get the orders ready for Christmas.'

'The Christmas Day matins will be at 10 of the clock. Perhaps I could accompany you?'

'Yes please, that would be most helpful, especially as I haven't been before.'

'I will call round about 20 minutes before the hour and we can all walk across to the church together.'

'Thank you. I will look forward to that.'

'I will say goodbye for now, then.'

'Goodbye.' Jenny watched as the old man left the shop, and noticed that he turned into Miss Carter's shop instead of his own.

On the morning of Christmas Eve, Jenny took a soft white shawl from the display cabinet and wrapped it in her distinctive paper. She slipped next door to Miss Carter's shop and waited for her to appear. 'Ah Miss Mitchell, how can I help you, my dear?' Goodness, thought Jenny, what a change from the first time I met her. She proffered the package to Miss Carter.

'This is just a little token to thank you for helping me, and sending so many of your customers to me. It has made a real difference.'

'Think nothing of it, my dear. And you shouldn't have bought me anything. You are so kind. I believe you have even asked Mr Forbes in for the Christmas repast. I know how it feels to be alone at the Christmas season.'

Jenny's heart sunk. Why hadn't she asked Miss Carter as well? She lived alone since her sister had married.

'Would you like to come too, Miss Carter?' There was a tinkling laugh.

'Goodness me, no. That wasn't a veiled hint. I am going to my married sister's home in Accrington. But it is kind of you to ask. I do hope that you have a lovely time.'

'I'm sure that we will. It's the first time that Marian and I have ever spent a Christmas in our own home. Well, the first that we remember, that is.'

'Then it will be all the more special.'

'I had better be getting back to the shop. I didn't tell Marian or Sarah where I was going. Goodbye, and do have a lovely time over the Christmas season.'

'Thank you my dear, I am sure that I will with my sister's young family.'

Jenny walked briskly back to her shop and started making a list of all the goods that they would need after the holiday, to replenish their stocks. When Marian came down, she asked her to add all the other accessories that she would need, that she couldn't get in Clitheroe. It took quite some time, as customers coming in for last minute presents interrupted them.

At long last, the shop closed. Sarah had taken George into the town to get all the fresh food that they would need for the festive season. She had managed to arrange a lift home at eight of the clock, and she was very excited about having five days holiday over the Christmas period.

As the carrier arrived, Sarah turned shyly to Jenny and said 'If you go into my bedroom, you will find some small gifts for you all to open tomorrow morning.'

'Sarah, you shouldn't have bothered. You have so little money, with sending it all to your mother.'

'She lets me keep sixpence back for myself. I am ever so lucky, aren't I?'

'Well, it is very kind of you. And by the way, if you reach under the counter, you will find a parcel with your name on.'

Sarah bent down and grabbed excitedly at the parcel. 'Ooh, this is big. Whatever can you have got me?'

Jenny laughed. 'You will have to wait until tomorrow to see. Now hurry up, or the carrier won't wait for you.' With that, Jenny pushed Sarah out of the door, closed it, and then locked it behind her.

Worn out by the previous few hectic days, Marian and Jenny went to bed early and were soon fast asleep.

Chapter 17

Jenny and Marian were both up early next morning. They had a light breakfast and then Jenny started to get ready for church. Marian had decided not to go. She wasn't sure that George would behave himself, and she didn't want to get disparaging looks on her first visit. Marian had decided that she would make the meal ready for them to come back to.

A knock on the door announced Mr Forbes.

'The Season's Greetings to you both,' he called loudly.

'And to you,' they both replied. Jenny got her coat, hat and gloves and set off towards the church. They had to go down the main street, then up the hill to the parish church of St Mary Magdelene.

It was a fine old church, which had been the only one in Clitheroe for many years, although St Paul's had been built recently to cope with the increased numbers of people coming to work in the mills. There had also been a growth in the non-conformist churches in the town, too.

Mr Forbes led Jenny into a pew that was situated half way down the church. Jenny was aware that there were a few curious glances as they walked into the church, but Mr Forbes said nothing. He merely smiled courteously to all of the people.

The beautiful story of the Nativity left Jenny with a wonderful sense of peace and calm. She felt that God had indeed been good to her, giving her many other gifts besides the gift of His salvation, which he did by becoming a baby on earth.

She reflected on the last two months of her life and still couldn't believe what had happened. She had a very full and grateful heart as they sang the last carol.

On the way out, Jenny was able to speak to some of the people that she knew. The Cannings were there and they kept waving at Jenny, until she realised who they were. She made her way over to them. Mrs Canning was wearing her second dress, designed and made by Marian. It was a deep russet colour with a warm cloak to match and looked perfect on this bright and crisp morning.

At the entrance to the church, Mr Forbes introduced Jenny to the parson. He commented that he hadn't met Jenny before. She explained that she had only recently taken up residence in the town and it had been the first opportunity that she had had to visit the church. He wryly commented that he hoped that it would not be long before he saw her again. She assured him that it would not.

On return from church, the smell of the roasting turkey came through the door. Marian hurried to put the kettle on the fire, to make them both a drink.

'There is a lovely smell of roasting meat, Marian, what are we having today?' asked Mr Forbes.

'Turkey. We developed a taste for it whilst we were in service. We only got goose in the workhouse,' laughed Marian. 'It is lovely to be able to have what you want to eat. I really enjoyed planning the menu. And I'm not going to tell you what else we are having. You will just have to wait!'

'Oh dear, I feel like a little boy who has just been told off,' said Mr Forbes in mournful tones. 'I won't ask any more questions.'

The three of them sat before the fire companionably, talking of other Christmases and watching George play with a baking tin and wooden spoon. Marian, though, kept popping in and out of the kitchen to check on the meal. Mr Forbes told them about his lively Christmases at home when there had been eleven children.

'It was very noisy, but mamma and papa soon got tired of us, and we were packed off up to the nursery with nanny.'

He was sad to hear about their Christmases in the workhouse, but happier when they told of the lovely times that they had had at Ormerod Hall. They told of the plenteous food, and the balls, which were held for all the staff on the day after Christmas Day. Even Lord Ormerod had helped serve their food that day and he had danced with all the senior staff.

When all the preparations were ready, Marian called them into the small dining room. Jenny gasped when she saw what Marian had done. The room was trimmed with holly, with bright red candles on the table and in the holders instead of the usual plain ones. She had embroidered red candles on to a new tablecloth with matching serviettes. She had also got the best china cups, saucers and dinner service out.

Marian brought the food into the dining room and Mr Forbes carved the turkey. Piles of steaming vegetables were placed on to their plates, along with crispy potatoes. At the end of the meal, Marian went into the kitchen and returned this time with a flaming plum pudding. George cried out with excitement when he saw it, and they all laughed.

'This is a present from Mr Forbes,' said Marian. 'He brought it in when you were upstairs last night.'

'It is my way of thanking you for asking me to come to your repast. I have had a lovely time. I bought it from Miss Carter's shop. She gave me the lovely mince pies for you as well.'

'And it is not over yet. We have to give each other presents now. That was something that we were never allowed to do in the workhouse, so we will really enjoy it now. Here you are George, this is for you.' Jenny gave George a large parcel. Marian objected. 'Jenny, you have already given him that lovely velvet suit; you shouldn't have got him anything else.'

'A velvet suit is not exciting to a child, this is just for him.'

By this time, George was ripping open his parcel and pulled out a big red shiny ball. He was mystified by it and pushed it round the room, although he did keep stopping to play with the paper that it had been wrapped in. He seemed as keen on the paper as he was on the ball.

'And here is another present for George,' said Jenny handing him a smaller present. 'This one is from Sarah.' George soon demolished the paper from this present, too. It contained some toffees. His mother promptly rescued these from George, but he was quite content with the paper, not having realised what the toffees were.

'And the next one is for you, Marian,' said Jenny. This was a very large parcel and Marian was amazed to find a thick, winter wool coat with matching hat. It was very fashionable, with a neat nipped in waist and velvet trim. Marian put it on immediately and hugged it to herself.

'This is the most beautiful coat I have ever had, Jenny. Well, for that matter' she laughed, 'it is the only one that I have ever had, so it is especially beautiful. Thank you so much.' She hugged Jenny, as she had hugged herself. 'And now it is your turn Jenny. Here is mine and George's present to you.' She handed Jenny a parcel. It was an exquisitely embroidered white blouse, with a plain, navy skirt.

'I thought that you should have a change from brown and cream,' she quipped.

'It's beautiful. I am ever so grateful. You're right. I spend too much time in my brown and cream.'

'Here is Sarah's present for you.' It was a pair of navy gloves.

'Well, what a coincidence, Sarah has bought the same shade of blue gloves to match my skirt.' Marian laughed.

'I am afraid we have colluded on your present, Jenny. We are both so grateful to you. You have changed our lives.'

'Don't be absurd, Marian. You would have done the same for me,' but Jenny turned away to hide the tears in her eyes.

Sensing the emotion in the room, Mr Forbes jumped up and said 'And now it is my turn.' He produced four parcels from under his chair. They were all, obviously, books.

'First of all, young George.' They watched as he ripped the paper off once again and looked at the book contained within. It had strong hardback covers, with a picture of a cat on the front.

'Puss, puss,' lisped George and they all laughed. Suddenly he noticed his ball again. He shuffled across for it, the book temporarily forgotten.

'I do apologise,' said Marian, 'I know that he will receive a lot of pleasure from this book in the years to come.'

'Think nothing of it. Now here is yours, Miss Marian.' Marian opened the book reverently. It was a book by George Elliot, called Middlemarch. 'This is a fairly new author; I hope that you like the book. It has been well received by the press.'

'As it is the first book that I have owned, I shall treasure it forever. Thank you Mr Forbes.'

'And now, Jenny,' Mr Forbes handed Jenny a small package. 'A much older author I am afraid, but one which I think you will approve of.' Jenny opened the package and found a leather bound book of Shakespeare's sonnets.

'That is beautiful. I too, will treasure my first book.'

'I have bought Sarah the fairy tales by the Brothers Grimm. I hope that she won't be offended? She is still only a child, despite the work that she does.'

'I try my best to improve her load,' said Jenny sharply.

'My dear,' Mr Forbes interrupted quickly, 'that is by no means a criticism of you. Her life has improved dramatically since you arrived. No, I was merely thinking that it is sad that children have to go out to work in the poorer classes. Childhood should be for exploring and learning.'

Slightly mollified, Jenny sat back into her chair, but a little coolness of atmosphere descended over the room. Marian jumped up from her chair.

'Shall we play Charades? That would be good fun.'

'What a good idea, Miss Marian,' replied Mr Forbes, glad that someone had relieved the atmosphere, that he had unwittingly caused. 'I will be first.' He started to dance around the room, until all of them were laughing at his antics.

The day passed quickly until Mr Forbes took his leave. George had already fallen asleep on the settee, so Marian and Jenny also went to bed early. Tired but happy, their first Christmas day of freedom ended.

Chapter 18

At the beginning of the New Year, Mr Briggs came round to make his monthly check of the books. He was very pleased.

'Well, Miss Mitchell, even though you did not have any business acumen, you have made a healthy profit. My congratulations.'

'I know, it is hard to believe, isn't it? Especially after the shop was making a loss under Mrs Bruce.'

Mr Briggs smiled at her naivety. 'It just confirms what I always suspected about Mrs Bruce. She was not keeping her records correctly and making some considerable amount of money for herself. I think that you are going to be in a better position than I thought you would be. You are obviously giving a good service.'

'It is all due to Marian. Not only is she the most wonderful seamstress, she has a knack of knowing just what will suit a person.'

'Yes, I am aware of that. I heard all the gossip about Mrs Canning's dress at the ball, and actually saw it, too. I suspect that by giving service like that, you will soon get a reputation in Clitheroe and the surrounding area.'

'All I hear about is the ball. I would love to go to a ball. How would I go about it next year?'

'You would need an escort and a ticket. I could arrange both of those for you, if you should wish. In fact, I would take great delight in escorting you myself, if you would do me the honour.'

'Why thank you kind sir,' laughed Jenny with mock severity, 'it would give me great pleasure to accept.'

'No, mine would be the pleasure, Miss Mitchell,' replied Mr Briggs. Jenny then told Mr Briggs about the bereavement that she attended to at Langho.

'That was good business practice. Making yourself available and working extra hours to hurry the order. People will remember that and come back to you.'

'I received a lovely Thank you letter from her,' said Jenny, 'but now that we have mentioned them, I would like to ask you about something else. Something that I am a little shy of mentioning.'

'Oh dear, Miss Mitchell, whatever can that be? I hope that I am a suitable person for your confidences.' Jenny blushed.

'It is a matter of money. Although I did Lady Carroll good service at Langho, and she wrote to me, she did not send me the money owing, even though I had sent her an invoice. What should I do?'

Mr Briggs laughed loudly. 'Oh my dear girl, you will have to wait a little longer to get your money. The gentry are not known for paying their bills too quickly. In about three months, if you are fortunate, you may get paid. Some houses are very reluctant to pay, I am afraid.'

'Well, what can I do?'

'You will find out which houses are not good at paying and eventually, refuse to give services. It is the only way. The newly rich industrialists are much better payers. Cash on the nail is their motto. I suppose they are not so far removed from poverty themselves, so being able to pay for goods and services is pleasurable. Besides,' he laughed, 'they have the money. Many of the landed gentry are now struggling to keep up their wealthy lifestyles. No, don't worry my dear. The money will come in eventually.'

Somewhat reassured, Jenny went to make a cup of tea for Mr Briggs, quietly pleased that she had passed the first hurdle of keeping accounts. After he had gone, Jenny went into the kitchen and asked Sarah to make something special for tea, with a promise to tell her why they were having a special meal at teatime.

It was a pleasure to see Sarah blossoming. She had come back from home after Christmas full of life and joy. Jenny realised that she had missed her over the Christmas period, or missed her giggling, if she was honest. She had such a happy demeanour at all times; she was a pleasure to have around the house. She was certainly good for George too, who was developing well.

'Were you sorry to have to come back to work, Sarah?'

'Oh no Jenny! I was glad. It was ever so noisy back home. And I had to share a bed with my sister. No, Jenny, I was glad to be back. Besides, I missed young George.'

'And he missed you, too. We all did. Now I must go and get on. I'll see you at teatime.'

That teatime, Sarah had made a sumptuous meal for them all. Jenny kept them in suspense about the reason for the treat. At the end of the meal, she got up from the table as if she was going to her room.

'Jenny,' said Marian sharply, 'stop teasing. What is the treat for?'

Jenny laughed. 'Oh yes, the treat. Well, I am pleased to say that we have made a profit in the last month, and Mr Briggs is pleased with the work that has been done. So I think that we all deserve an increase in salary? What say all of you?'

'No, Jenny,' said Marian, 'we do not need an increase. We are happy enough. We have food and lodgings as well.' Sarah was nodding.

Jenny was visibly moved. 'You are both so good to me. I know that the shop will work, because I have two faithful friends to help me. And now I must go.' She hurried out of the room wiping the tears from her eyes as she got into her own room.

The weeks passed, and the business continued to progress. Marian and Jenny were making names for themselves amongst the ladies in the town.

Eventually, despite her fears, the bill was paid from the Carroll family at Langho, along with others that were outstanding. It was just a question of waiting, which she was more able to do now that she was getting regular orders. She couldn't believe how much the shop was making, and how much people would pay to be dressed in a unique style.

They were all getting busy, and Jenny was thinking that she might soon have to get more help in the shop. She could certainly afford it.

One cold morning in March, as Jenny was opening up the shop, she heard a banging on her door. It was Mr Forbes.

'Miss Mitchell, could you come and help me? Come quickly.' Jenny followed him next door, after telling Sarah where she was going.

They got into the shop next door where Mr Forbes took Jenny into the back kitchen. By the roaring open fire, sat a dirty old woman, huddled into her cloak and shaking.

'I found her in my doorway this morning when I opened the shop door for some fresh air. I think that she is very ill. I have sent for Doctor Higson, he should be here soon.'

Jenny looked at the woman. She looked as if she had not had a good meal in a long time. She made a decision.

'Mr Forbes, this lady is going to need nursing for some time. I will take her into my shop, as we can look after her better than you could.'

'Why no, Miss Mitchell, there are places where they look after people like this who are ill.'

'Yes, I know. I was brought up in one,' replied Jenny tersely. 'I will look after her.' The doctor arrived at that point. He placed the old lady on a couch and after Mr Forbes had left the room, Jenny helped him to undress the woman.

'She has severe malnutrition,' the doctor said. He placed a tube against her chest and listened for some time. 'She also has the pneumonia. We'll get her into the workhouse.' The old lady, who had made no movement or sound before, suddenly reared up and tried to speak.

'No. No workhouse,' insisted Jenny, 'I will nurse her in my own home next door. Kindly help me to remove her. I will of course pay all your bills.'

'There may be little hope. It could be quite some time before she recovers. There could be a considerable burden on your time. Are you sure?'

'Quite sure,' replied Jenny. 'Now please help me.' The two of them helped the lady to get dressed again and wrapping her cloak round her, took her into Jenny's shop.

Marian and Sarah looked on in amazement, until Jenny barked orders at them.

'Quick, get a dry nightdress for this lady. She is unwell, and needs care. We will put her in the spare bedroom. Sarah, go and make a bed up for her and light a fire. Then you will have to go to the doctor's surgery for some medicine. He is going to come back and put a poultice on her soon, so we will need a pan of boiling water keeping hot on the fire.'

When Marian returned with the nightdress, Jenny and Marian carefully undressed the lady and washed her in warm water with some soft soap. Whilst they had been undressing the lady, Jenny realised that she wasn't very old, more a case of being poorly nourished and a lack of care. The lady moaned at times when they moved her, but said nothing.

Once she was clean and dry, they put her into the nightdress, and lifted her into the spare bedroom, which was already warm, a glowing fire blazing in the grate. Sarah had lifted some of the kitchen fire into the bedroom for quickness. She had also put a lot of candles round the room.

'I put a lot of candles in, if doctor was going to be doing things,' explained Sarah.

'Well done, that was very sensible Sarah.' Sarah looked very pleased at being praised. 'Now could you bring her a cup of tea? I am not sure about food yet. I didn't get chance to ask the doctor.'

Sarah soon returned and the lady was gently raised to sip at the steaming fluid. The effort seemed to weary her and she soon fell back asleep.

When the doctor arrived, he put the poultice on the lady's chest, but although she moaned when she felt the heat of the poultice, she did not speak. The doctor spoke to Jenny on his way out, in the shop downstairs.

'I think that you will need some help with this lady, if you are determined to go on caring for her yourself. It is going to be a long illness. Shall I recommend a nurse to you? You have to be careful. Some of them are not very respectable.'

'No, I will find my own nurse, Thank you. I have thought of someone who may be able to help.'

'Well, I will leave it up to you. By the way, Mr Forbes caught me earlier, he will pay for all my costs, so there is no need to worry, my dear,' he said patronisingly.

'I am quite able to pay all your costs, thank you very much,' Jenny said sternly. 'I shall speak to Mr Forbes later. Goodbye doctor.' And held the door open to him.

'Very well. I will return in the morning to check on her progress.'

Jenny shut the door and ran back upstairs.

'Marian, could you look after the shop for me? I have an errand to do. I have decided to go and get Susy out of the workhouse to come and live with us here. She can look after the lady.' With that, she dashed out of the shop, grabbing her cloak as she ran.

'Who is Susy?' asked Sarah.

'A close friend of Jenny's in the workhouse.'

'I thought you were Jenny's close friend in the workhouse?'

'Well, yes, I was. She looked after me when I first came in. But Susy was her first friend. She won't be able to come. Sometimes Jenny doesn't think. Susy has a mother who is not all there in her head. You know what I mean?' Sarah nodded. 'She will never leave her mother. No, I think that this is one of Jenny's less well thought out ideas. She does tend to jump in. Anyway, we'll wait and see. We'll certainly need some help with this lady. So I hope that is does work out.'

Meantime, Jenny was having a similar conversation with Susy. The Matron of the workhouse had not been too pleased when Jenny demanded to see Susy on a weekday, reiterating that visiting was only on a Sunday. But she was persuaded when Jenny said that she was offering Susy a place at her shop.

In the end, in desperation, Jenny told Susy that she could bring her mother too. In that way, she could look after both ladies. At long last, Jenny got a smile out of Susy. Jenny instructed Matron to get Susy and her mother's clothes together. She would take them both!

'Perhaps you could order us a carriage,' said Jenny to Matron imperiously, whilst laughing inside to herself. As soon as Matron went out of the room, Jenny and Susy hugged each other.

'We will be all right, Susy. And so will your mum. You'll see. They were going to send this poor lady to the workhouse, and I couldn't let them do it. I knew that she would die if they did. She is so weak, and I know that you are good at nursing people.'

Matron returned, saying that the carriage would be along in fifteen minutes, and would she like some tea whilst she was waiting? Jenny agreed that tea would be lovely, and then trying to keep the smiles off her face; she made small talk with Matron. Jenny noticed however, that there wasn't a cup for Susy, but decided to say nothing. She would make it up to Susy and her mother later.

When the carriage arrived, Jenny, Susy and Mrs Marshall all got on board, and drove the short distance back into Clitheroe to the shop. Marian couldn't believe her eyes when all three of them got out of the carriage.

'Now stop staring, you two. I couldn't bring Susy without Mrs Marshall, could I?'

'Where are they all going to go?' asked a practical Sarah.

'I have thought about that. I have the biggest bedroom and there is only me. If Susy and her mum and the lady all share my room, I can have the room where the lady is now.'

'Are you sure?' asked Marian slowly.

'Quite sure. Now let's get on with things. We'll not move the lady until we get the rooms rearranged.' Everyone started bustling about, whilst Mrs Marshall sat in the corner of the room, not speaking, but watching what everyone was doing. Slowly, she got out of her chair and walked over to the stove. She started making the preparations for a pot of tea. She was just pouring the boiling water on the leaves when Susy returned.

'Mum, what are you doing?' she asked with concern in her voice.

'Making tea. Nice tea. Lots of new tea leaves. Not old ones.' Susy stared at her mum and shouted for Jenny.

'Jenny, Jenny, look, my mum has made some tea. That is the first time that she has done anything on her own for a long time. And she has spoken too. Back there, she just did what she was told and rarely talked,' said a radiant Susy.

Jenny picked up a cup of tea, and thanked Mrs Marshall. She was rewarded by a lovely smile, one that had been rarely visible in Mrs Marshall ever since she had gone into the workhouse.

By night time, all the moves had taken place. Three small beds were placed in Jenny's old bedroom, whilst Jenny had moved to her new smaller room. Susy had managed to spoon some thin broth into the lady, as instructed by the doctor.

As Jenny got into her new bed, she wondered how she was going to manage. Suddenly, she had three new people to look after, all who wouldn't be able to contribute to the shop for a long time, if ever. No matter, she thought sleepily to herself, if profits keep going up, I would be able to afford servants soon. With that laughable thought, she slowly drifted into sleep, after thanking God for His goodness.

Chapter 19

Slowly, but surely, the lady started to recover. The doctor made daily visits for many days to apply the poultices. The weak broth was replaced with light food, followed by a return to normal food. Many times, she grabbed hold of Susy's hand and smiled her thanks, still unable to speak.

After a particularly bad night, where she had tossed and turned and moaned, the doctor was sent for again. He shook his head when he saw her, and warned Jenny and Susy that this could be the end. Her dull rasping breath cut through the air, seeming to fill the room with its intensity.

After he had gone, Jenny and Susy took it in turn to wipe the sweat off her brow. Early in the morning, Jenny went to bed, leaving Susy to care for her alone.

Susy fell asleep through sheer exhaustion. She woke with a start, with the sudden realisation that the rasping noise had stopped. She jumped up, feeling guilty that she had fallen asleep, only to notice that the lady was breathing easily, and her colour was back to normal.

Susy felt her forehead, and it was cool for the first time in days. 'Thank God,' said Susy out loud, and hurried to find Jenny.

When the doctor arrived that morning, he was very pleased. 'She has had a crisis from what you describe. She will be all right now. Have you found out who she is yet?'

'No, she doesn't seem able to talk,' said Susy.

'Well, keep up the good work. You would make a good nurse. If ever you want work as a nurse, just ask me. I will highly recommend you. I'll say goodbye for now.'

Eventually the lady was able to tell them her story. She was called Edith and had been widowed some years ago. All her children had died from various aliments and she had struggled to get regular work.

Her mother had died in the workhouse and she was determined that she would not go in there, if she could help it. Then she got a bad cough. She vaguely remembered arriving at the bookshop, but could remember little else since.

'We are so pleased that you are better. And you say that you can remember nothing?'

'I think I remember a man, am I right, or 'ave I dreamed it? I 'ave 'ad many dreams whilst I've bin ill.'

'Oh, that will be Mr Forbes next door. It was his shop doorway where you were found. He called for me to help him, and as he is a bachelor, I thought that it was more appropriate for you to come with me. I didn't want you to go to the workhouse, either; I used to live there. So did Susy and Marian.'

'Thank you all. I must thank this Mr Forbes.'

'He has been round to enquire after you every day. He sent those flowers round for you,' said Susy, pointing to the daffodils on the dresser. 'We will ask him to come in today if you feel you could manage.'

'Yes, I'd like ter thank 'im.'

Later in the evening, when Mr Forbes called round, he was very glad to see that Edith had recovered. She thanked him for helping her, and they had a chat about how she came to be in his shop doorway.

'An' soon, I'll be on mi way. I'll 'ave ter find a job. I'll never be able ter repay all of yer fer what yer've done fer mi.'

'I have had a thought about that,' said Mr Forbes. 'I live alone, and I find it quite difficult to keep the house and shop and myself for that matter, clean and tidy. Would you accept a post of housekeeper with me?'

'Oh yes, Sir, that I would. I'd like ter 'elp yer, cos yer 'elped me. Thanks.'

'Well that's settled. I will look forward to seeing you when you recover. I will wait for Doctor Higson's permission for you to commence work again.'

This seemed to be the stimulus for Edith's recovery to rapidly progress. Obviously, the threat of being turned out had been worrying her. Within two weeks of this conversation, Doctor Higson declared that she was fit to work again.

Jenny provided her with two new dresses of dark grey cotton, a pair of shoes and some underwear, so that she had a good start. A happy Edith went off to start her new life next door, but often popped back for a cup of tea, with Susy and her mum.

During Edith's illness, Mrs Marshall had also slowly improved as well. She would never be back to her former self, but she had become very useful around the shop. She had taken over the cleaning of the shop and would mind George if Sarah was busy.

Jenny needed to make a decision about the future. She sought out Susy on the morning after Edith left.

'We need to talk about you and your mum's future, Susy.' Susy froze in her tracks, looking petrified.

'Er, what do you mean, exactly? Are you sending me back to the workhouse, now Edith has gone?

'Susy, don't say that. Of course not. I need you, and anyway, I would never send you back. I mean that we need to discuss your job here. Are you still good at sums? You always were at school.'

'Yes, why?'

'I would be very grateful if you would work in the shop, but also be responsible for looking after the accounts. As Marian is getting busier, I need someone who can do the accounts, so that I can concentrate on the shop. Could you do that for me?'

'Oh course, I am just so grateful that you don't want to send me back there.'

'Not if I can help it. None of us will ever go back there. It still makes me shudder. But the shop seems to be going quite well, and I can afford to keep you on, although I can't pay you very much.'

'Whatever you pay me, will be more than I got at the workhouse,' quipped Susy. 'But what about my mum. Can she stay here, too?'

'Certainly. We couldn't do without her now. She does so many of the little jobs around the place and she never complains. Of course she can stay. Are you happy continuing to share a room?'

'More than happy. Thank you so much.'

'Well, I had better get on with some work, or we will all be back in the workhouse.'

Just before Easter, a lady walked in to the shop rather nervously. Her clothes were expensive, but not in a style that suited her. It was when she opened her mouth that Jenny got a shock. She talked like a poor person.

''Ello Miss, I'm 'avin' a dance for th' posh folks, and I want a frock fer me and me daughter. She'll be along in a minute. She's just gone ter get a book. She's gone all soppy. Think's she's in luv. He he he,' cackled the lady to herself. Jenny pulled herself together.

'Good morning madam. Of course we can help you. I will just get my seamstress to come down and discuss your requirements with you.' Jenny rushed upstairs and told Marian about the lady.

When Marian entered, she gave a warm smile to the lady who introduced herself.

'I'm Mrs Duxbury. Wife of Jeremiah Duxbury of Low Moor Mill.' Jenny suddenly remembered the lovesick young man and his handkerchiefs, and wondered if this was the same family. She could hardly imagine a peer of the realm marrying into this family.

As she was thinking this, the door opened and the most exquisite creature breezed through the door. She was blond where Mrs Duxbury was dark, and slim where her mother was more generously proportioned. Even her speech was different.

'Mama, I am sorry that I took so long. I had a lovely time with Mr Forbes in the bookshop. He is a most learned man. I have ordered a new poetry book. You said that I may.'

Jenny and Marian glanced at each other, not believing that this child could have come from this mother. She had obviously been away to school, to be able to speak like that. Her mother quickly introduced her to Marian and Jenny.

'Has Mama told you that we both want a ball gown? We have wanted to come to your shop ever since my birthday. A certain young man bought me some exquisitely embroidered handkerchiefs, and said that he had them made at this shop. Is that so?'

'Yes,' said Marian, 'I made them. I'm glad that you liked them. What sort of ball gown were you thinking about?'

'I would like a white one. Very simple lines, with not a lot of frills or flounces. And I would like some flowers in my hair to match the dress.'

'Well, that will be easy to manage. Now what about you, Mrs Duxbury?'

'Oh, I do want frills and flounces, the more the better. And I'd like a bright colour. Bright pink, I think.'

Marian was astounded. The thought of the plump Mrs Duxbury in a bright pink, frilly dress appalled her, but how could she tactfully make her change her mind without offending her?

She took a deep breath. 'Mrs Duxbury, I have had a bolt of material in for some time, and I have never found the right person for it. I am sure that it would suit your colouring perfectly. It is not pink, but a lovely purple. And I have the most delicate lilac that it can be trimmed with. Let me show you.'

Marian went for the material and draped it round Mrs Duxbury. She sketched a ball gown that was simplicity in itself, but with fussy sleeves trimmed with the lilac. The rest of the gown was in smooth flowing lines that flattered her figure. A neat bustle at the back completed the outfit. Mrs Duxbury wasn't convinced. Her daughter came to the rescue by enthusing over the gown.

'You will be the height of fashion, Mama, in London gowns have become much more simple now. Just let Miss Marian make it, and if you don't like it, you could have another made. Papa wouldn't mind.' Mrs Duxbury obviously adored her daughter, as she acquiesced and the order was made.

The week after the ball, Miss Duxbury came into the shop chatting excitedly.

'Miss Marian, your magic worked. He proposed to me. I am now engaged to be married. I am so happy. In a way, you have been a link in our romance. First the handkerchiefs, then the ball gown. I now want you and nobody else to make my marriage gown.' Marian looked excited. She had longed to make a marriage gown. At that moment, a man came into the shop.

'Oh Papa, this is Miss Marian who made my gown, and Miss Jenny, the proprietor of the shop.' They both said hello, gathering that this was Mr Duxbury. He was tall, slim and so full of energy that he couldn't keep still whilst he was talking.

''Hello lasses. Well I'm glad that my wife and daughter came here. You did them up grand. They looked a lovely pair of pictures. Now, you may have guessed that we're not top drawer. Well, my Ethel is worried to death about this wedding do. 'Cos our girl's the bride, we have to arrange the whole thing, and we haven't a clue what to do. Can you help my wife? Money's no object. Nothing is to good for my only girl.' He looked fondly at his daughter.

Jenny stepped forward. 'Yes, I think we can help you. When Marian and I were in service at a Lord's house, they had a wedding and we were involved in it, so we know what would be expected.'

'That's grand. Well here's the money for them last two frocks and here's £300 on account for the wedding do. But think on, there's plenty more when that runs out. I might not have much style, but one thing I have got is money. Now I'll tell the wife to come down tomorrow. The wedding's in June by the way.'

With that he put a handful of banknotes on the display cabinet, and walked out, leaving Jenny and Marian gasping. His daughter followed him, after confirming that she would bring her mum the following day. Jenny pressed a receipt into her hand, to give to her father.

'June,' gasped Marian when they had gone, 'and it's the middle of April. I think that we're going to need some more help Jenny.'

'Yes, I think that you're right. I'll think about that tomorrow, when we know how big the wedding is to be.'

That night, as Jenny was locking the outer door, she was startled to see a man peering in through the window. She jumped back in alarm.

'Please Miss, do not be alarmed. I'm only looking for my sister. Susy Marshall. Is she here, or do you know where she might be? The workhouse said that she got a job here, but I see that you are shutting the shop. Has she gone home?'

During this long speech, Jenny looked at this young man, and rather liked what she saw. He was so earnest and forthright. He obviously wanted to explain what he was about so that she got the full picture, and was trying to reassure her, all at the same time.

He had rather a nice face, now she looked at it. He had a high forehead, with his brown hair sweeping back from both sides of the middle parting. His hair was worn just a little long, and it curled round the base of his ears. He had a strong, firm jaw and shapely nose.

He was only a little bit taller than her, not very tall for a man, but he was stocky of build. His clothes were those of a workman, but they were clean and tidy, and he smelt pleasantly, not like many workmen.

'Well, Miss? Are you all right Miss?'

Jenny was startled out of her reverie. She had been fascinated in looking at this man. What an embarrassment. She didn't even know what he had asked her.

'I am sorry; I just became a little faint. What did you ask me?'

He was all concern, wanting to help her and take her inside to sit down. That just made Jenny worse. She began to fluster.

'Well, er, I er no. I will be all right. Do come inside. I don't know what overcame me,' she said to the young man. Humph, she thought to herself. Pull yourself together, girl. So busy looking at a man, that you don't know what he asked you.

'I asked if my sister worked here, Susy Marshall.'

'Oh yes, of course. And your mother.'

'My mother?' The young man gasped. 'The workhouse never mentioned my mother. I thought, well, I thought that perhaps she had passed away. She was so ill when I saw her last.'

'Your mother is here, too. I will call them.' She went to the back of the shop and called for Susy and her mum, only saying that they had a visitor.

Susy came first and let out a scream when she saw the young man. She ran across the room and flung her arms round him.

'Jonny, Jonny, we thought you had gone forever. It's so good to see you.' Light dawned in Jenny's brain. This was Susy's brother who had been in the workhouse. She had been so busy studying him that she hadn't recognised him. How embarrassing! At that point, Mrs Marshall came slowly in and also ran across the floor to Jonny. She cried bitterly, hugging him and rocking him, all the while.

'When did you come back to Clitheroe?' asked Susy.

'Yesterday. I got a job at the stables. I get to live above the stables in a sort of all in one room. It's very warm and very handy. Don't have to walk too far to get to work,' he quipped. 'I went to the workhouse this afternoon with a delivery and got quite a shock when they said that you'd left and got a job in a shop. How did you get this job? You were lucky to get out of the workhouse weren't you? And to get mum a job, too. She is so much better, Susy. I can't believe the change in her.'

'It was all through Jenny.'

'Jenny?'

'Yes, Jenny Mitchell. Surely you remember her from the workhouse. My best friend.' Jonny looked slowly at Jenny.

'Jenny from the workhouse?'

'Yes, you silly man. Stop repeating what I say.'

'Little Jenny. Susy's friend.' Light seemed to be dawning on Jonny at last. 'And how did you get a job here?'

'I didn't. I own it.'

'Own it?'

'Look, he's repeating what you are saying now,' said Susy in exasperation. 'She inherited a shop, and she doesn't know why or who from. All right. Understand?'

'Well, I'm pleased that you have done well for yourself and grateful that you gave my sister and mother a home. I'll look after them now, as it's my responsibility. Thank you.'

'Don't be daft, Jonny, we're happy here. We're not coming to live in your one-roomed place. We have our own bedroom here, all meals provided, and we get wages as well. We have never been so rich. And mum has come on a treat here. So don't talk about taking us away.'

'We never liked charity, Susy,'

'This isn't charity. We are all working girls. Anyway, you were happy enough to leave us in the workhouse, when it suited you, after that row with the charge hand. Went off to make your fortune. Where is it then?' said Susy bitterly.

'Please, don't argue. I couldn't do without your sister and mother now. They are an important part of my staff. Feel free to come and visit anytime you like, but they have a home here with me.'

There was silence all round.

Eventually Jonny broke the silence. 'All right. As long as you need them, that seems satisfactory. Well, I'll be getting along then.'

'Oh please don't go yet,' said Jenny, just a shade too quickly. 'Please come and have some tea with us,' she said to cover herself.

'I will then. Thank you Miss.'

'It's Jenny, not Miss.'

'Jenny, then.' Jenny shivered at the way he said her name. He seemed to linger over the 'J' making it a much longer name. Oh dear, she was being really silly now. She led the way upstairs to the kitchen and they sat down to their evening meal.

Jenny sat furthest away from Jonny, so that she could have covert glances at him, without anyone else noticing. She really would have to take herself in hand. She had never behaved like this before. Some of the other servant boys at Ormerod Hall had teased her and asked her out, but she had never been interested. And you are not interested now, Jenny Mitchell. You have too much to do at present, she chastised herself. But there was no harm in looking!

Soon after the meal, Jonny excused himself, and left the shop. Susy and her mother talked at length about old times, and about the surprise they had just received.

Jenny was content just to listen to their talk about Jonny. Only one letter difference in their names, she thought. Jenny and Jonny. Jonny and Jenny. How nice they sounded together. Even his name was nice she thought as she drifted to sleep that night.

Chapter 20

Next morning, Mrs and Miss Duxbury arrived early at the shop.

'Good morning to you both. I will just get Miss Marian down to assist you.' She led the two ladies to the settee. 'Susy, could you bring a tray of tea, please? And could you ask Marian to come to the shop. The Duxbury's have arrived.'

Jenny returned to the couple then pulling up a small table, placed her notepad, quill pen and ink on to the table. 'Now tell me about the marriage. When is it to be? How many guests? Where will the marriage be performed? Where will the wedding breakfast take place?'

'The marriage will be on the 12th June, at St Paul's church. The wedding breakfast will be at our home. And there will be two hundred guests. Was that all the questions?'

'Yes, I am sorry, I did ask you rather a lot all at once. But these are questions that I need to know before I start planning. Your husband says that you would like advice on how to go about planning the wedding. Am I right? I don't wish to interfere if you would prefer to do some of it yourself.'

'No, yer right. I'd like yer to do as much as possible. I wish I could wake up and find that it were all over. I'm fair dreading it. And yet, I want it ter be the best day o' th' lasses life. Oh, I'm fair weary of it already.'

'Don't despair. I will help you as much as I possibly can. Now, first of all, let us discuss the bridal gown. Over to you Marian.'

'Right Miss Duxbury, what ideas have you got?'

'Please call me Bethany. I feel as if we are friends already.'

'That is a lovely name, Bethany. Quite unusual nowadays.'

'Yes, it was my great grandmother's name. They were very religious.'

'Well, Bethany, you must call me Marian if I am to call you Bethany.'

'Right, Marian. What do you think would suit me?'

'I received a book from London through Mr Forbes next door, with some fashion gowns in. They have given me some ideas. You will want white or ivory, won't you?'

'I think ivory would be nice. Sometimes I look better in ivory than white. It's gentler. And I don't want a low cut dress, rather a more demure style.'

'Yes, I agree with you there. What about fabric?'

'What do you think?'

'Leave it with me, and I'll sketch you some designs, and see what you think.'

'Will you have done them tomorrow? Or the next day? I am so excited.'

Marian laughed. 'Yes, come back tomorrow, and I'll have something ready for you.'

In the meantime, Jenny and Mrs Duxbury had been discussing other facts about the wedding. Jenny had agreed to ask about the cake being made at Miss Carter's, and the invitation cards being printed at Mr Canning's, as an urgent priority. Jenny had suggested the wording of the invitations, as Mrs Duxbury had no ideas of her own.

'Now what about yourself, Mrs Duxbury? Have you thought about your own outfit?'

'No ideas, you surprise me termorrow.'

'Have you thought how many bridesmaids there are to be?'

'Only three. I have no sisters, but I have a cousin and my husband to be has two sisters.'

'Well, I will do several drawings for tomorrow. Will the young ladies be able to come in for fittings?'

'Oh yes, they live locally. When would you like them to come in?'

'Not for a while yet,' Marian said laughingly. 'Give me time to get some ideas together. I know we haven't much time, but I need to have something to fit on to them when they come for a fitting. I will of course need them to come in for measurement before that. They could come in quite soon for that. Then I could get a better idea of how they would look.'

'I could bring my cousin tomorrow. And I'll try to get the others to come in too.'

'We need to plan the menu, and discuss the catering for the wedding breakfast, Mrs Duxbury. Are your staff able to manage, or will you need to arrange caterers?'

I think that me staff'd prefer ter 'ave folk coming in ter do the work. They'll be all right with most stuff, but a big wedding breakfast, well; I think that'd be a problem. They gets nervous enough when we 'ave dinner parties. I 'ate 'em too,' said Mrs Duxbury. 'I end up talkin' even more common when I'm flustered, and I get right proper flustered when we 'ave company.'

'Oh Mama, stop worrying, I will help you with your speech. It is easy if you speak slowly and think about what you are saying at all times. I had to learn when I went to boarding school. The girls teased me terribly. I soon learned. We shall have lessons every day, starting from now. We only have two months to the nuptials, so we will have to work hard.'

'Thanks, luv. Yer are good ter me.'

'Pardon?'

'Oh yer, I mean, thank you my dear,' said Mrs Duxbury in very clipped tones. Everybody applauded.

'We know how you feel,' said Jenny. 'We were made to speak properly when we went in service. It is hard at first, but you do get used to it. I am so glad I did, because now I can hold my own with the people who come in here, and don't feel embarrassed.'

'Well, we'll see yer, I mean you, tomorrow. Goodbye for now, and thank you. I feel better already,' said Mrs Duxbury.

They didn't arrive until mid-afternoon, and they all came together. Lord Hastings had brought his carriage containing his two sisters, along with Mrs and Miss Duxbury. They were a lively bunch.

'Here you are then, Miss Marian. I suppose you want me to conveniently disappear for a few hours, whilst you sort out the outfits. I am believe that I am not supposed to see the bride's gown before the marriage ceremony,' laughed Lord Hastings. 'Well, I will go and come back for you all in two hours. Will that be long enough?'

'Just about,' replied Marian just as quickly. 'It's a very serious event that we're preparing for.'

Still laughing, Lord Hastings left the shop, suggesting that it would amuse him to go and look at Cosgrove's outfitters shop for men and perhaps plan his outfit, although he promised not to outshine the bride!

The women and girls sat around a small table and Marian showed Bethany the sketches for her dress first.

'You wanted a plain demure gown. How does this look? It is actually a two-piece garment, made of ivory, corded silk. The bodice is tightly fitted with a round neck, which is trimmed in

Honiton lace. There will be a long row of tiny silk covered buttons, all down the front of the bodice.'

'The sleeves are gathered at the shoulder, but taper down to the wrist, where there is Honiton lace again to match the neckline. They would also have the same tiny covered buttons, like the bodice.'

'The bodice comes to a point in the front and covers the skirt. The bodice would be boned and lined with cotton for comfort. The skirt would be covered in pleated bands of the same silk, and a small bustle would be in place at the back. A long train would develop from the back of your gown. It would be very elegant and fairly plain, but I think that it would match your loveliness and fair colouring.'

'The main feature would be the lovely long veil, which would be made of Honiton lace. There would be roses and other flowers within the lace pattern. I would suggest a circlet of apple blossom flowers made in wax in your hair, which could be matched by carrying apple blossom flowers as your bridal bouquet.'

'Your slippers would also be in satin with a small heel, with ruched bows of satin on the front. They would also have a tiny sprig of apple blossom and a tiny covered button in the middle of the bow.'

Everybody fell silent. Marian began to look worried. 'If it is not to your taste, I can try again,' said Marian nervously.

Bethany turned very slowly towards Marian. 'Oh, it is to my taste, Marian. Very much to my taste. I couldn't have designed it better myself. I like the idea that the only fussy parts are the veil and the train. Yes, I like it very much. Now what about the maids of honour?'

'Again, I would like to try a new idea for them,' said Marian.

'Tell me about it, then,' replied Bethany.

'What about having virtually the same gowns as you for the two big maids of honour, but in a different colour? Of course, they wouldn't wear a headdress and veil, but would wear more formal hats, as befitting their position. I thought of a lovely rich medium blue silk for them, with pale blue trim.'

'Yes, that would be nice, but it wouldn't suit the little bridesmaid.'

'No, I would suggest that we are more traditional with her. The usual frilly gown in a much lighter material than silk, but in a pale blue to match the trim on the big girl's outfits, with a deep sash in the medium blue. She could wear a smaller version of the hat. And her little shoes could be dyed to match the gown.'

'Oh yes, I want to wear a gown like that Bethany. Do say yes, please?' piped up the little maid of honour. Everyone laughed.

'What do you two think about the suggestions?' Bethany asked the other two girls.

They both agreed that the gowns would be a refreshing change from the usual frills and furbelows that brides and maids of honour were usually made to wear.

'Like my mama would have me wear, if she got her own way,' whispered Bethany to her cousin. Fortunately Mrs Duxbury was heavily engrossed with Jenny at this point, so missed the aside.

The girls were all measured for their outfits and Marian made copious notes.

'And now it is your turn, Mrs Duxbury. The mother of the bride must look especially lovely. I thought that we could stay on the same colour scheme, and have your dress in dark blue silk, with a plain under gown and bodice, but overlaid with patterned brocade in the same shade, to give it richness.'

'There would be a small bustle under the skirt; the bottom of the skirt would be ruched and have small bows, on the edge of each ruched section. And the small bows could be sewn on the top of each shoulder and on the front of the bodice.'

Marian thought that the mention of bows would appease Mrs Duxbury, as she knew her penchant for all things frilly and fussy. The small bows would hopefully satisfy Mrs Duxbury without making her look overdressed and silly.

Fortunately, the sketch was approved, and Marian was commissioned to make all the gowns according to her suggestions. After the ladies had left, Marian turned to Jenny.

'I'm really going to need that help that we talked about yesterday. This is a really big order, Jenny.'

'It certainly is, and I'm very proud of you. Where do you get your ideas? You are so good. You even convinced Mrs Duxbury that she doesn't want frilly gowns anymore. You are amazing! Now, about your help. Is their anyone that you can think of?'

'There is someone, but she would need somewhere to live as well.'

'Who?'

'Mrs Hartley, who taught me how to sew in the workhouse.'

'What a good idea. I want to employ people from the workhouse where I can. Yes, Mrs Hartley would be excellent. I shall go and see Matron today. I do love seeing Matron's face when I go and get someone out. I must be honest; it gives me a good feeling inside. Perhaps I'm being too proud. I should repent or God might punish me.'

'Well, I will always be grateful to you, and I thank God that you saved me. So I am sure that God won't think you too proud.'

'Would you like to come with me to the workhouse?'

'Not this time,' laughed Marian, 'I have too much to do. Such a slave driver of a boss I have!'

'Humph, you brought this on yourself by designing such beautiful gowns. You have only yourself to blame. I'll be off then. Can you and Susy re-arrange the bedrooms, yet again?'

'Yes. We're going to be bursting at the seams soon, if we take anymore people in.'

Jenny was only away a little over two hours returning with a very happy Mrs Hartley. She soon settled in, and Marian had her at the sewing machine by the next morning. Marian came to see Jenny next morning whilst Mrs Hartley was busy sewing. She looked as if something was worrying her.

'Come on Marian, what's the matter?'

'I know that you've got a lot of expense, especially with Mrs Hartley coming to stay, but it would be much easier if we could have another Singer sewing machine. Don't worry if you can't manage it at this time. We'll just have to take turns at sewing and trimming. But if we could both sew, Susy could trim as well.'

Jenny threw back her head in laughter.

'Marian, this order for the wedding alone would buy several sewing machines. Look, Mr Duxbury popped in again at closing time. He seemed very pleased with how the planning session had gone. He slapped another £500, in banknotes, in my hand towards the cost of the wedding. Of course you can have a sewing machine. This time, you can go out and buy one. Here, take some money.'

Jenny peeled off some banknotes as Marian stared at her.

'Oh, and get a receipt. Susy will be cross if I don't account for all the money.' Jenny set off upstairs to Susy with the rest of the money. When she talked to Susy, she mentioned about the need to expand the business.

'Do you think that we could all fit into the bedrooms on the third floor, and then we could open up the second floor for more areas to shop. We could have racks of dresses downstairs, with all the accessories upstairs. What do you think?' Jenny turned, as Susy had gone quiet and not answered.

'Susy, what so you think?'

'Now you've mentioned it, I wondered if I could have a word with you about us living here.'

'Yes, what about it?' said Jenny breathlessly. Perhaps they wanted Jonny to come and live here as well, so that the family were all together. Jonny under the same roof, it would be so exciting, she thought to herself. Her heart was beating rapidly. But she was wrong and her hopes were dashed.

'We wondered if you would mind if we all got a house together in town. I mean mum, Jonny and me. It would be nearby so that we could still both work for you.'

'Are you not satisfied with living here?'

'Oh yes, but it is just that we haven't lived like a family for so many years. And now that we have found Jonny, we don't want to let him go.'

Yes, thought Jenny, I can understand that. I wouldn't want to let my family go if I was in the same position. And I wouldn't want to let Jonny go either.

'That's all right if you wish, but there is a condition.'

'Yes, what is that?'

'That you invite me to tea when you are settled.'

'Oh Jenny, thank you. Of course you can come. You will be our first guest.'

'I suppose that helps my situation now. I could start planning the second floor much earlier than I intended. Perhaps your going will help me as well, although I will miss you.'

'No you won't. I will still be here all day. So get on with your planning.'

Jenny realised that she had started to look forward to Jonny's visits. Well, she remonstrated with herself, that is the end of that. She would hardly see Jonny now.

Chapter 21

The shop was a hive of industry for the next few weeks, with everyone working towards Bethany's wedding. They even borrowed Edith from Mr Forbes to help with the sewing.

Jenny spent many a long hour closeted with Mrs Duxbury, explaining how the gentry conducted themselves and what they would expect. Mr Duxbury also came in to ask advice at times and they both seemed grateful for the help given.

At last, everything was ready. The cake was taken down to the house a few days before the wedding, then the gowns, accessories and shoes the day before. Marian and Jenny had a dress rehearsal with the main party, but no one else was allowed to look in.

Marian had also organised the flowers for everyone to wear, as well as those for the house. These were delivered directly to the house the day before the wedding. The brides' favours were also delivered from the shop. They were delicate little bookmarks embroidered by hand, with the young couple's name on, along with the date of the wedding.

On the day, Mrs Duxbury had asked that Marian would attend the dressing of the bride, both at the house and at the church. Despite the bride's last minute nerves, everything went according to plan. The sun even shone beautifully to help the occasion.

It was not only the bride's mother who had a tear in her eye that day, as the radiant bride seemed to glide, rather than walk, down the aisle on her father's arm to make her vows with her besotted groom. The wedding over, the families went back to Irving Hall for the wedding breakfast.

Sighing to themselves, Jenny, Susy, Sarah, Mrs Hartley and Marian all walked slowly back to the shop, which had been closed for the hour of the wedding. George was delighted when they returned, as if he knew that he had been left out of a treat. But as he had been left behind with Mrs Marshall and a dish of sweets, he hadn't really been neglected.

Jenny decided to close the shop early that day, as none of them felt like working. After the shop had closed, Jenny and Sarah moved the furniture around on the second floor, to make it look more like a shop.

Mr Aggett had been in to decorate the second and third floors, as Jenny realised that once the new floor opened, there would be little chance of doing any decorating.

The second floor still had the main colours of brown and cream, but was dressed in a different style. The curtains for the fitting rooms were made out of brown and cream brocade, giving a lighter feel to the room.

Because it was an upstairs room, it was a little darker than downstairs and Jenny wanted to make it look brighter. The walls were painted in cream, with brown woodwork. The chairs were in a similar material to the curtains. Jenny also had more candelabras dotted about the room, to give extra light.

The second floor was solely for the accessories. A new girl, Janet, was brought from the workhouse to help in this new venture. She had worked in a shop previously and soon fitted into the group of women, who incidentally, were beginning to be talked about in the town.

This was largely due to the Duxbury wedding and Jenny knew that she had experienced an increase in sales since the wedding.

Many of the new customers mentioned the wedding and said how lovely the bride had looked, almost with a note of surprise in some of their voices, as if a little provincial gown shop was not quite the thing for a Society wedding. But the Duxbury wedding also brought a surprise to Jenny.

On the Tuesday after the wedding, Mr Duxbury came in to settle his account. Jenny explained that he had given more than enough money already. He threw an extra bundle of notes onto the counter.

'This is to be shared out amongst you all as a gift. I have never been so proud of my girl. And even those gentry were impressed. You could tell they were looking down their noses at the wife and me, but not at our Bethany. She looked a right treat. Like she were born to it. And her a Lady now. Who'd have thought that my daughter would marry a Lord. She's gone all over Europe as well. I'll miss her though.'

Mr Duxbury stopped suddenly, looking quite crestfallen. Jenny was at a loss what to say, but there was no need to worry. As fast as he had appeared upset, he recovered again.

'Well, no point getting maudlin. The time will soon pass, and then she'll be back. I'd better be getting back to the factory or else they'll be standing around idling away. Oh, by the way, here's a little something as a thank you. You'll tell whose is whose.' With that, he threw a box on to the table and left.

Jenny opened it carefully. Inside the box were four packages with names on. She called down to Marian, Mrs Hartley and Susy, to give them their packages.

'What are they?' asked Susy mystified.

'I have no idea. I haven't opened mine yet.'

They all opened them together. Marian was the first one to open her package, upon which she gave a small gasp. The others looked at her. She was drawing out a large gold locket from the package. It was beautiful. It had delicate scrolling on one side, with a large 'M' engraved on the other. Marian started to cry.

'What's the matter, Marian?' said Jenny. 'You should be happy.'

Marian sobbed. 'I have never had any jewellery before. I'll treasure it for all of my life. I'll put a picture of George in it.'

By now, the others had opened their packages. Jenny had an identical locket to Marian's but with a 'J' engraved on hers. Susy and Mrs Hartley had been given smaller versions of the locket, with their own initial engraved upon it. Inside the package was a note for each woman, thanking her for her part in making the wedding perfect.

They all discussed whom they would put in their locket. Jenny was silent. She did not have a picture of anyone to put in her locket.

Eventually, Marian asked whom Jenny was going to put in. Jenny said that she wasn't sure yet.

'Only, I wondered if you would like a picture of George to go in yours?' Bless her, thought Jenny, she has realised my dilemma.

'Thank you Marian. That would be perfect.' The moment passed and the women went off to their work, stunned by this generous present from the Duxbury's.

Jenny then remembered a conversation that she had engaged in with Mr Duxbury about suitable presents for the maids of honour. Jenny had suggested lockets and had said that any woman would be pleased to receive a locket. Oh dear, she hoped that he didn't think that she had been hinting. But it was too late now. And Bethany had bought a locket each for the maids of honour.

Perhaps it had been a genuine enquiry, which then gave him the idea for their presents. Whatever the reason, Jenny was grateful that she had received her first piece of jewellery, just as Marian was. If only she had some pictures of her own family to put in it.

The shop continued to make an impression in the town and Jenny couldn't believe the amount of profit that she was making. She now had a healthy bank account and was relieved that she would meet one of the conditions of the legacy. She was making a profit of the business, even though she was employing several people.

Jenny gave generous wages as well. All her employees had said that they would work for her for nothing. They were just so glad to get out of the workhouse, but Jenny didn't abuse their generosity and gave each of them a fair wage.

The year flew by and it was soon the anniversary of the opening of the shop. They had a little party to celebrate. All the staff and friends such as Messrs Briggs, Shoesmith and Forbes were invited, as well as Miss Carter and the Canning's. Jenny thanked them all for their individual help in making the business a success.

In the New Year, Marian asked if she could have a quiet word with Jenny.

'I would like to buy my own house, if you wouldn't mind. One has just come up for sale three doors down from Susy and Jonny. It's very cheap because it's run down and neglected. I've been saving my wages and I can afford to buy it now.'

'Of course, Marian, that will be great. It will be another house where I can come for tea,' she laughed.

'It will mean a lot to George and me. We can be our own family there. Sometimes, I feel that he belongs to Sarah more than me. He took his first steps to her and said his first words to her. I'm not complaining, she is very good, but I do want him to myself more. Am I being selfish?'

'Not at all. I understand how you feel. I hope that you will be very happy.'

Marian soon had the house looking spic and span. Everybody helped with the painting and Jonny found her some second hand furniture that was in good condition. He did many of the harder jobs for her too, but Marian made all the curtains and cushion covers herself. She was very proud of her little terraced house and invited everyone to tea.

The shop remained busy. At their busiest times, they all helped to serve in the shop and with the sewing, but they all had their own special tasks as well.

Susy's was the accounts. One day, as Jenny was working in the office, Susy exclaimed as she was looking at the accounts.

'What's the matter, Susy?' asked Jenny.

'The bill for the carter is £4 16 shillings this week. That's a large amount.'

'It certainly is. But then, we have given them a lot of things to deliver this week. Everybody who bought something this week seemed to live out of town. There isn't a lot we can do. We have to have things delivered. That is the way most of our customers shop. They will come into the shop, but won't take the shopping home with them. Well, I must get back to Marian. She wanted to discuss our next wedding.'

Whilst she was talking to Marian, Jenny told her about the cost of the carter.

'I don't know why you don't have your own carter. You do enough business now,' said Marian.

'It would be far too expensive.'

'Once you had bought the horse and cart, it would only be the cost of keeping the horse and the man's wages, wouldn't it? Would that be very expensive?'

'I suppose not. Not as much as our carter is costing. I'll get Susy to work some figures out for it. Yes, I'll go now.' Jenny went back upstairs and outlined Marian's idea to Susy.

Two days later, Susy asked Jenny if she would come to tea that evening. Jenny was delighted. The small terrace house was pleasant and relaxing and she enjoyed going there. Besides, she could see Jonny as well!

Jenny arrived punctually at six of the clock. Jonny himself opened the door and Jenny felt herself blushing as he took her coat.

Even though he only gently touched her arm as he took her coat, it was enough to send shivers up and down her spine. She had a sudden longing for him to touch more than just her arm and then was shocked by her own thoughts.

She hurried into the sitting room, greeting Susy and her mum warmly. Mrs Marshall served a delicious meal and then they sat by the fire, having a welcome cup of tea.

'Jenny,' said Susy in a wheedling voice, 'I know you don't like to talk about the shop after it's closed, but I've had an idea. You may not like it, and please say so if you're cross with me. I don't want to offend you.'

'Well tell me, Susy. I am intrigued at what you may have to say that may offend me – I am your longest friend after all.'

'It is about the carter.'

'Yes?'

'I was wondering if you would like to see the figures for the costs of having your own carter.'

'I suppose so, but I usually like to keep business separate from pleasure.'

'I had an idea that you could have your own carter's carriage. It could be made in brown and cream paint, and have a covered top to protect both the driver and the goods being delivered. It could have 'Mitchell's Modes' painted on the sides, with our address. I have got some prices for you here.' Susy passed a piece of paper over to Jenny.

'Yes, these all seem reasonable prices. Go ahead and order it, please. But why tonight?'

'Er, that is the rest of the plan. That is why I needed you to be here tonight.'

A mystified Jenny waited to see what Susy would say.

'We would need a decent, trustworthy driver for the cart. Someone who is able to work on his own and look after a horse as well.'

'Yes,' replied Jenny cautiously, not understanding where this was leading.

'Jonny would like to apply for the job of being your carter,' Susy gasped out suddenly.

Jenny froze. She couldn't speak. Susy could bear the silence no longer than a few seconds.

'Have I offended you? Never mind, forget what I said. It was only an idea. I'm sorry.'

Jenny waited for the rapid beating of her heart to subside.

'No,' she said slowly, 'you have not offended me. In fact, I think that it's a very practical idea. Yes, why not? What do you think Jonny?' she held her breath whilst he replied.

'I would like the job, Jenny,' he replied equally slowly, drawing out the 'J' of Jenny as usual.

'Well, that's settled then. How long will you have to work before you can come to me?'

'Just a week. I could start for you next Monday.'

'Good. I will look forward to that.' Yes, indeed I will, thought Jenny, without saying anything. Seeing Jonny every day. What more could she ask for?

'Perhaps you could arrange an outfit from Cosgrove's, the Gentleman's Outfitters. If you order it tomorrow, it might be ready for when Jonny starts.' She turned to Jonny. 'I am afraid it will have to be a uniform in brown with cream braid trim. You know I like everything to match,' she laughed.

'With one brown shoe and one cream shoe, Jenny?' he quipped back.

'No, don't be silly, brown shoes during the week and cream shoes on Sundays,' she replied. Jonny looked crestfallen.

'Sunday's? Cream shoes?' he asked.

'Not really, I'm just teasing. You can wear what you want on Sundays. That will be your day off like the rest of us.'

'Jenny, I am so grateful. I will work hard for you. Believe me.'

'Good. That's what I like to hear. And now I must make my way home. If I'm to employ yet another member of staff, I'd better get home, so that I can be up bright and early tomorrow to make some more money.'

'It's quite late Jenny, please let Jonny walk home with you.'

'I'll be all right. The lamplighters have been round,' said Jenny half-heartedly, but Jonny was already getting his coat. Taking her by the arm. Jonny led Jenny out of the house and back up to the shop.

Jenny wished the walk would last forever. She had left early because she wanted to go home and savour the fact that Jonny would be working for her, but here he was walking her home.

All too soon, they reached the door of the shop. Jenny would have liked to linger, but as she was stood in the middle of town, she thought it better to go inside. Once the bolts had been shot, she made a drink and went up to her bedroom. She got into bed, blew out the candle and sat sipping her drink by the light of the streetlamp, dreaming about Jonny.

Chapter 22

The following Monday brought a new era in Jenny's life. She had daily contact with Jonny, as she gave him orders for the day. Sometimes he would pull his forelock, and say 'Yes Miss', which was always guaranteed to get her laughing.

Some days, Jenny would go out with him to deliver a big order, as she said that she liked to give personal service to her customers. Marian and Susy would nod wisely and agree to her face, but then wink to each other after she had gone out with Jonny.

After a few months it was patently obvious to everyone that Jenny loved Jonny and vice versa, but nothing seemed to progress. Marian and Susy plotted as to how they could help the star-crossed lovers, but couldn't think of a plan.

The shop however, continued to progress, unlike the romance. New customers were coming in daily, as well as all of the original customers, consequently Jonny was kept very busy. Eventually he had to take on a young boy, Robert, to help with the deliveries. He jokingly called him his apprentice.

The year went quickly by. Many more weddings were ordered and provided for. The notion of Jenny arranging the whole wedding was a popular idea with a lot of mothers in the Ribble Valley. They were only too keen to let Jenny have all the worry and also give them some ideas. Between Marian and Jenny, they produced some spectacular events and outfits.

The fathers' of the brides' were also happy, as Mitchell's Modes prices were a lot less than some of the costumiers in London, or even worse, Paris.

Despite the spate of weddings, Jenny and Marian were always able to come up with an original idea to make each wedding special to the family.

The local balls were another event where their ingenuity was taxed. So many different gowns had to be made for the same event. There had to be not even a hint of similarity between the gowns, or they would have lost business and credibility in the town. It was a tall order!

The second Christmas that the shop had been opened, Jenny invited all the staff to a Christmas meal. Here, she announced that she had been reading about a co-operative system in Rochdale where the local shoppers got some money back for buying from certain shops.

Jenny explained that she was going to do a similar arrangement for all the staff; not according to how much money they spent, but rather on how much money the shop was making. They were to get half of 1% of the profits each as a bonus on top of their wages.

There was a stunned silence.

Jonny was the first to recover his voice. 'But you can't, Jenny. It's your money. You shouldn't give us any.'

'Why not?'

'Because, er, because, well, you shouldn't that's all. Because you are the boss,' he said at last triumphantly.

'That is correct,' said Jenny rather haughtily, 'and as I remember, what the boss says is the rule. Am I correct in my assumptions?' There were a few sheepish nods.

'Right then, we will hear no more about it. Mr Briggs will prepare the system with Susy and ensure that it is correctly administered.'

'What about me?' said Sarah in a quiet voice. 'I don't make any money in the shop. I only look after George.'

'Only look after George? Isn't that one of the most important jobs in the shop? How would Marian sew if you didn't mind George for her? Don't be silly, Sarah. Of course you will get your share. And your mum too, Susy. She has an important job here, helping in the kitchen.'

'But then we'll get three shares at our house, that's not fair,' said Jonny.

'Why not? You do three people's work. Stop arguing and get back to enjoying the Christmas celebration. I wish I hadn't told you now. You all seem miserable, when I thought you'd all be delighted.' Jenny looked pretty ruffled.

'We are very grateful Jenny,' said Marian. 'Thank you. It will make a difference to all of us.'

'Right, who is for a game of charades?' The moment passed and everyone seemed happy again.

The rest of Christmas sped by and soon they were back into the throes of winter, trying to cope with getting deliveries out in the deep snow. Jonny and Robert often came in frozen to the marrow, but Mrs Marshall always had a pan of hot soup ready and the kettle on the boil.

But the customers managed to get in despite the snowdrifts. One of the new customers was Lady Morag, Lord Jeremy's older sister. Lady Morag recommended a lot of her friends to the shop.

Jenny could see that they were curious about this young woman who had been a servant in Lady Morag's home, but was now a successful shop owner, who was the fashion talk of the Ribble Valley and beyond.

Lady Morag had never forgotten the way Jenny had looked after her when they visited Ormerod Hall. She recognised Marian as well, but made no comment when George came into the shop one day, merely stared after him.

Jenny could only think that this was the reason for what happened later. One quiet afternoon, the bell rang when Jenny was in the downstairs shop. The rest of the staff were either upstairs, in the town or on a day off. Jenny turned to see who had come into the shop, her usual smile fixed on her face. Her smile froze, though. It was Lord Jeremy Ormerod.

'Good afternoon, Lord Ormerod. How may I help you.'

'Ah Mitchell, I need some help.'

'Miss Mitchell, Lord Ormerod,' Jenny corrected.

'Quite. Now where is that brat that had my child?'

Jenny tried to pretend that she didn't know what he was talking about. He got angry.

'Come on woman, stop fooling. Where is she?'

'Surely there is no woman who had your child, Sir; you denied all knowledge of it at the time. What right have you to come in and demand to see her?'

'Never you mind, just get her for me. I am in a hurry.'

'Well, I am sorry, she is out at present. You will have to make an appointment to see her another day.'

'Make an appointment?' he exploded, 'I will do no such thing. I will wait here until she comes back.' As if on cue, the door opened, and in walked Marian with little George. They had been having a rare stroll out together. Marian gasped when she saw Lord Jeremy and hurried into the back of the shop with George.

'Come back,' he ordered. Marian came back into the shop alone.

'Where's the boy?'

'It s none of your business where he is. He is my son.'

'Ah, but he is my son as well. And I need a son. That bitch only gives me girls, and they usually die. I need a son, don't you understand? I have come to tell you that I am taking him back. I can get a magistrate to say that you are an unfit mother, so that will be easy. Now come on, give him to me.'

'Over my dead body, said Marian with venom. 'You weren't interested in helping me then, so I won't help you now.'

Lord Jeremy started to bluster. 'But he even looks like me. It is obvious that he is my son.'

'More's the pity,' said Marian. 'Thank God that he hasn't your nature.'

'Well, I will be back, and with a magistrate. I'll soon have him off you.' He was stood menacingly near to Marian whilst he was saying this. She even thought that he was about to strike her, as he raised his arm, but just at that point, Jonny returned from his deliveries.

'What's going on here?'

'Oh Jonny, thank goodness you are back. Lord Jeremy was just leaving. Please could you show him to the door?' Lord Jeremy stood his ground for a few seconds, then glaring first at Marian and then Jenny, he strode out of the shop, pushing Jonny out of the way.

Jenny and Marian both burst into tears at once. Jonny didn't know who to turn to first.

'What was going on? He looked very threatening.'

'He was trying to take George away from Marian because his wife can't give him a son. It was awful,' wailed Jenny. 'He won't get him. I won't allow it. I am going to go and see Mr Shoesmith and see what rights Marian has. Will you stay here with her, Jonny? She is really shaken up.'

'Of course, but will you be all right too, Jenny? You seem shaken up too?'

'I'll be fine. I must go and see Mr Shoesmith or Mr Briggs. They will know what to do.' Jenny hurried upstairs for her bonnet and cloak and set off down the hill to the solicitor's office.

She came back in a much happier mood. Mr Shoesmith had reassured Jenny that Lord Jeremy had no rights on George, as the name of the father on the birth certificate was left blank, as was the usual case with illegitimate children.

'Also,' Jenny reassured Marian, 'Mr Shoesmith will sign a letter to say that you are a good mother, so a magistrate won't be able to force you to give George away.'

'I may have not wanted him when I knew I was to have a child, but I love him so much now. I could not bear to be parted from him,' said Marian tremulously.

'You go and have a special time with George, now. I will look after the shop.'

When Jonny returned from the stables, Jenny thanked him for helping her with Lord Jeremy.

'It gave me an awful fright when I saw you with him. I thought he was going to hurt you both. I was really frightened that he would hurt you.'

'Oh Jonny, that's so kind of you to care.'

'I do care Jenny. More than I should. I know that it's not my place to say anything, but I do care about you very much.' Jenny's heart was pounding until she thought that it would burst.

'Why should you not say anything, Jonny?'

'Because you're my employer.'

'But I'm a woman too,' said Jenny softly.

Jonny stared at her, as if she had spoken in a foreign language.

'You mean, you have a woman's feelings for me?' he asked disbelievingly.

'More than that, Jonny Marshall, I love you, and have since you came to the shop that night to find Susy and your mum. Now how do you feel about me? I seem to be saying everything here.'

'Jenny, I also have loved you from the night that I returned, but I felt that because you were Susy's employer, and then mine, that we could never be more than friends. I can't believe this. Here, let me hold you.' He moved towards her, but Jenny backed away.

'Not in broad daylight in the shop window. What will people think? Come into the back room, and you can kiss my cheek.' He kissed her cheek in the back room.

'Jenny, will you marry me, or is that too much to ask?'

'With pleasure. When? Soon?'

'Soon,' said Jonny as he slowly enveloped her in a warm hug.

Mrs Hartley coming downstairs to ask if she could go home interrupted them. She was worried about Mr Forbes, who hadn't seemed himself that morning. Mrs Hartley had moved in next door with Edith to share lodgings there. Jenny allowed her to go home, especially after Mrs Hartley had commented that Jenny looked all flushed, and she hoped that she wasn't coming down with something too.

As soon as she had gone, Jonny mimicked her voice, saying he hoped that Jenny wasn't coming down with something, as well. They both laughed and were disturbed this time by Marian and Susy.

'Well, they are both here together. We had better say something,' said Jenny. 'We would like to announce that we are engaged to be married,' she said looking very pleased with herself.

'Who? When?' asked a bemused Marian.

'Me and Jonny. Who did you think?' laughed Jenny.

Susy and Marian hugged them both and then each other.

'At long last! Can we be maids of honour?' asked Susy.

'Oh, I only want a quiet wedding. But I suppose you can. But no frilly gowns, mind. I'll just have a winter suit that will wear again. We thought we would get married nearer Christmas in the Parish Church. That will be close to the time when it is three years since I inherited the shop. Just think, by the time I get married, I may know more about my benefactor.'

Jonny looked at her in amazement. She had such a quick mind. He hadn't got over the fact that she loved him, and there she was, coolly arranging not only the date of the wedding but also where it would take place and what she would wear.

'Isn't that right, Jonny?'

'If you say so Madam, I am only the groom. Do I have any say?'

They all laughed.

'Not with this bride,' quipped Susy, 'you won't get much say with this bride. Oh, can I go and tell mum? She'll be delighted.' Susy dashed off home to tell her mum.

On the surface, to her friends, Jenny didn't seem to be overjoyed at the prospect of being a bride, but underneath she was ecstatically happy. She couldn't believe her luck. In rare moments when she and Jonny were alone, they embraced, and eventually kissed on the lips, feeling very daring for an engaged couple.

Jonny insisted on buying her an engagement ring. Jenny didn't want one, but he stood his ground, saying that they wouldn't be properly engaged if she didn't have a ring.

She hadn't wanted to put him to the expense of buying a ring and was trying to choose a ring with only a tiny diamond stone. But he wouldn't have any of it.

He bought her a ring with three diamonds in a row, in a twist of gold. The ring suited her perfectly and she had to agree that she loved it. It cost him three weeks wages. Jenny offered to help him, but he was offended and said he didn't need her help.

Jenny managed to offend Jonny about another matter as well, soon after their engagement. She asked Jonny if he wanted a manager's role within the business, now that he was going to become her husband.

'Certainly not. What do I know about running a gown shop? I prefer doing my deliveries. That's enough to be going on with. I don't want to be a boss.'

'Are you sure?'

'Quite sure. Besides, we have enough with you being a boss, without me being a boss as well,' he grinned cheekily.

'What do you mean by that?' asked Jenny in a rather haughty manner.

'Just that. Sometimes, you do get bossy, my dear.'

'I'm sorry if I'm bossy, I don't mean to be. Especially not with you,' said Jenny taking the huff.

'It's not important. I'm happy as I am.'

'Do you want to be a partner then, even if you don't want to be a manager?'

'No. Just leave me be. I'm going back to the stables now. Is there anything else you want at present?'

'No thank you,' replied Jenny in a cool manner.

The atmosphere remained cool between them for a few hours, but they couldn't stay cross at each other for long. Their romance was too new, and they were soon making up again.

At the beginning of the next month, Marian happened to be out of the shop when Mr Williams came with the order. He kept looking round the shop as if he was looking for something.

'Is Marian not here, today then?'

'No. She has had a few days holiday. She's going to take George on a train ride tomorrow. He loves trains. He runs round, making 'shoo shoo' noises. He is really funny.'

'He is a lovely boy. They're not alike though. Jenny is so auburn and yet he is so blond. I suppose he must be like his father.'

Jenny quailed at the word 'father'.

'Please, don't mention the word 'father' to Marian, and she proceeded to tell Mr Williams all about how Lord Jeremy had tried to take her son away.

'Why should a Lord be interested in Marian's son?' asked Mr Williams innocently. Jenny realised that she had set herself a trap. She deliberated what to do, but then in the end, decided to tell Mr Williams the whole story.

'That explains a lot,' he said, when Jenny had finished her tale.

'What do you mean?' asked Jenny.

'Over the last two years I have made good friends with Marian and I would like to take it further. But just when I get close to her, and think of declaring myself, she seems to freeze up, and goes very distant again. Now I understand. But what can I do? She has obviously had a bad experience of our sex, and will be wary of men in the future.'

'Why don't you talk to her? Or better still; go on the train with her and George tomorrow. She would love that. I know that she is frightened of seeing Lord Jeremy again, and would welcome a man's presence just at the moment.'

'A good idea. I will go with her tomorrow and tell her that all men are not alike, and that she would be safe with me. Thank you for being so candid with me Jenny. I can't tell you how much I appreciate it, even though I know you hesitated in telling me the story.'

'I want what is best for Marian. But I think that you are the best for her. I wish you well. Oh, and by the way, she and George like liquorice comfits!' said Jenny laughing as he left the shop.

The plot paid off. A very happy Marian came into the shop a few days later, saying that Mr Williams had proposed and she had accepted. They were to live in Marian's new house, and would also be married before Christmas.

'Good Heavens,' said Jenny, 'that was quick work. Shall we have a double wedding Marian? It would save a lot of money. Only one lot of guests and one lot of clothes to make.'

'Oh yes, I would love that. When shall it be?'

'I was planning the Sunday before Christmas. By then we will have done all the Christmas ball gowns.'

'Good idea. Will you book the parson, Jenny?'

'Yes. I wonder if he will just want one fee if it is a double wedding,' schemed Jenny, and they all laughed.

'We will have to plan our outfits so that we don't clash. What colour do you want Jenny?' asked Marian.

'Anything except brown and cream. I think I am getting slightly fed up of that now!'

Their hilarity was soon stopped when Mr Briggs came into the shop, his face grave.

'May I speak to you, Miss Mitchell. I have some bad news.' Oh no, thought Jenny, not now. Not when I am so near to the three years. I suppose something has gone wrong with the inheritance. But her selfish thoughts were totally on the wrong track.

'I am afraid that I have to tell you that Mr Shoesmith has passed away.' Jenny was bewildered.

'When? How? I don't understand? I saw him this week. He was fine.'

'He had a seizure last night and passed away just before midnight.'

'I am so sorry. Is there anything that I can do?'

'Not really. Everything has been taken care of. You will come to the funeral, though, won't you? I know most ladies usually stay behind, but that fashion is changing now, and ladies are perfectly acceptable at the church service. I will let you know the arrangements.'

'Of course. Thank you. May I get you some refreshments?'

'No thank you. I have a lot to do, but Thank you all the same. I will bid you good day.' A subdued workforce carried on in the shop that day and the shop was closed during the funeral, such was the importance that Mr Shoesmith had been in Jenny's life.

The week seemed to go from bad to worse after that. Mr Forbes also suffered a seizure, but he recovered from his. Yet it was sufficiently frightening enough for him to sell the shop. Jenny made him a bid and was accepted gratefully. He offered it to her at a lesser price, as he wanted to sell it quickly, but Jenny said that he needed the full price. He was to go and live in Bury St Edmunds with his sister and her family.

As soon as was decently possible, Jenny converted the next-door shop into several departments, having to employ extra staff to help. Again, she employed girls from the workhouse. Indeed, one day whilst she was in the bank, she overheard some businessmen talking about her. They said that she was taking on so many staff from the workhouse, that the workhouse was making a profit, as it had so few mouths to feed.

The other man laughed and said that was good, because it would mean less tax for them. Jenny was furious, and let them know that she had heard their snide comments. They had the grace to look sheepish and raise their hats to her.

But the following week also brought a near tragedy. Sarah had been taking George for a walk in the castle grounds. They were on their way home and were almost back to the shop when a rough looking man tried to snatch George away. Sarah screamed and two men grabbed hold of the man, whilst one of the men's wives comforted Sarah and George. The policeman was called for, and he took the man to the police cells.

Next day, the policeman came to the shop to tell Marian that the ruffian had confessed that he was told to snatch the child by a 'rich looking blond haired toff, who promised him a lot of money.'

'Lord Jeremy Ormerod,' said Marian bitterly.

'What makes you say that?' asked the policeman.

'He tried to take my child away once before, but I refused.'

'Well we will look into this for you, my dear.'

'Yes, but you won't get anywhere, will you? He's gentry, isn't he? Can do what he wants,' said Marian, still in a bitter mood.

'Not abducting a child. But I suppose you are right. It wasn't him who tried to abduct your son, and that is what he will argue. But we will try, and I will let you know if there is anything to tell you. I will leave you now, Miss.'

After that episode, the staff were all a lot more wary of strangers, and always wanted to know where George was. Slowly, they got back into the routine of the shop, partly because they were so busy.

The double shop just seemed to make more business and profits soared. The girls were kept busy at all times, just keeping the shop well stocked. It also made an excuse for Marian to see her Mr Williams, or Will as she often called him.

Jenny had built up a reputation for planning and providing everything for the perfect wedding. It meant that Jenny got all the custom, and the customers had only to make one visit to plan the whole wedding rather than visits to many shops to order each separate thing.

With all her contacts, she was able to arrange everything for the entire wedding from the rings to the cake. Shoes to parasols. Hats to underclothes. For the bride and her entire family. It made things far easier for the families.

It was a sound business venture.

Part Four

The Key

Chapter 23

Jenny sat nervously outside Mr Briggs' office. So much had happened in the last three years. She could feel her heart was pounding, just like the first time that she came to see him and Mr Shoesmith. But now the three years were up and she was going to find out who her benefactor was. It had been such a strange legacy; even Mr Briggs had said that.

Even more nerve-wracking was that she was going to be able to open the upper floor of her premises. What would she find up there? Most of the time she forgot about the upper floor, except when Mr Briggs came to undertake his regular inspection of the lock.

There was no danger that she would ever have interfered with the lock, as it would have invalidated her claim to the property. Whatever problems she may have had paled into insignificance compared to going back into service, or even worse, the workhouse.

She was pleased with how well she had managed the shop and how it had expanded already. She had great ideas to expand even more, perhaps open another shop in another town. Jenny was so busy with her grand ideas, that she didn't notice the door opening.

'Miss Mitchell, would you be so good as to come into my office, please.'

Jenny smiled graciously and slowly entered Mr Briggs office, where he led her to a comfortable chair.

'I have taken the liberty of preparing a cup of tea for you. I trust that you will partake of some little refreshment?'

'Indeed I will, Mr Briggs, how kind of you to ask.'

Jenny watched Mr Briggs fumbling with the delicate china and pouring out the tea. She tried hard not to smile as she thought of the first time that she had come up to this office. She had been plainly terrified.

It saddened her that Mr Shoesmith was no more, and she felt sad that he wasn't here to share in the final revealing of her mystery. Although she felt sure that Mr Shoesmith could have told her more about her mystery benefactor, as Mr Briggs had never met him.

But over the years, Mr Briggs had come to see how much Jenny had improved the business, and she now used him as her solicitor. She had brought quite a lot of business to his doors, either directly or through her recommendations.

Overall, she had become quite a person to reckon with in the town. Part of the attraction was that no-one, not even Jenny, knew exactly who she was, and the air of mystery lent a little romance to her, not to mention the continuing success of her shop.

Mr Briggs walked slowly across the room with the cup balanced precariously on his outstretched hand. It was obvious that he wasn't used to this role, but then what man was? mused Jenny.

'There you are, Miss Mitchell. I trust that this is to your liking?'

Jenny smiled graciously and murmured her thanks.

'So today I get to see the upstairs of my house at long last, Mr Briggs. I cannot deny that I am quite excited about it.'

'Well, er, actually, Miss Mitchell, you do have a further delay.' Jenny's heart sank.

' Delay, what delay Mr Briggs?'

'Well, when I opened the outer covering of the package, there was a letter of instruction for me, also. It says that I have to give you this letter to take home to read, when you have read it, you can come back and get the key, tomorrow, or at your earliest convenience.'

'Believe you me, it will be tomorrow. I am so anxious to learn something about my life and I believed that it would be today. Why did you give me this false information, Mr Briggs? I am not best pleased,' Jenny burst out in an unusual show of anger.

'Upon my soul, Miss Mitchell, I had no idea. The whole case has been unusual. I have no idea what is in this letter either. I thought the package just held a key. That is all we were told at the time when the gentleman left the package.'

'And you say that you have no idea who the person was who left the package?'

'None at all. Mr Shoesmith said that one day he would tell me the whole story, so he obviously knew more than I did, but as we know, that day never came. Jenny pondered on how many other secrets Mr Shoesmith had taken to the grave, never to be revealed.

'And he didn't give his name?'

'No Miss.'

A silence fell between them. Jenny sat pondering, whilst Mr Briggs looked anxious.

Suddenly Jenny stood up, gave the teacup back to Mr Briggs and grasped the package in her hand.

'Well the sooner I get home and start reading it, the sooner I can get on with my life. I'm a busy woman now and do not have time for games.'

Mr Briggs followed her out of the door and down the stairs, offering his services for anything that may be needed once she had read the letter.

Jenny gave him a curt nod and left the premises. She walked briskly back up the town to the shop. Thank goodness this was her early finish in the shop today and she had no major fittings or appointments still to attend to.

The day wore on, and Jenny tried to be her usual self, but the package in her pocket seemed to be weighing heavy against her leg. The hours seemed to drag by until two after the clock, when she could close the shutters and have some peace.

She was grateful now that no one lived on the premises with her, and yet she felt safe because Susy and Jonny lived not far away if she needed anything, as well as Marian and George.

Jenny forced herself to make a pot of tea. She laid the tray with a light fruitcake and Lancashire cheese before she started reading the letter. It felt quite bulky and she didn't know how long it would take her to read through it all. She opened the outer coverings of the package and drew out the letter.

The writing on the envelope was in a very spidery handwriting that she didn't recognise. Her heart was pounding as she started to open the letter. It was on expensive vellum paper, but had no crest upon the top of it. Indeed, there was no address at all.

'My dear Girl'

Jenny started to read, barely believing how it was addressed. She was no ones dear girl. Who on earth could have written this? She read on.

If you are reading this letter, it means that I have been dead for more than 4 years and it is now time to tell you things that I could never have shared with you in my lifetime, however much I would have liked to.

'Four years, Four years, who do I know that has been dead for four years,' thought Jenny, but in her feverish state she couldn't think of anyone.

The shop belonged to your mother and I left instructions that after she died, the shop had to be kept in trust for you until after my death. I also insisted that a length of time should pass before your inheritance was revealed to you.

Jenny was getting angry now; who was this person who knew her mother had a shop, but wouldn't let Jenny claim her inheritance until they had died themselves. What a selfish person, I bet they were getting the profits for years, in collusion with that evil woman. In desperation, Jenny turned to the back of the letter to see who had written it, and was stunned at what she found. At the end of the writing was a simple signature.

From your ever loving father

Jenny sat rooted to the spot. Father? Father? Who on earth could it be? She never thought about her father, only her mother. But there was just the bleak inscription, giving no clue as to who her father was. She would have to be patient and read through the whole letter. She turned back quickly to the front page and carried on reading.

I want to say first of all my dear, that I loved your mother very, very much, and if things had been different I would have married her. When she passed away I was unable to adopt you without making a lot of trouble for myself and possibly for you. Your mother's seamstress, Bruce, didn't let me know when she died and when I next visited, you were already in the workhouse. I could do nothing about it for many years. At the first possibility I made sure that you got a decent position where you would be cared for.

I'm sorry if Bruce gave you any trouble, she was very jealous of your mother and did try to blackmail me at one stage, but I made sure that she would be compromised herself if she ever gave any of our secrets away. It was her who abandoned you at the workhouse, saying you had no family, and your mother had just died in childbirth. She also said that she didn't know your surname, only that you were called Jenny. She even denied you your own real name

– *Genevieve. She always said that it was too fancy a name for a child born out of wedlock. But your real surname is Barnes, or should I say your mother's was. And I suppose because of your birth you will have to keep that name until you marry. Would that I could have acknowledged you and given you my own name.*

I couldn't help falling in love with your mother, she was so slim and pretty, always a smile on her face. Her thick black hair was so shiny and there were always little tendrils of hair escaping from her cap. She never said a wrong word about people she knew, and would do anything to help anyone. She was too obliging perhaps and that is where the trouble began. I'm not proud of what I did, but things were difficult for me with my wife being an invalid.

Your mother had a room of her own at my home, and inevitably, I started going up to her room. At first, it was just so that we could be together and talk privately, but our fierce love for each other overcame sense, and we became lovers. When she found out that she was with child and my wife learned of it, she made me ask your mother whom the father was, but of course we couldn't tell. Your mother invented a follower from the village but said that she couldn't marry him. My wife sent her away without a reference that would have been disastrous for your mother. But I knew I couldn't just abandon her to her fate, or you, for that matter.

So I bought her the business and got away to visit her as often as I could. It wasn't very satisfactory for either of us, but it was better than nothing. When her time came near, I booked her a nurse to stay with her, until she was ready to pick up the reins of the business again. I also appointed Bruce to help her in the business, and that is where I made a grave mistake. Unfortunately, Bruce found out who I was and held that as a threat to me, but she seemed to have a good knowledge of business and your mother needed help.

I used to love playing with you when you were small and we had a very special relationship, which I am sorry we were not able to carry on. You used to love to climb on to my knee, and play at Ride a Cock Horse using my knee as a horse. Or you used to cuddle up in my arms. It was very special, as with my own children I never got near to them. They were always looked after by nannies and were only brought down for short interludes at teatime. I never got to know them like I did with you. I hope you can believe how very special you were to me.

I hope you will forgive me for all the subterfuge, but I didn't want to harm you. Also, I wanted to make sure that you could run the business yourself before you found out who you really were. That is why I insisted on three years passing before you read this.

I also hope that you will forgive me, and perhaps even love me a little, as I loved you. Pity me as a weak man, who should have known better. I should not have abused my position of trust and claimed undeserved privileges. I hope also by now that you are a successful business woman who has no need of a man to protect her, unless you so wish. Thus you will never be in the vulnerable position that your mother was.

At least I can say I loved both you and your mother until my dying breath, albeit from a distance.

From your ever loving father.

Jenny dropped the letter in to her lap. She still didn't know who her father was, and not much else about her mother. How could he? Giving her this entire letter to read, but still not revealing who he was. I wonder why? Jenny mused to herself; did he think I would know who he was?

All I know is that he was a typical Lord of the Manor who wanted his cake and to eat it, she thought bitterly. And he said that her mother was small and dark haired, with tendrils. Jenny's hair was a mousy colour that had never seen a tendril in her life. So I must look like this unknown father, she thought.

Terrible feelings of anger raged through her body, alternating with tears of frustration. She would have preferred not to know about anything. She was grateful enough for the shop, but what else was going to come with it? Was there more knowledge that she couldn't bear to face? And Bruce. How could she have abandoned her at the workhouse saying that she didn't know her surname? And given the wrong first name, too.

That reminded her that her real name was Genevieve. She tried it on her tongue. Genevieve Barnes. Yes, she supposed it was a fancy name for working class folk. It didn't really go with Barnes. Still she would continue to use the name of Jenny Mitchell. It was good enough for her.

The full knowledge slowly dawned on her that she was after all born out of wedlock. She had suspected as much anyway, but that would no longer matter when she married Jonny. 'JONNY!' she gasped to herself. 'What would he think about all this? Would he still want to marry her knowing that she was a bastard?' Although Jonny's parents were poor, they were honest and respectable.

Jenny read and reread the letter until she almost knew it by heart. She looked at the clock and realised how late it was. Her head was aching and she knew she had to be up early to open the shop.

She also had to go to the solicitors to get the key. She would rip the lock off that door in sheer frustration because of what her unknown father had put her through. Her evening ablutions were almost automatic, as she pulled her nightgown over her head and got into bed. Sleep was difficult, as her mind kept going over the facts that she had just read, but eventually her eyes closed and she slept.

Chapter 24

A hammering on the front door of the shop brought Jenny instantly awake next morning. As she jumped up out of bed, the throbbing in her head was like a loud drum. Jenny staggered down to the front door to find Marian peeping through a small crack in the curtains, a worried expression on her face.

'I'm so sorry, Marian, I must have overslept. What is the hour?'

'It's nine o' the clock, Jenny. Does anything ail you? You look quite fatigued this morning.'

'Just a slight headache, Marian, don't fret yourself. I will be better as soon as I get a cup of tea inside me.'

'I'll put the kettle on the hob for you.'

'Thanks Marian,' Jenny replied whilst walking away rubbing her temples.

'Why don't you go back to bed for a while, until your headache passes? I can manage the shop.'

'No, I have too much to do today. But I do need you to mind the shop, as I have to go to see Mr Briggs this morning. In fact, I'll go and get ready and go now without tea, if you don't mind.'

'I thought you went to see Mr Briggs yesterday?'

'Yes, but I have to go again today. On second thoughts, I will have that cup of tea. I don't think I could face going out without one.' Jenny hurried upstairs to wash quickly and put on her brown work gown. Instead of keeping the sleeves turned back, she left her sleeves fastened at the wrist.

She checked the cuffs to make sure that they were as immaculate as usual, no speck or stain marring their pristine cleanliness. Going through the routine of dressing calmed her thoughts a little as she knew that today she would find out more about herself. She only hoped that there was something to give her more details, rather than the unsatisfactory letter that she had received from her so-called father.

Jenny sipped the tea that Marian had made for them both. As she finished the drink, she hurried back upstairs and then having got her outdoor cloak and her gloves, she left the shop.

When she got to the solicitors office, Mr Briggs was only just arriving himself. He ushered her up the stairs to his office.

'Well, my dear, tell me all,' Mr Briggs started, with a smiling face.

'I would if I knew all,' replied Jenny tartly, 'I am not much wiser. Unless you think that the fact that my parents loved each other is all there is to know.'

Mr Bridge looked mystified. 'Would you like me to accompany you when you open the lock then?'

'No thank you. I have asked Jonny to be present to help me with the lock.'

'Of course, your fiancé will help you,' replied Mr Briggs looking disappointed. Jenny laughed at him.

'Do not worry, I will tell you all when I find it out. You deserve that much for being part of the mystery,' replied Jenny.

'Was there no clue at all in the letter?'

'Well, I now know my real name. It's Genevieve Barnes. Can't say I am over enamoured about it. I've been plain Jenny Mitchell for so long that I think that I will keep the name. I can also confirm that my parents were not married and my father was some person from the gentry or upper classes. The letter was actually from my father, who died about four years ago, but he did not give his name.'

'Then how did you know that he was your father?'

'He simply signed the letter - *'from your ever loving father'*

'Well,' said Mr Briggs meaningfully. But he only looked pensive and didn't continue speaking.

'It's all a mystery,' replied Jenny. 'I had built up to reading the letter yesterday and I was so cross when it left me still not knowing. I will let you know as soon as I can.'

With that, Jenny left the room and hurried out of the office. She walked back up the hill to the shop and hurried inside. Janet smiled as Jenny walked through the door and gave her a polite 'Good Morning', almost as if she was a customer. Jenny returned the greeting and went through to the back of the shop. Susy was at the office desk, preparing the accounts when Jenny arrived.

'What time is Jonny coming in today?'

'At about ten of the clock, I should think. He was going to make deliveries to Lady Jolley at Holme Manor at Waddington, and then go over to see Lady Shuttleworth at Gawthorpe Hall with the new uniforms that she ordered. We finished them yesterday.'

'I would have liked to go over with him and ensure that they were all satisfactory myself. Why did he not ask me?' Jenny said with a little trace of annoyance in her voice.

'I asked you yesterday, and you said that Jonny could go himself. You said that you were far too busy to bother about a few uniforms,' Susy replied with an aggrieved tone.

There was a stony silence. Susy sat with an air of self-righteousness in front of the desk.

'I'm sorry, Susy. I remember now. I was a little pre-occupied yesterday. No order is ever too small for me to deal with. Just remind me of that next time.' Susy sniffed.

'I am sure I only try and please you Jenny.'

'Oh Susy, this is me you are talking too. Not Lady Muck of Muck's Hall. We have been friends for too long to fall out. Come on, let us forget any unpleasantness and have a cup of tea. I'll get young Maisie to go to the bakery and get some of those lovely coconut buns that you all like. How does that sound?' Susy tried to look aggrieved for a while longer, but the promise of coconut buns soon won her over.

'Yes, that sounds like a nice idea. I'll tell Maisie now.' Scooping some coins out of the petty cash drawer, Susy went downstairs to ask Maisie to go to the shop.

In the silence of the office, Jenny felt in her pocket to check that the key was still there. She longed to go and open the door now, but knew that she would have to wait until everyone had gone home tonight. She must try and take her mind off it. She bent down to the bottom drawer and reached for her notepad. Walking over to the window, she sat down on the chair and rested her notepad on the small occasional table where she did her sketchings and plans for wedding events.

Her latest plans were for the wedding of Mrs Duxbury's young niece. It reminded Jenny of the previous wedding that she had arranged for Mrs Duxbury. It had given her the idea for the integrated shop that she now had. In fact, Jenny owed a lot to Mrs Duxbury and she silently thanked her.

Jenny began to plan the wedding from the notes she had taken during the interview with Mrs Duxbury and her niece Anne. She would make sure that this was the best wedding that the county had ever seen.

Completely engrossed in her work, she didn't notice the passage of time. It was only when Susy came back in and reminded her that it was past their usual lunchtime that Jenny broke off and went up to the dining room.

'Where is Jonny? Has he not been in?' asked Jenny.

'Yes, but I told him you were too busy to be disturbed. I know what you are like when you are making a plan.' In actual fact, Susy had warned her brother that 'Jenny had a mood on her' and advised him to wait until later.

'Has he had his luncheon yet?'

'He has just gone for it now.'

'Well, I will go and have mine, and then perhaps we can have a talk and catch up on news. I will be back later to go through the accounts for the end of the month.'

Jenny hurried round to the dining room and found that it was quite busy. Janet, Maisie and Marian were all in having their luncheon, as well as Jonny. So much for a quiet chat with Jonny. They got so little time together as it was. She joined them at the long dining table and the waitress hurried to serve her.

'What can I get you, Miss? There is a lovely Lancashire Hotpot, or a nice piece of liver and onions. '

'I will have the Lancashire Hotpot please. Jonny, I need to speak to you afterwards. I need you to do a little job for me.'

'Certainly, Miss, whatever you say, Miss,' Jonny replied with a manner that was far too ingratiating, pulling his forelock at the same time. He loved to tease her like this in front of the other staff. Jenny gave him a dirty look and he turned away smiling.

'Did you manage to get the orders to Lady Jolley?'

'Yes, Lady Jolley was out, but I saw Mrs Metcalfe, the housekeeper. She said to thank you for the uniforms and that her Mistress would settle the account shortly.

'That will be unusual,' remarked Janet cynically. 'The gentry are not known for their prompt settlement of their accounts.'

'That will do, Janet,' replied Jenny sharply. 'As it happens, Lady Jolley's household are very prompt at paying. Not as good as the 'nouveau riche' families like the Duxbury's, who always feel that they have to pay immediately. But certainly better than some of the gentry locally.

Janet and Marian finished their cups of tea and hurried back down to the shop. Jenny declined a sweet after her Hotpot and told Jonny that they could have a cup of tea in her office and she could explain what she wanted doing. The waitress brought in a tray of tea with two china cups, and Jenny carried the tray to her office, whilst Jonny opened the doors for her.

When they closed the door, Jonny went straight to Jenny and enveloped her in a strong bear hug.

'Oh, Jonny, behave yourself. I have a lot to tell you. Just sit down and listen. I don't know whether you'll like what I have to tell you.'

'Why, have you now found out that you are a Princess and were betrothed to a handsome prince at birth?'

'Do be serious. I do not jest. It has quite upset me.'

'What has upset you, my love?' Jonny was now all tender concern, holding her hands gently in his and stroking them.

'I have read the letter from the solicitor and it was written by my father.'

'Then you did have a father after all, and all those worries about you being illegitimate were unfounded.'

'Well, no, not really. I did have a father, but him and my mother were not married. So I am definitely a child born out of wedlock.'

'I have told you before that this does not matter, Jenny. You will become legitimate anyway when you become my wife next month. I cannot wait. I just long to stay with you at nights now. So tell me, who are you? Who was your father?'

'That is the annoying part. I have read the letter from my father and he has just signed the letter

'from your ever loving father'

I still do not know who he is. It is almost as if he thought I would know who he was when I read it. But I have no idea. There are no clues. It is so frustrating. I will not know the answer until I can open the door of the upper floor.'

'When do you intend to open the door?'

'Tonight. I cannot bear the suspense any longer. Please will you come and help me?'

'Of course. What time will you need me?'

' After the shop closes and everyone has gone home.'

'Fine. I will go and check up on young Robert in the stables and then go and get some feed for the horses. Also, old Spirit has shed a shoe, so I will take her to the blacksmiths down Parsons Lane. That will tide me over until you need me. I am feeling quite excited after all this time.'

'I'm not. I am a little apprehensive after the delay. But whilst you are at the farriers, could you pay our account? Susy will prepare the money for you.'

Jonny nodded his assent on his way out. As he walked through the doorway, he turned and whispered 'Until tonight!' with a leer on his face. Jenny looked thunderous, so Jonny hurried through the door, whistling a cheeky tune to himself as he went.

'Men,' exclaimed Jenny. They only have one thing on their mind, she thought. Mind you, it had been in her mind also of late. She blushed as she remembered the feelings that Jonny had aroused in her lately. She felt quite a hussy. It was a good job that they would soon be married.

Jenny went back to the accounts office to continue with the plans for the Duxbury wedding, and tried to take her mind off her own wedding, and more importantly, the first night of her marriage.

Chapter 25

After the shop closed, Jenny locked the doors and slid the bolts across. Jonny had gone to the back of the shop and made the back doors secure. There had been a spate of burglaries in the town lately, and the shops had been the main targets. Only those where the owners lived on the premises had been untouched. Although Jenny lived in the shop, Jonny was taking no chances. He checked the windows as well, on his way around the shop.

He went back upstairs to Jenny's sitting room, but she was not there.

'Jenny? Where are you?' he shouted.

'I am here, just in the kitchen. I thought that you might like something to eat and drink before we start.'

'Yes, that would be good. We may feel too tired later.'

'I have made you a pressed brawn sandwich and some cake. Will that be sufficient?'

'Fine Thank you, but where is yours?'

'I could not eat a thing tonight, I feel so anxious about the whole situation.'

'Well the sooner I eat this, the quicker we can get started,' replied Jonny. He chomped his way through the snack whilst Jenny nervously sipped her tea.

'All ready then?'

Jenny took a deep breath and then nodded.

'I will go and get some tools from the storeroom and meet you at the top floor. Cheer up, Jenny, it cannot be as bad as you imagine.'

Jenny smiled nervously, but her smile disappeared quickly once Jonny had left the room. She walked slowly up the stairs until she came to the ugly doorway that barred the top floor. Leaning against the opposite wall, Jenny stared at the doorway, wondering what there was behind it, thoughts that had plagued her greatly in the early months of her inheritance.

'Ready?'

'Ready'

'Have you got the key?'

'Yes.' Jenny put her hand into her pocket and slowly drew out the key. She gave the key to Jonny, a frightened expression appearing on her face. Jonny kept hold of her hand and squeezed it before taking the key off her.

'Do not worry, little Jenny Wren. Whatever we find out, I will be here beside you.'

Jenny gave a tremulous smile as Jonny turned away to the door. He placed the key into the lock and turned it slowly. Surprisingly, the key turned easily in the lock.

'I thought that the lock would have been rusted and difficult after so long,' suggested Jenny.

'Well, it would have been, but I have been oiling it for the last week. I did not want there to be any further delay for you.'

'You are so thoughtful, Jonny, what would I do without you?'

'Nothing. Because you are never going to be without me for the rest of your life.'

Jenny smiled gratefully, her heart swelling with love and pride for this lovely man that she was to marry. Her attention was soon arrested when she heard the grating of the door. She looked expectantly as Jonny opened the door. As he fully opened the door, Jonny started laughing.

'What is the matter? Why are you laughing?' Jenny pushed Jonny out of the way, raised the candlestick, and then started laughing herself. There was a large solid second door behind the first one. No wonder she hadn't been able to see anything when she had peeped through the keyhole. Whoever ordered the closing of this upper floor must have known how inquisitive she was!

'Is there a lock on this one as well?'

'No, it has just been nailed together. It will just take me a short time to remove the nails.' Jonny started to work on the nails and soon removed the second inner door.

'There you are, it's all yours now.' Jonny stood back to let Jenny go through first. 'Do you want me to come with you or do you want to go upstairs alone?'

'You stay here, please. I have got to do this myself.'

'Well, I will be waiting here in case you need me.'

Jenny walked slowly up the steep flight of stairs, a musty smell drifting around her as she went further up the flight. The steps reminded her of the ones going up to the servant's attic quarters at Ormerod Hall. At the top of the steps was another door. Jenny carefully opened the door and found herself in a dark passage. She held the candle higher to get a better impression of the passage. It was long and narrow, with doors leading off along both sides.

She opened the first door and found herself in a fully equipped, yet small kitchen. There were shelves all around the walls and although it was obviously dusty through years of not being used, it had an air of being cared for. Just dusty rather than dirty and neglected. There was a large window high up near the ceiling that let in a lot of light, making the whole room look airy.

Looking at the shelves, it was obvious that the person had good taste as the foodstuffs were of the highest quality. Jenny approved of this small neat kitchen.

And then she realised. This was her mother's kitchen and perhaps she liked it because this was just how she would have planned the kitchen if it had been her own. Jenny felt an uncanny bond with her unremembered mother, desperately trying to remember what she looked like.

Jenny then turned to the next room on the same side of the corridor. The room was enormous and took Jenny's breath away. It was a drawing room that was long and narrow, rather like a gallery in a rich man's house.

There were several sumptuous armchairs and settees, with rich flocked wallpaper in a burgundy colour, on the wall opposite the windows. Her eyes were instantly drawn to the ceiling, which had three marvellous chandeliers spaced out along the roof. Each chandelier had thirty candleholders in it, and Jenny could see how rich and elegant the room would be when they were all lit.

There were very large windows all along the side of the room and the curtains were heavily decorated with swags and tails, in a combination of burgundy and cream brocade. The armchairs and settees were all in cream with cushions in cream, which were trimmed with burgundy. The carpet was mainly cream, but the burgundy colour was also picked out in small swirls.

It was obvious that whoever had planned this room had great taste, not to mention wealth. No expense had been spared, and it was uncanny that Jenny felt that if she had been asked to design this lovely room, she would have chosen the self same colours.

There were small occasional tables, a large bookcase, and a lovely writing desk, making the room look very comfortable, but still gave the impression that it was used a lot and well loved.

A great deal of care had been taken in furnishing this room, not to mention a great deal of money. Her mother's 'protector' had obviously been a wealthy man.

It was then that she saw the fireplace and gasped. The fireplace was a large marble surround, grey streaks being shot through the white marble. But it was not the fireplace itself that caught her attention, beautiful though it was.

It was the portrait over the fire. It was of a man and woman. The man was sat on a chair and the woman was stood up. The woman had one arm round the man's neck and the other hand was holding his hand.

The man was looking up at the woman with a look of raw naked love. Jenny went nearer to the picture and as she did, she inadvertently screamed.

'What is it? Are you alright?' Jonny shouted, 'I'm coming up.'
Jonny bounded up the stairs and ran to where Jenny was stood, rooted to the spot, her hands covering her face and mouth, to stop the screams erupting.

'What is the matter? What have you seen?' Jenny did not reply, not even when Jonny held her close and gently tried to shake her out of her almost trancelike stance. She pointed to the picture, with trembling finger.

'What is it? Please tell me' Jonny cried desperately.

'It's Lord Ormerod. That is him in the picture.'

'Why is he here, then?'

'I . . , er . . he. .' Jenny stuttered incoherently. Jonny rocked her, trying to comfort her. 'I think that he is my father,' Jenny eventually burst out. 'How could he? I lived at Ormerod Hall all those years and he never said a thing to me. And he let me look after Lady Ormerod, knowing full well that I was his mistresses' daughter. Oh, I cannot bear it. It is too awful. I hate him. I hate him. How could he do that to my mother as well?' Jenny rocked against Jonny, as she gripped him tightly.

'There, there. It doesn't matter who your father is. You are still you, and we still have each other.' By now Jenny was sobbing loudly, her whole body shaking.

'I hate him, I hate him,' Jenny screamed again.

'It is too late for hate. At least he seemed to stand by your mother. This is a very sumptuous room. No cost has been spared. She obviously lived very well. And they do look like they love each other. Look at the expressions on their faces.'

Jenny turned slowly to face the portrait again, and started to look at her mother. No sudden feeling of recognition happened, and Jenny was distraught that she felt nothing for this woman who had borne her.

But there was the thick dark hair that her father had described in his letter. Her father. Her heart sunk again. How could she live with the knowledge that she was Lord Ormerod's daughter? She would never acknowledge it in public, ever.

So her mother had been seduced at her workplace by the Lord of the Manor, just like Marian. But as Jonny had just said, at least he acknowledged her, and provided for her. Not like they treated Marian. A sudden thought hit her.

'Jonny, if he is my father, then George is my nephew. No wonder I felt such a bond with him. I thought that it was just because I saw him growing up. Oh no,' her face took on a look of terror. 'The current Lord, Jeremy, is my half brother. Oh, Jonny, how can I bear being related to this family, even if it is out of wedlock.'

The sobs overwhelmed Jenny again. Jonny held her closely, making soothing noises, whilst kissing the top of her head. He was a little overwhelmed by the news himself. To marry a Lord's daughter! Well, that was a tall order. Even though she was illegitimate.

Perhaps she would want to release him from the engagement now she knew who she was. He wouldn't be good enough for her. Once she was calm again, he would suggest it to her. His heart would break, but he knew that he would have to be brave and start the conversation, as Jenny would be too embarrassed to start it herself.

Jenny suddenly jerked herself away from his arms.

'I never want anyone else to hear about this. Do you hear? You are the only person who knows and I do not want anyone else to know. Ever. Do you hear?' Jenny repeated herself. Jonny nodded, too full to reply verbally. 'Let us get out of this room, now. I have seen enough of it for one day. I will look at it in the light tomorrow, when I am calmer.'

'Shall we go back downstairs now?' asked Jonny, managing to recover his voice.

'No. We will look at the other rooms,' Jenny said quite forcibly, 'I want to see the rest of this floor. I have waited long enough.'

Jonny and Jenny walked slowly out of the drawing room, without a backward glance, and moved to the first door at the other side of the corridor. It was a bathing room, with a toilet and a bath and a sink. The sink was set into a table of mahogany, with drawers underneath. The bath had a mahogany cover over it, with a shield rather like an arbour round the top, so that bathers were not visible from the doorway.

The bathroom was quite large and airy, with a small room leading off. It was a kind of dressing room, with lots of shelves. The shelves were covered in stacks of beautiful towels, and bedding and the room seemed to be a general storeroom of all kinds of bric a brac. Large mahogany wardrobes lined one of the walls.

'This is so elegant. It quite puts our own bathing room to shame. And I thought that I was so modern when I had it installed,' Jenny commented to Jonny. 'I wish that I had known about this luxury before. I think that I would have broken the door down.'

Jonny thought about the strict rules of the inheritance, but did not mention them. He was so pleased that Jenny seemed to be on an even keel again, and seemed to be more in control. He wasn't going to upset her again. He merely smiled, and squeezed her hand.

Suddenly Jenny stopped in her tracks.

'Lady Morag,' she said, totally inexplicably to Jonny.

'What about her?'

'That is who I look like. Not my father or my mother, but like . . er. like my sister, I suppose she is. That is why her hair is like mine. I suppose I've got her slim build as well. Not like most of the Ormerods. They tend to be heavy in build.'

Jenny went off into a reverie again. Jonny gently pulled her hand, more to distract her thoughts than to make her move. It worked.

Jenny abruptly left the room to look in the second room on the other side of the corridor. Again she gasped as she entered this room. It was almost as large as the drawing room. It was a very large bedroom. Or she thought that it was a bedroom. She had never seen anything so erotic in her life, and she blushed as she looked round the room. Jonny too, was speechless.

In the centre of the long wall, near the windows, was the largest four-poster bed that she had ever seen. It was covered in a large lilac silk counterpane, which came down to the floor.

The back of the bed was trimmed in a paler lilac shimmery material, and there were folds of the same material making a canopy over the bed, falling in folds down to the floor. Deep purple cushions were scattered haphazardly over the top of the bed.

All the furniture in the room was of a pale cream colour, all matching, with cameo insets of entwined lovers on each piece of furniture. Besides wardrobes, there were chests of drawers, and dressing tables.

Jenny could hardly take it in. She turned slowly to face Jonny and then realised what was on the other long wall facing the bed. Most of the wall was made of mirrors. Jonny saw her eyes widen in surprise and turned to see what she was looking at. He too gasped when he saw the mirrors.

'Looks like they spent a lot of time in here,' Jonny said, with the merest hint of a twinkle in his eye.

'Well, I think that it is unseemly,' Jenny snapped and hurried out of the door.

Jonny caught her by the arm and turned her round to face him. 'Do not be afraid of this room, Jenny. It is a testament to your parent's love. Come. Let us look at the other rooms.' Jonny quickly drew her out of the room and opened the third door on the other side of the corridor. They were both unprepared for what they saw.

This room was obviously a nursery. It had a tiny bed, which was fussily trimmed in pink tulle. It had toys everywhere and a smaller cradle over by the window. There were chests of drawers and wardrobes, all matching.

Jenny went towards one of the wardrobes. There were racks of clothes, all to fit a small toddler. Gowns that were of the latest mode and obviously expensive.

Over the fireplace was a portrait of a little girl, with very straight mousy coloured hair. She was running towards someone, her arms outstretched, a look of sheer delight on her face.

Her dainty little feet were encased in soft kid leather slippers, the gown that she had on was a feast of ribbons and trounces, in sunny yellow and palest green. It was obviously her best gown, and she had worn it to have her portrait painted.

In the bottom of the picture, there was an inscription

'Genevieve on her second birthday'

As she read that, Jenny broke down into tears.

'That is me, when I was a little girl,' she sobbed. 'That was the lifestyle that I was used to. I was loved and adored. Pampered even. Beautifully gowned. And I think of the clothes that I had to wear in the workhouse, and even when I was in service. And the treatment I was given. Oh, I cannot stand the pain.'

Jonny held her close. He was out of his depth and did not know what to say to Jenny. The change in her circumstances was so different to what she had been born to, that it must have been terrible for her to live in the workhouse.

It had been better for him, as his parents were desperately poor anyway. Just getting some food every day felt a bonus to him when he went into the workhouse, however bad the food had tasted.

Eventually the sobs subsided and Jonny suggested again that they finish the tour for today.

'There is only one door left. I will finish it tonight. Come Jonny, let us look.' They moved onto the last room, only to find that it was less sumptuous than the rest of the upper floor. It appeared to be a workroom. There were bobbins of cotton, swathes of material, needles, pins and dressmakers dummies. Shelves covered the whole of one room with a variety of dressmaking equipment and materials.

'This was probably where my mother worked at night when she was on her own with me.'

'Yes, it is a much more practical room,' replied Jonny. 'I wonder what is through this door?' and opened the door at the back of the room as he said it. 'Oh, it's a kind of apothecary. There are lots of bottles and herbs and things.'

Jenny entered the room after him and was instantly struck by the smell.

'Oh, I can smell lavender. It is so beautiful. Oh. Jonny, I remember this room. I remember the smell of lavender. My mother always wore it. I remember. I remember.' Jenny's face was animated as she turned to Jonny.

'What can you remember?'

'Only that. A lady holding me, cuddling me, that smelled of lavender.' The sobs were threatening to reappear, so Jonny firmly grabbed her hand and pulled her back downstairs. He locked the door, and said, 'that is enough for one night. Come, we will have a drink together and then I must go home.'

Jenny let herself be taken back downstairs. She was barely able to walk and looked as though she had been given a potent medicine.

Jonny took her into the lounge and sat her down in a chair whilst he went into the kitchen and made her a drink of tea. She remained silent. Jonny put the teacup down on the small table next to her, and sat on the settee near to the chair.

The minutes ticked by. Jonny was becoming increasingly anxious about Jenny and yet was reluctant to break the silence. She was obviously trying to absorb all the new things that she had seen tonight. Pictures of her mother, her father, and finding out just who she actually was.

Eventually, Jonny broke the silence. 'Jenny' he said softly. There was no answer. He tried again, speaking a little louder, but got the same result. He leaned over to the chair and shook her arm gently, to bring her out of her reverie. 'Jenny, speak to me, tell me what you are thinking and feeling, please,' he pleaded.

Jenny very slowly raised her eyes and looked at Jonny, her eyes dull and barely focused. 'I don't know what I think. It is all too new for me. I have had so much of a surprise today.' Suddenly, Jenny burst into tears. Jonny jumped up from the settee and took hold of Jenny, and led her back over to the settee, so that he could comfort her.

'I'm glad that I now know who I am, but I'm not sure that I'm comfortable with those facts yet. What must you think of me, Jonny, born of parents like that?'

'The same as I thought of you before, you silly goose. You know that I loved you the first time that I saw you. Not that I would have dared say anything at that stage. I was just so grateful that you had rescued my sister. And even more grateful when you rescued my mother. Her life was so different after that. How could I not love you?'

Jenny looked up sharply. 'So you only loved me because you were grateful for what I did, then?'

'You know better than that. And now all I want to do is marry you as soon as possible and look after you for the rest of your life.'

'Well, it is not long to wait now, only six weeks to the wedding. And so much to do.' Jenny suddenly sat up as if thinking about the wedding and her business had put some life back into her.

'Wait until you tell everybody about who you are tomorrow,' said Jonny. Jenny looked angry.

'No, I've already told you, no one will know who I am tomorrow. I am not going to tell anyone. And neither must you. Promise me

Jonny. Nobody must know. I don't want people finding out about any of the upper floor and my parentage. We must make a plan. Decide what to do with this upper floor and what we tell everyone. Now, do you think that we should open this floor up to be a new department?' Jonny stared at the sudden change in Jenny as she became the businesswoman again.

'You are not going to destroy all that your parents created, surely?'

'Why not? Would you live up there?'

'I would love to live up there, Jenny. I think that it's a lovely suite of rooms, and it could be ours for when we are married. It would be so private. The staff are always drifting in and out of your rooms on this floor, aren't they? We would not get much privacy. Besides, you were only saying recently that you were getting more concerned about burglaries in the shops which were empty at night. This would make sure that we were protecting the shop as well.'

Jenny sat forward on the settee, her head resting in her hands. Eventually she spoke, slowly.

'Would you really like to live up there, Jonny. You are right, we would not get much privacy down here.' She went quiet again, Jonny could almost hear her brain working, and he watched the changes in her face as she worked things out in her mind.

'You are right. We will live up there. But what about all those mirrors in the bedroom?'

'What about them?'

'Well, er, they, er,' Jenny stopped in mid sentence, unable to frame the words that were in her mind. Nor could she keep the flush from spreading up her face.

'Why don't you make some curtains and cover the whole of the mirrored wall, then it wont be so obvious?'

'Mm, we could do. Yes, that's a good idea, Jonny. Now, what shall we tell the others about this upper floor? I had been planning several things for up here. I will have to let Mr Briggs know a little of the story, but shall we just tell everyone that the rooms were another suite of rooms, and we are going to continue using them, but they will be private. No staff will be allowed up there. The door will remain locked.'

'Good. I am glad that that is settled. What will you say about your parentage?'

'I will just tell them that my mother was a widow, who had been left the shop by a grateful employer. I will not mention my real name, or who my father was.'

'I really must go home now; it is getting very late. Susy will wonder where I am. Will you be alright if I leave you now?' He got up and started to walk towards the door. He was half way across the room when he heard a little voice.

'Jonny'

He turned towards Jenny again.

'What?'

'Thank you for today.'

'It has been a pleasure. I wanted to be with you today and with all the revelations that you have had, I'm glad that I stayed.' He turned back towards the door.

'Jonny,'

'Yes?'

'Don't leave me tonight. I'm frightened.'

'What is there to be frightened of, Jenny? You have lived here on your own for ages now. Why are you suddenly afraid?'

'I don't know, but I don't want to be alone tonight.'

'But what will people think? It would compromise your reputation if anyone found out.'

'Who will find out if we do not tell anyone?'

'Well, Susy for sure.'

'We can explain to her tomorrow. She will understand. Besides, what reputation have I got? The illegitimate daughter of a Lord and a servant. Not much reputation there to despoil. Please?'

Jenny looked at Jonny with such pleading in her eyes that he could not refuse her this wish. His Jenny, who had been so strong all her life, who had made a success of this business, who bossed everyone around, including him, was now pleading with him to stay. He smiled and nodded his head.

'I'll sleep on the settee in your office.' She smiled and ran towards him, giving him the largest hug and squeeze he had ever had from anyone.

'Now then Jenny' he said huskily, 'hold me like that and I may forget myself.'

'Good,' said Jenny, whilst Jonny looked aghast, 'I hope you do. I don't want you to go home and you're not sleeping on the settee. I've made a decision. We'll use the rooms for our own, and we'll start from tonight. I want to go back to my mother's bedroom, with you, and learn about the love between a man and a woman. Now. Tonight.'

Jonny was speechless.

'Jenny, we can't, not yet, we are not married,' he eventually spluttered.

'Well, it didn't stop my parents, so why should we let it stop us? Are you refusing me?'

'No, of course not, I would like to stay with you more than anything in my life, but are you sure?'

'Never been surer, so hurry up before I change my mind. It's not long to our wedding anyway, and we do not have the time or money to go on a bridal tour, so we will have our bridal tour here, tonight.'

Jonny took hold of her shoulders, pulled her towards him, and gently kissed her. The kiss deepened and became more passionate.

'Not yet,' cut in Jenny, as she pulled away. 'In the bedroom, please. And I want you to blow the candle out as soon as we get there.'

'Why I do believe you are blushing, Jenny,' Jonny laughed.

'Well, it is the first time that I have asked a man to take me into his bed, so I am bound to be a little nervous.'

'It is your bed, not mine,' replied Jonny, very conscious always of the riches she had compared with him.

'Our bed from tonight onwards. So hurry up or it will be night no longer.' Jonny laughed and taking the candle in his hands he led a nervous Jenny back up the stairs to the bedroom. He opened the door, led Jenny towards the bed, and then blew the candle out, as promised.

Chapter 26

Jenny woke up suddenly next morning. She looked around the strange bedroom, and for a moment, she wondered where she was. Then the memories of last evening came flooding back and she stretched luxuriously in her bed, remembering all that had taken place last night.

How could she have been so brazen, because in all honesty, she had made the first move to Jonny. Jonny. Where was he? The bed was cold next to her, so he had obviously been gone a while. Perhaps he was being discreet. That would be so like him. She only hoped that he wasn't disgusted by her behaviour last night and thought her too fast. Jenny reflected that perhaps he might not want to marry her now.

Jumping out of bed, Jenny hurriedly got dressed and went down to the old kitchen, carefully locking the door to the top floor. Fortunately, the stove was still warm and she kindled the fire until it got warmer. Putting the kettle on the griddle, Jenny went downstairs to take the bolts off the front doors before the staff arrived.

She released the bolts automatically and it was only on the way back to the kitchen that she realised that the bolts should have been off if Jonny had gone home. Mystified, she thought perhaps that Jonny had not gone after all, but had simply gone somewhere else. She called his name, several times, in different areas of the shop and old living quarters. There was no reply.

Jenny made herself a cup of tea and set out the trays for the other staff to have a drink when they came in. Susy and Jonny were the first to arrive.

'Good morning, Jenny, did you have a nice night? Jonny certainly looked worn out when he came home last night, or should I say the early hours of this morning. You must have found some interesting things up on that top floor. When do we all get a look?' Jenny turned away to the kettle to try and cover her blushing face.

'Actually, it was just another set of private quarters. I've decided to keep it that way. It will be mine and Jonny's home when we get married.'

Oh, so you're not going to get a house separately from the shop, then?'

'No, I want to use the suite of rooms, it makes so much more sense than buying something, and then having to have a person like a night-watchman on duty every night. You can't trust these burglars nowadays.'

'Well, that is a turn up for the books. I can't see the point of living all the way up there. You'll need more space when the babies come along, as they certainly will, once you are married.' Susy walked away towards the office door.

Babies. Jenny nearly choked on her tea. She had never given it a thought last night. What if she was with child? She fervently worked out how long it was before the wedding. Six weeks. It couldn't come quick enough now. What would she do if Jonny wanted nothing further to do with her?

'I will be with you shortly Susy,' she shouted after her, 'I just want a word with Jonny.' After Susy had gone, Jenny turned furiously to Jonny.

'What did you tell her last night? I was so embarrassed.'

'Nothing. I didn't speak to her. But I must have disturbed her when I came in. Are you alright?'

'Never better,' she grinned, 'and you?'

'Come here and I'll show you how I am.' He leaned towards her, as if to cuddle her, but she bypassed him.

'Behave yourself, we're not married yet.'

'I don't remember you saying that last night?'

'Oh, go on with you, let me do some work.'

'So we are not going upstairs to the new quarters to do some work, then?'

'No. Not today. You can wait until we are married. That is if you still want to marry me.'

'After last night? Why would I not want to marry you?'

'Well, perhaps because of last night,' Jenny said with embarrassment, struggling to put her thoughts into words.

'Do not worry. I too, cannot wait for our wedding day.'

'What if I have begun a child? What will we do?'

'I will think that we are the cleverest couple in Christendom.'

'Really?'

'Really.' Jonny hugged her tightly. 'And I would be the proudest man alive. I do hope that we have children quickly, Jenny. I do so want to be a father. I want to do for my children what my own father could not do.'

'Well, I would rather wait to start babies until we are married, Thank you very much, so there won't be a repeat performance of last night until we are married. I don't want people talking.'

Jenny looked at Jonny's crestfallen face and started laughing.

'It's not long to wait now, Jonny.'

'It will feel like a long time, Jenny, especially after last night.'

'Well, we will see how it goes. I will have to give you lots of deliveries to do to keep you busy and then you will be tired.' Jonny laughed and bowed down low to Jenny.

'Yes, Ma'am. I will go and do your work now, Ma'am.' Jenny threw the dishcloth at him as he hurried out of the door.

She ran after him.

'Jonny?'

'Yes? Changed your mind?'

'No, a thought has just returned. How did you get out last night? The bolts were still on the inside of the door this morning.'

'Oh yes, I forgot about that. Do you remember when we opened the door, we went straight down the corridor?'

'Yes, what about it?'

'Well, to the right of the main door, sort of behind it, there is a curtain. Do you remember?

'Yes, but what has this to do with how you got out?'

'Patience, Jenny. Behind the curtain was another door. I found the key cleverly hidden on a false ledge at the side. The door opened into a flight of dark stairs. I went down them and found another door with a similar key. When I eventually got that door opened, I found that I was in a narrow little ginnel, which led into a back street. I followed the back street and came out in Lowergate. No one would guess that you had just come out of this building. Clever, isn't it?'

'That must have been how my father got in and out. Keeping himself hidden in case anyone knew him. I know that he lived a fair way away from here, but he would not want to be found out, I don't think. It looks like he went to elaborate lengths to be discreet.'

'I must admit, I felt like a sneak thief going home last night. But perhaps it is a good idea. We could open this up and use it for when we want to go out, without everyone in the shop knowing our business. It will also keep our rooms more private.'

'Good idea. I am glad you found it.'

'Now I am going. I promised to be over to the wholesalers early this morning. I am usually well on my way by now. Well if they complain, I'll tell them that my boss wouldn't let me go. Wanted to keep kissing me,' laughed Jonny, as he left the room.

'Don't you dare,' she shouted after him, trying to be cross, but not succeeding. She couldn't be cross this morning, in fact she felt wonderfully happy and gloriously alive. She would look forward to married life if last night was a foretaste.

She hadn't really known what to expect, as she had only heard some of the old women in the workhouse talking crudely about bed matters. And she remembered the state of Marian after the rape. But she definitely liked what had happened last night. She blushed to herself, but then hearing the rest of the staff arriving, she went downstairs to meet them.

The weeks coming up to the wedding flew by. Being the Christmas season kept her mind off worrying about everything. Marian had made her a lovely two-piece suit in dove grey with pale pink trim.

Marian had made herself a suit in palest blue with darker blue trim. Both had matching hats, as Jenny wanted the outfit to be useful for going to church in afterwards.

For about a week prior to the wedding, Jenny was excruciatingly tired, and complained to Jonny.

'I can't keep my eyes open, I'm really tired.'

'It's all the extra work you have had this last few weeks. It must be wedding day nerves,' he laughed, as he went out of the door. Jenny too, laughed. She was getting an old woman before her time. She would be glad when the wedding was over and she could relax.

At long last, the wedding day dawned. Jenny felt queasy; she was so excited that the Friday before Christmas had at last arrived. When she was bathed, she put her dressing gown on and went downstairs to where Marian had put all the clothes ready.

Marian and Susy were coming in early to help each other get dressed. Jenny went to the fitting room to start putting her clothes on, but couldn't find her outfit anywhere. After a fruitless search, Jenny was beginning to get agitated, when Marian and Susy arrived.

'Marian, where is my suit? I can't find it anywhere.'

'Oh, I put them away safely. We didn't want anyone to see them, did we?'

'Well, it is no big secret. Only a plain suit.'

'Here it is then. Your plain suit,' laughed Marian.

Jenny gasped. Marian was holding a sheer gown of ivory lace over silk. It had a tight waist, with puffy sleeves, with long tight cuffs. It had a long straight skirt, with the tiniest bustle at the back.

Susy followed carrying a gossamer veil and headdress. The headdress was made of holly leaves, intertwined with mistletoe.

'Where has this come from? What is happening?'

'It's your bridal gown. You didn't think that I was going to let Miss Mitchell of Mitchell Modes wear a plain grey suit for her wedding, did you? That would really disappoint all the local ladies,' laughed Marian. 'And I have a reputation to uphold as well, so I won't be wearing blue. They will be our going away outfits instead.'

'But we aren't going away.'

'I know, but I had to make the suits to keep you from guessing. We can either use them ourselves or sell them, it doesn't matter.'

'I can't believe that you have made all this without me knowing. I wouldn't have let you if I had known.'

'That is exactly why we didn't let you know,' said an excited Susy. 'Come on, Jenny, try it on.'

Jenny slipped the dress over her underwear. The dress was boned so that she didn't need to wear a corset underneath. It fitted perfectly. Marian put the veil in place along with the seasonal headdress.

Then she slipped delicate pale green slippers on her feet. It was then that Jenny noticed the tiny green flowers round the hem of the dress, tucked between the folds of silk and under the lace. Jenny cried when she caught a glimpse of herself in the mirror. She looked a truly beautiful bride.

She turned to thank Marian and Susy but was too full to speak. It was Susy who spoke first.

'Come on Marian, now it is your turn. I hope you like what I've designed for you. Mrs Hartley has made yours.'

Another dress was brought into the fitting room. That too, was in ivory, but a delicate satin material. It was plain in the bodice and sleeves, but all the skirt was gathered to the side to reveal a patterned brocade underskirt.

The sleeves had tiny covered buttons all down the side of the length of the sleeves. It was very feminine and made Marian look taller and elegant.

Her veil was plain lace, with small green flowers at the edge of the veil. Her headdress was similar to Jenny's, reflecting the Christmas season.

A knock at the door brought Sarah and Mrs Hartley in. Sarah had moved into a small house with Mrs Hartley and Edith after Mr Forbes shop was converted. Sarah was carrying two large bridal bouquets, containing Christmas roses and mistletoe. They were beautiful arranged.

The next person to arrive was Mr Briggs. Because both Marian and Jenny had no parents, Mr Briggs had agreed to give both the girls away in marriage. He had been delighted to be asked and had given them both a substantial wedding gift.

By this time everyone was ready, so Jenny started getting busy trying to organise the walk up to the church. As they came out of the front door, Jenny noticed her own delivery carriage, all trimmed up with holly, with young Robert sat on the front seat, grinning broadly. Even Susy and Marian gasped.

'Whose idea was this?' asked Jenny.

'Jonny's. He didn't like the idea of you walking to church. He said all the toffs go to church in carriages, so why shouldn't you?'

'Are there going to be any more surprises today?'

'Don't know, Miss. I only know about this one.'

Robert got down from the seat, and lifted the side of the carriage down. They had made some seats that had been covered with white material, so that the girls didn't get dusty.

He helped both girls up into the carriage, then told Susy and the others that they would have to walk. 'This is only for the brides,' he said importantly. They all laughed, but did as he said.

When she arrived at the altar, Jonny looked at her long and lovingly, as if he couldn't believe his eyes. He squeezed her hand gently and whispered 'Forever, my love.' Jenny felt as though she was going to faint, she felt so much love for him.

The wedding went off perfectly and Jenny was amazed to see how many of her customers and the townspeople were there to see her. Even Martha from Ormerod Hall had come.

After the wedding, they all returned to Miss Carter's next door. She had put on a lovely wedding breakfast for Jenny and Marian as her wedding present to them.

Before the food was eaten, another surprise was in store. A photographer arrived to take some pictures of the happy couples.

'Now you will have someone else to put in your locket,' whispered Jonny in Jenny's ear, whilst they were waiting for the picture to take.

Jenny felt choked with emotion. He had remembered a careless comment that she had made so long ago.

'Thank you my dear, I will wear your photograph for evermore.'

After all the excitement of the photographer, everyone tucked into the delicious meal that had been prepared. There was a final surprise.

Miss Carter wished the happy couples a long and happy marriage, with plenty of little ones to follow. Both the brides blushed at this, but everyone else laughed.

'I also have an announcement to make. I am going to sell my shop. I have decided to retire early to the seaside.'

'May I buy your shop?' asked Jenny quickly.

Jonny groaned. 'When will my wife stop working? Even on her wedding day, she is doing business.' Jenny noticed how proudly Jonny had said 'my wife'. Oh, she was lucky. He was a fine man.

Miss Carter said that she could buy the shop, but perhaps today was not a good time to discuss it. The party began to break up and everyone went home.

'Thank you for a lovely wedding day, Jonny. It has been lovely. It couldn't have been more perfect.'

'Well,' said Jonny as he pulled her close, 'I can think of something else that would make it even more perfect.'

'So could I,' replied Jenny huskily, as she drew him towards their private quarters, 'so could I.'

Chapter 27

Saturday dawned bright and clear, a warm day for December. Jonny was hurrying Jenny to get dressed as if she was going to be late.

'What is the hurry, Jonny? I'm not working in the shop today, we could have had a longer time in bed.'

'Mm, that sounds inviting. Do you want to go back?'

'No,' said Jenny pretending to be scandalised. 'What are we doing today?'

'Wait and see.'

'Why can't you tell me?'

'Secret.'

'I'm your wife now, you shouldn't have secrets.'

'Oh, I shouldn't? You've changed your tune. You keep secrets from me.'

'I don't. Tell me one.'

'Can't think at the moment.'

'Oh stop being so annoying.'

'You are annoying me too.'

'Are we having our first argument?'

'Yes,' Jonny laughed. 'I think we are.'

'We are a real married couple now,' replied Jenny.

'Time for a make up cuddle after the argument, then,' Jonny grabbed hold of Jenny to hug her.

They were interrupted by a knock at the door. It was Marian and Will.

'Come on you two, we're going to be late,' said Will.

'Late for what?' asked an exasperated Jenny.

'Our joint bridal tour.'

'Bridal tour? Where are we going, round Europe?' said Jenny sarcastically.

'No. It's only for the day, we couldn't afford any longer.'

'We are going on a day trip on the train to Blackpool,' laughed Marian.

'Oh, so you knew about this as well?'

'No, only on the way here, because I nagged Will so much.'

'Only married a day and nagging me already,' said Will with a mournful tone.

'Well, you look good off it,' quipped Jenny.

'We are probably going to be the most nagged husbands in Clitheroe,' commented Jonny, equally mournfully.

'You just needed two such women as us to take you in hand. I am sure there will be a great improvement in both of you, soon,' said Marian. Jenny stared at her friend. She was usually so quiet, and never made such acerbic comments.

They all went out of the shop together and walked down King Street to the station. Jonny walked in front with Will, leaving Jenny and Marian to talk behind.

'Was everything all right last night, Marian? You know what I mean?'

'Oh yes,' replied Marian with a happy smile on her face, 'it was fine. Will was very patient with me. I was worried before though, weren't you?'

'I suppose I never thought about it,' replied Jenny, desperately trying to think of something else to say, in case she let slip that last night was not the first time.

'What do you think we should do about Miss Carter's shop? Have you any ideas?'

'Not really, but I'm sure you have,' laughed Marian.

By this time, they had got to the station and waited patiently for the train. Marian was an old hand at going on trains, but Jenny was a little wary. They seemed to go so fast, complained Jenny.

But she was persuaded to get on the train, clutching Jonny's hand all the way to Blackpool. Her face was a picture when they eventually got down to the seaside. She had never seen the sea or sand before and she was like a small child.

Because it was nearly Christmas, Blackpool was quiet, but the girls dragged their husbands round the shops, to give them a chance to buy some presents, they claimed.

Secretly, Jenny wanted to look at other shops, especially as she was going to be able to expand again, courtesy of Miss Carter. They had a meal in a large hotel on the promenade, and even had a walk on the pier.

On the way home, Jenny sighed loudly. 'Oh it has been a wonderful bridal tour. Thank you so much. I'll remember this when I am an old lady and will bring my grandchildren to Blackpool, to show them where I came on my bridal tour,' mused Jenny.

'Might I be allowed to come as well, my dear?' asked her husband, somewhat aggrieved.

'Oh of course! I didn't mean particularly on my own. I was just being foolish. Of course you will be coming.' Jenny laughingly shook her head.

Once they got back to work, the time flew by. Jenny was increasingly feeling unwell in the mornings, though it was Mrs Marshall that asked the blunt question one day, fortunately whilst they were on their own.

'Are you in the family way, Jenny?'

'Oh, I don't know for sure,' stammered Jenny, blushing furiously.

'Well, you have been sick quite a few mornings that I know of. And you have got the look in your eye.'

'What look?'

'Oh you know, the look.'

'No, I don't know. What look?' said Jenny hurrying over to the mirror. She searched her face in the mirror, but couldn't see anything different.

'Well, I think you should go and see someone.'

'Surely it is too soon?'

'Might be, but best be safe than sorry. It's my grandson you have got in there,' she grinned sheepishly.

Jenny blushed. 'I will go and get advice, then, if you think so.'

Next day, Jenny had her pregnancy confirmed by the doctor.

'It is a little early to say when you may expect the baby, but from what you tell me about your monthly flow, it may be around July or August. Congratulations Mrs Marshall.'

Jenny thanked him and walked out of his surgery. July or August! She was horrified. She must have conceived the baby that first night when she and Jonny had . . well, er, oh dear. Everyone would know what they had done. How embarrassing. She hoped the baby would be late. At least she had heard mothers say that first babies were usually late. She would just have to pretend that the baby was early.

That night, she told Jonny and he was delighted. Jenny told him not to tell anyone yet, but it was too late. The proud grandmother to be was hinting to all and sundry what might be about to happen.

Jenny also told Jonny the date that the doctor said the baby might come, and asked that Jonny told people that the baby was due in September.

'What's the point? They'll know when he's born.'

'You are as bad as your mother. She talks about 'he'. What if it's a girl?'

'That will be great. A baby version of you. The next one might be a boy, anyway.'

'Next one? Can we get this one born before you talk about the next one, please?'

Jonny went out then to make a delivery. Whilst he was away, Jenny pondered on what she had heard about her mother. She had died in childbirth. Jenny began to fear that she might too die in childbirth. She talked about her fears with Mrs Marshall, but she reassured her.

'Eh lass, it's much safer nowadays. They wash their hands and things like that.'

Jenny wasn't convinced, but left it alone and put it to the back of her mind, and worried whilst she was alone.

Just after Easter, Marian also shyly told everyone that she was expecting a baby in October. She was delighted. Jenny was also pleased for her. It would be good that their babies could grow up together.

The two pregnancies gave Jenny an idea for her shop. Now that she would have three four-storey shops, she would leave the front of Miss Carters shop as a café and put the kitchens for both the shop workers and the café at the back. The second floor would be given over to shoes, handbags and accessories.

She would build a play area in the courtyard at the back of the shop, so that the children could play outside. A small bedroom would be put on the top floor so that the babies could have a sleep during the day.

An alcove was built through from the first shop, as there had been one built through into Mr Forbes' shop. Then the customers could walk through all of the different departments and come back down the stairs at any level.

A special room had been built at the top of Mr Forbes shop. It was set out like a drawing room, with several chairs and a low table. When Jenny had been choosing her wedding ring, Mr Nettleton, the jeweller from three shops away, had brought a tray of suitable rings into the shop.

Never one to waste a business opportunity, Jenny asked him if he would do this service for all the brides that she was planning weddings for.

He readily agreed, and even gave Jenny's business card out when a couple bought an engagement ring. It was mutually convenient and brought even more business both their ways.

Working in the shop, meant that Jenny and Marian had to have new gowns made to accommodate their increasing girths. This gave a new idea to Jenny and Marian, who very discreetly advertised that they would make gowns for the expectant mother, which were flattering and helped to hide the bump.

Most women avoided going out once the pregnancy was obvious, but Mitchell's Modes new gowns meant that they could socialise a little longer than usual. They were very popular.

Her next idea was to open a baby wear department. She stocked all kinds of clothes that a baby would need for a layette. Bethany, now back from her long bridal tour and expecting her first baby, was one of the first people to make use of both the discreet gowns and later the baby clothes.

Jenny was asked if she was going to give up work when the baby was born, causing much scandal amongst the local women when she said that she was going to come back to work afterwards.

She promised Jonny that she would only work in a very part time capacity, more as a supervisory role, but she knew in her heart, that she wouldn't let go.

As her girth increased, Jenny found it more and more tiring. She seemed quite a lot bigger than Marian, but then of course, she was a lot further on in her pregnancy than Marian, but couldn't say anything.

Jenny got into the habit of having a rest in the afternoons. She called it her thinking time, but Jonny often found her asleep in the little room that was to become the nursery for both her own and Marian's baby.

Jonny tried to persuade her to give up work until after the baby was born but he gave up asking when he got nowhere.

Chapter 28

In early July, Jenny was having one of her 'thinking rests', but she couldn't get comfortable. She had been plagued by a dull, nagging backache all day. Just as she was drifting off to sleep, a sharp pain stabbed her in the back and came round to the front. She sat up sharply. No, she must have dreamt it, or perhaps it was because she had slept in an uncomfortable position.

Just as she was settling back in the chair, the pain came again. Stronger this time and beginning to hurt. This was it then. It must be labour pains. In July. Far too early. Everyone would know that the baby had been conceived before her marriage. There could be no pretence now. But wait, she thought, perhaps this is something else and not the baby.

The next few minutes left her in no doubt. The pains got stronger and were coming more frequently. She got up from her chair easing her way slowly to the door; having to stop each time the pains came. She knew Maisie would be on the next floor, so she shouted to her. Maisie took one look at her Mistress and ran downstairs for help.

The rest of the day went by in a blur of pain for Jenny. She felt as if her body was going to be ripped apart. Jonny had been banished from the room, as all husbands were, although he wanted to see how she was.

The doctor had arrived at the point when Jenny felt that she couldn't take any more. She was too exhausted. Then the pains mysteriously changed in nature.

'I want to push,' groaned Jenny through the haze of pain. The nurse that the doctor had sent examined Jenny and nodded to the doctor.

'You are ready Mrs Marshall. You can push with the next pain,' said the doctor.

Jenny pushed until her body felt as though it were splitting. She seemed to have been pushing for a long time and had no strength left. Perhaps she was going to die like her mother.

'Just another push, Mrs Marshall, we can see the baby's head now.'

That was enough for her to give one last almighty push; again she felt something change within her. The baby slithered out onto the bed and started to cry. A lusty, loud cry straight away.

'It's a girl, Mrs Marshall. Everything looks normal. Well done. She has certainly got a good pair of lungs, but she is smaller than I expected. But she is early after all,' said the doctor. Jenny weakly smiled.

She had a daughter; she could not believe it. The nurse was cutting the cord, and Jenny was keen to hold her daughter in order to take a long look at her. Suddenly, the pains came back again.

'Oh, I've got another pain. I want to push again. Oh, it's just as bad as before,' gasped Jenny.

'Don't worry my dear, that will be the afterbirth. It will all come away very soon,' reassured the doctor.

The nurse lifted the sheets to get a better look.

'Doctor, come here,' she said, trying to keep the urgency out of her voice but not succeeding. 'Look!'

The doctor looked aghast.

'What is the matter, Doctor?' asked Jenny but was ignored.

'Just push my dear,' the doctor said eventually. Jenny did as she was told. She felt the afterbirth come out but was shocked that it felt as big as the baby.

She got an even greater shock when she pushed out not the afterbirth, but another baby.

'Ah, that is why this first baby was small, her brother was waiting to come into the world,' laughed the doctor.

'Brother?' gasped Jenny, trying to sit up.

'Just lie down, Mrs Marshall. We will let you see your son in a moment. And now we will get the afterbirth, unless there is another one in there!' quipped the doctor.

A bang on the door at that point was followed by Jonny bursting into the room.

'What's the matter?' he said. 'Is Jenny alright?'

'Yes Mr Marshall, and so are both your babies.'

'Both? Babies?' repeated Jonny incredulously.

The doctor laughed. 'Yes, your clever wife has just given birth to two babies, a girl first and then a boy.'

'Two?' repeated Jonny, and promptly sat down on the chair near the bed.

'Yes,' said a weary Jenny, 'two. Aren't we clever?'

Jonny rushed over to where his wife was in bed in the small nursery and hugged her.

'You are very clever. Both a boy and a girl all at once. Thank you Jenny. My life is complete now.'

'Come along Mr Marshall, this is no place for a man. We need to sort your wife out, cleanse the babies and get them dressed properly. I don't suppose you have any extra things for the second baby, do you?'

'That is the advantage of living in a shop. We have lots of baby things. My clever wife opened a baby goods department once she found out that she and Marian were both having a baby. We have lots of things, fortunately.'

He left the room, promising to return when the doctor and nurse had finished. Trays of tea and biscuits were sent up for all the people who had been involved. Jenny drank hers down thirstily.

The babies were then put into her arms, one by one. She looked at the wonder that was her daughter. The little girl looked up straight into her mother's eyes and stared at her, as if she too was appraising this mother of hers.

Jenny gently touched her face, stroking her cheek, and the baby turned hungrily towards her finger.

'Looks like she wants something to eat. Do you feel up to feeding, Mrs Marshall, or are you having a wet nurse?'

'Certainly not. I shall feed my child myself,' Jenny replied indignantly.

'Yes, Mrs Marshall, but there are two of them.'

'Oh, I forgot. Will I be able to feed both of them?' she asked naively.

'Yes, you should be able to,' reassured the nurse. 'Here, let me show you.' She manoeuvred the baby into position at the breast and got her to latch on to the nipple.

Jenny gasped at the feeling as the baby sucked vigorously at the breast, seeming to know right away what to do.

'I think that one has been here before,' laughed the nurse. 'And now for the other one.'

The nurse took the little girl away and brought Jenny's son. My son, thought Jenny. He was much sleepier and had to be persuaded to latch on to the breast. He was also much smaller and quieter than his sister.

'What are you going to call them?'

'I'm not sure. I will check with my husband. We didn't choose any names, it seemed to be tempting providence.'

'And here he is. We were just talking about names. Any ideas?' said the nurse.

'I would like to call the baby after my father if you don't mind, Jenny. He was called Benjamin. We could call him Ben for short.'

'Ben Marshall. That sounds grand, Jonny. Yes, I like that.' Jonny smiled distractedly. Jenny knew that he was remembering once again that his father had never come back for them. He assumed by now that he must be dead, for they were sure that he would have returned if he could have done.

'And what about his sister? Shall we call her after your mother?'

Jenny burst into tears. 'I still don't know my mothers name. What can I do? What can I call my daughter?'

Jonny cuddled her and could have kicked himself for being so tactless.

'What about Martha, after your friend at the house?' he suggested brightly.

'Martha Marshall? No, it doesn't sound right. I think that I will call her Rachel. That's a lovely Biblical name. What do you think?'

'Yes, Rachel. Rachel Marshall. That's lovely. Both have Old Testament names. Now, you need to get some sleep. The nurse will be shooing me out again if I stay any longer. Are you coming up to our quarters tonight?'

'No, let's keep them private. We don't want the doctor and nurse coming in. I'll stay here until I am up and about again. It will be easier, as we have cots and plenty of things in here.'

'Good thing we got two cots. We'll have to get another one for Marian's baby now. I hope that she doesn't have twins; we'll have to build another floor for all these children! By the way, my mum wants to come in and see them. Do you feel up to it yet?'

'Yes, it will do her good. She was fretting when I went into labour.'

The proud father returned with an equally proud grandmother, who fussed and fretted over the babies and Jenny.

Chapter 29

The babies soon settled into a vague routine. Jenny seemed to spend all her time feeding, washing or changing their cloths. George was a frequent visitor to the room, along with Sarah who helped Jenny as much as possible.

George sat and stared at the babies, and said 'Babies. Two babies,' with wonder in his voice.

'Yes, George, two babies. And soon there will be three, when your mummy has a baby too,' said Jenny.

'Two babies,' repeated George.

'I hope not,' Jenny laughed. 'Only one for your mum.'

In preparation for another new baby coming, Jenny had employed another girl to help with the babies. This time, she had suggested one of Sarah's sisters, Mary Jane. They were both delighted. They shared a bedroom at the top of Mr Forbes side of the large shop, next to the 'jewellery room' as it had become known amongst the staff.

Jenny laughed to herself as she heard Sarah lording it over Mary Jane, whilst explaining her duties. She would have to watch that Sarah didn't make life too hard for her little sister.

After three weeks, Jenny was straining to be back in the shop. Jonny forbade it, but as soon as he was out next day, she got dressed, kissed her babies tenderly, and handed them over to Sarah and Mary Jane, who were both delighted.

Most of the shop assistants gasped as Jenny came downstairs in her brown and cream working outfit. She smiled at them all and answered their queries.

Susy was a different matter. She loudly berated Jenny for being back at work too soon.

'Oh Susy, I feel fine. Some of the mill women are back at work the day after their babies are born, because they need the money. I am young and fit; I want to work.'

'Well, wait until Jonny finds out. He won't be pleased.' Susy was right.

Jenny and Jonny had the worst row of their married life. He said that she mustn't work. She said that she must. She had been given this shop to work in and work she would. What about the babies? Jonny had asked. She replied that they were well cared for.

For the first time ever, they went to bed without making up. They even slept at the furthest ends of the large bed, to avoid touching each other.

The following morning, however, as Jonny awoke, he reached over to Jenny and started touching her body gently, a usual routine for them each morning. It was only after they had made love that Jenny remembered the row they had had the day before.

'Oh,' she said angrily, 'I forgot, I'm not speaking to you,' and pulled away from his grasp.

'Bit late for that' replied Jonny laughing and hugging her.

Jenny then laughed and the row was over. They both compromised and agreed that Jenny could work in the shop every morning, but had to rest or play with the children in the afternoons, or vice versa.

A few weeks later, Marian went in to labour. Her birth was much quicker than Jenny's because it was her second child. She gave birth to a large boy, who was as dark as George was fair. They called him Luke. He was very vocal like Rachel and Jenny could foresee arguments in the nursery, when these two tried to be the boss of their little games, and also of young Ben.

When the twins were nine months old, Jenny realised that she was expecting again. She was quite embarrassed about it.

'What if I have twins again? What will people think? What shall I do?' she complained to Jonny.

'Don't be silly, Jenny. No one will think anything. For me, I think you are a clever girl. I want to have lots of children, and have them whilst we are young.'

'Yes, but we will have three babies under two years old. Or even four,' said Jenny with a look of dread on her face. 'Jonny, what if it is twins again?'

'It's too late now. We'll have to take what we get. But at least we are not poor anymore. We can give them a good standard of living. Not like our childhood.'

'I suppose so. But we will have to see about not having any more after this for a while.'

'That sounds a bit drastic. I quite like making babies.'

Jenny blushed. 'No, I don't mean not make love, just not make babies.'

'That's not always easy, my love.'

'But I have heard about things. Things to prevent babies.'

'Really Jenny. I don't know where you have heard these things. I am surprised at you.'

'Well, I don't want to stop loving you, but I don't want to have ten babies,' wailed Jenny. 'It's all right for you; you don't have to carry them or give birth. Or look after them.'

'Well, we will talk about this when we have had six babies, then. Will that do?'

'I suppose so,' said Jenny glumly, thinking how on earth she would run the business as well as have six babies.

Jonny was finding that he and Robert were always being asked to transport other items, whilst they were delivering their own goods. He talked to Jenny about the possibility of expanding the delivery side of the business.

'If we could have another carriage and horses, I could be doing one delivery whilst Robert was making another. He has really come on in the business. I can rely on him to make deliveries on his own, now. Then we could develop a business of deliveries throughout the town. We could even deliver our own goods, whilst charging other customers for their deliveries, which would make our own deliveries cheaper.'

Jenny nodded, as he outlined his business plans. She was pleased to see that Jonny was taking responsibility for his own business, even though he wouldn't get involved with hers.

'Just get what ever you need and I will pay for them.'

'I'd rather borrow the money, and then pay you back when I can.'

'You don't have to borrow it, Jonny.'

'I know, but I want to.'

'Of course,' replied Jenny, knowing that this was important to Jonny. He still felt that she was 'the boss'. This way he would have more control over his own affairs. He didn't like having to ask her for money.

'Won't you need a new boy or two as well, to train up?'

'That's a good idea. Can we afford them?'

'Yes, as long as you get them from the workhouse. You know the rules,' laughed Jenny.

And so Micky and Peter, two little waif like creatures from the workhouse, became the latest part of the workforce. They lived over the top of the stables which Jonny had bought nearby to house the carriages and the horses.

The business expanded, and became known as Marshall's Transport. Jonny became far more confident through running his own business. Jenny made him keep separate books from the shop, so that the businesses could be kept separate.

Working on the same fair trading ethos that Jenny did, Jonny also went from strength to strength with his transport business. Their bank balance was growing.

In due time, Jenny was delivered of another daughter. Thankfully there was only one child this time. They called her Ellen after Jonny's mum.

Jenny spent all of her time trying to juggle home, family and business. Her babies were very precious to her, but she did so love her business as well. She knew that she had to keep an eye on what was happening, or else the success that she had experienced could all go away.

Having lived in poverty in the workhouse, Jenny never wanted to be in that situation again. Nor did she want her children ever to be in that situation. She would always make sure that her family were provided for.

Her babies were developing their own little characters now. Where Rachel was domineering and wanting her own way, Ben was gentle, easy going and kind, like his father. He worshipped Rachel and followed her in everything she did.

Young Ellen sat in her pram and watched the two older siblings avidly. She looked as if she couldn't wait to get out of her pram or chair and be off into some mischief with them.

Marian's baby, Luke, was also quite a character. He was always laughing and could be persuaded into any mischief that Rachel was getting into. George was a big brother to them all. He especially cared for little Ellen.

'Those two are inseparable,' said Marian one day to Jenny. 'Look well if they marry each other when they are older.'

Jenny froze. She had never told Marian that she and George were related. What would happen if it should come to pass? Well if it looked likely, then she would have to tell Marian, but not now. She managed to laugh at Marian, and say 'What a thought. We would be related at last!' then changed the subject quickly.

As the nursery in the upstairs quarters was getting a little crowded, Jonny started asking Jenny to move.

'We could afford a nice new house of our own. Sarah and Mary Jane could come with us to look after the babies, and still look after them at the shop whilst you are working.'

'But I love our private quarters. I wouldn't want to spoil them or use them for the shop, now.'

'Neither would I. Perhaps we could keep them for when we were in the shop, but have another house as well.'

'I don't know. I'll have to think about it a bit more,' replied Jenny. 'Leave it alone for now. I will think about it.'

A few weeks later, Jenny and Jonny were taking the children for a walk on a Sunday afternoon. They took the Waddington Road, where Jonny pointed out the new houses that were being built.

'Those are nice houses, Jenny. Look at the big gardens. The children would like playing in those big gardens.'

Jenny looked. He was right. He was getting through to her about the children's need to have somewhere to play, more than the courtyard outside the back of the shop.

'Yes, they do look nice, I must admit.'

'They are very reasonable, too.'

'How do you know?' laughed Jenny.

'Oh I was talking to the builder when I was making a delivery to Lady Jolley at Waddington last week.'

'Mmm, I bet you were,' she said meaningfully. 'And did you order one by any chance?'

'No, not exactly.'

'What does 'not exactly' mean? Either you ordered one, or you didn't. Now come, on, what do you mean?'

'Er, I didn't order one, but I did say that we may be interested,' said Jonny sheepishly.

'And?'

'And what?'

'And what else did you say?'

'Nothing really,'

'Jonny?' said Jenny ferociously.

'Well when I said that we might be interested, he offered to show us round so that you could have a look.'

'And when was this tour to be?'

'Any time at your convenience.'

'Oh yes, well why is that man stood outside the house, waiting?'

'Er, well, he may be just checking up on the work being done,' said Jonny lamely.

'On a Sunday? A likely story! What is his name?'

'Bill Rostron.'

'Mr Rostron. Hello. How are you?' asked Jenny. He came over to the couple.

'Hello Mrs Marshall. I trust that you and yours are all well.'

'We are all well, thank you. Apart from my husband who seems to be suffering from a lapse in memory.'

Jonny and Mr Rostron looked equally uncomfortable.

'Well I suppose now that we are all here, we can have a look at one of the houses. I am not promising anything though, Jonny.'

Mr Rostron bowed and led them into the nearest house. Jenny was overawed with the size of the house. They entered through a very large hall. The house had good-sized rooms, with five bedrooms, an up to date bathroom, and a set of rooms on the top floor for the servants.

The house had piped water, which was a real bonus. There was also one of the new flushing lavatories with a bath, which had hot water as well as cold. Altogether a very luxurious house.

There were two large reception rooms with a very modern kitchen. The whole house was lighted by a gas supply, which also lit the kitchen stove.

There was even a small study, which could be used as a library.

'I could see you doing some of your business planning in there, my dear,' wheedled Jonny hopefully. 'Look, it overlooks the garden. You could get inspiration from there. Or watch the children whilst you were working.'

Jenny looked out at the garden. The study had French windows that led out into the garden. She opened them and the children followed her into the garden. They leapt about and cavorted around the garden, thoroughly enjoying themselves.

Jonny knew that he had a chance, when he saw Jenny watching the children playing in the garden. But she didn't let him off the hook even then.

'Thank you very much for showing us round, Mr Rostron. It is a lovely house.'

'I suppose it's hard to imagine what it will be like with furniture in, but we only finished the building last week. It could be ready for occupation in six weeks to two months.'

Jenny smiled but said nothing, then took her leave. In her mind's eye, she had already been decorating the place and planning furniture for each room, but she wasn't letting either of the men know that yet.

In the end, the children kept asking her if they could move to the nice house. She suspected that Jonny had put them up to it, but daren't ask.

They moved into the new house just before Christmas and Jenny had a lovely time buying furniture, pouring over material swatches with Marian for curtains, cushions and trimmings.

On Christmas Day, Jenny felt that her life was complete. She had a successful business, a good husband (who also had a successful business), and three lovely children. She even had a staff of servants to help her run the new house.

Jenny felt that her life had come full circle. From servant girl, to keeper of servants herself. And yet she knew that she didn't take any of it for granted. She thanked God for his goodness, as she fell drowsily into sleep.

Chapter 30

1892 was a busy year for Jenny. The shop continued to grow. She started new departments, having sections for household goods and curtains. Again, they made curtains and cushions to order from a customer's colour preferences.

The shop became known not only for its clothes, but also for its interior design. Jenny and Marian now employed a fleet of girls who were able to design and produce everything for the new ideas and looks that people wanted in their rooms.

And still, the staff received a percentage from all their sales, which made them the happiest and best-paid salesgirls in the town.

But despite the growth of the other departments, Jenny and Marian still loved the ladies clothes side of the shop best.

Jenny especially loved planning the weddings and being able to offer the whole wedding arrangements in her own shop, without the bride having to go anywhere else.

Young Sarah loved the shoe department best, as she had developed a penchant for shoes, of all descriptions. She was now engaged to be married and Jenny had offered to plan her wedding as a present. Young Mary Jane was to be her maid of honour and couldn't wait to be dressed up in her finery on the day itself.

Even Susy had a follower, although she strongly denied this most of the time and made light of the situation. Her suitor was a clerk at the local bank, where she went to deal with the financial accounts. He was said to have good prospects at the bank.

She was very ambivalent about getting married and would not name the day. Said she was frightened of having twins like her brother's wife!

On the following Christmas Day, Jenny told Jonny that she had a very special present for him. She was pregnant again. Jenny wasn't as overjoyed as he was, but welcomed another little one. She hoped for another boy this time, so that she had two of each.

Secretly, she hoped that this would be the final addition to her family, but knew she would have to go carefully about issues such as this with Jonny.

As it happened, Marian was pregnant again, too. At least they could have children growing up with each other. During this pregnancy, Jenny wasn't as big as she had been with her first pregnancy, so she hoped that this was a single baby again, as Ellen had been.

Marian wanted a girl this time and asked if she could call the baby Jenny, after her friend and protector. Jenny was touched by this, and hoped indeed, that Marian's next baby was a girl.

Jenny was beginning to find the premises in the shop a little cramped. She was looking round for bigger premises.

Jonny suggested that they get rid of their private quarters on the upper floor, now that they had their own house. Jenny refused. That was their own special haven.

Fortunately, the shop on the other side of Mr Forbes' shop came up for sale. Jenny snapped it up at once. When she went to see Mr Briggs to start purchase proceedings, he laughed.

'Are you trying to buy up the whole of Clitheroe, Mrs Marshall? There is a row of houses going for sale down Parson's Lane. Are you sure that you don't want to buy them as well? I could do the conveyancing all at the same time. Save you some money, too,' and roared at his own joke.

'What sort of houses? Are they just for sale, or are they to buy as landlord?'

'They are landlord houses. There are already tenants in them. I was only jesting really. Would you be interested in them?'

'I am not sure. What responsibilities would I have as a landlord?'

'From what I have seen of these properties, not a great deal. They charge high rents for very poor conditions. In fact, the houses have been up for sale for some time. I could perhaps get you a good price on them.'

'You could get me more details, I suppose.'

'I could do better than that. I could take you round. I have a set of master keys. I have the responsibility of selling them.'

'But aren't there people living there?'

'Yes, but part of their tenancy agreement is that the landlord can enter at any time.'

'Yes, take me down then. I am interested.' Jenny was secretly appalled at the tenancy agreement; that the landlord could just barge in at any time, but didn't say so.

Jenny and Mr Briggs set off down Parson's Lane. They went over the bridge and round to a mean looking row of terraces, that didn't look like they had seen a lick of paint in many years.

As well as peeling paint, there was a stale smell coming out of the alleyways that were interspersed after every four houses. The houses had three storeys above ground and a cellar below ground.

Mr Briggs knocked on the first door. After a while, a dirty looking, old woman shuffled to the door.

'I paid me rent, now get lost,' she said menacingly.

'Now, now, I am just an agent, not the landlord,' said Mr Briggs.

'What der yer want, then? Cum ter throw me out?'

'Not at all. This lady would like to look round the houses. Would you mind?'

'No option 'ave I?' She opened the door wider.

Jenny laid a hand on her arm.

'Yes you have. This is your house.'

The woman looked amazed but said nothing as she stood back to let them in. The stench was appalling. A mixture of stale cabbage, dried urine and faeces.

With being in the early stages of pregnancy, Jenny had to make a great effort not to heave, but merely fumbled in her pocket and found a handkerchief with some eau de cologne sprinkled on.

'What is the hardest thing about living here? Jenny asked the woman.

'Dunno. It's all 'ard livin' 'ere. Never got any water, 'aving no food, too many bodies. It's all bad.'

'How many live in here?'

'We're lucky. My son does well by us. There's me and 'im an' 'is missis, an' seven bairns. An' we 'ave two rooms, so we are lucky.'

'Two rooms?' repeated Jenny in disbelief.

'Yes.'

'Well who lives in the rest of the house?'

'There's the Wilson's i' th' top floor, and Barton's in the cellar. An' a nice young widder man and 'is bairns in the middle. I mind 'is bairns whilst he's at work.'

'So how many people live in here altogether?'

'Dunno. 'Bout twenty or twenty four, I think. Not that I'm any good at reckoning.'

'And how many toilets do you have?' The woman stared at Jenny.

'We have a privvy down th' street. The whole street shares at three privies.'

'What about water?'

'Oh yes, we got water. There's a pipe down t' street. We get it every mornin'. Well, those mornings when there is some.'

Jenny was becoming more appalled by the minute.

'Thank you for letting me look at your house. I will let you get on with your jobs now. Goodbye.'

She walked quickly back up to Parson's Lane.

'I have never seen anything like those houses. They are not fit to keep a dog in. I will buy them. But I will improve them as well. I thought I had a hard life in the workhouse, but at least it was clean, at least I had toilets of a basic kind, and running water.'

Mr Briggs hurried behind her, not speaking very much, as he puffed and panted up the steep part of Parson's Lane.

When they got back to his office, Jenny instructed him to buy the properties at the lowest price possible. She also asked for some figures from a builder to make the houses more habitable.

'They would have to move out if you were to make improvements. Also, they couldn't afford any more rent. They are all quite poor.'

'I know that. We could work it out somehow. But I wouldn't increase the rent. They are extortionate already.'

'I will get some estimates to you as soon as possible. Well that is after your bid has been accepted by the current landlord.'

'Thank you, I will look forward to them. I will bid you good day now.'

Jenny walked back the shop and asked that Jonny come to see her as soon as he returned from his deliveries.

He came through the door, tugging his forelock.

'You wanted to see me boss? Don't give me the sack, please. My wife is expecting and we already have three little ones to feed. And we have just bought a house. Please don't sack me, boss.' Jenny couldn't help but laugh.

'Don't be silly. I've got some serious news for you.'

'Let me guess. You have been invited to be Lord Mayor of Clitheroe next year. Or is it . .'

'Jonny, be serious. This is important.'

'Yes, boss, I'll be serious now.' But he pulled a funny face at the same time. Jenny stamped her foot.

'Jonny,' she screeched, 'listen!' This time Jonny knew that he had gone too far.

'Sorry Jenny, you know I like to tease.'

'I have put a bid in for a row of houses today.' Jonny laughed.

'Now who is teasing?'

'I am serious. Mr Briggs took me to see them. Jonny, I have got to buy them. They are awful.'

'Why do you have to buy them if they are awful?' Wouldn't that be a reason not to buy them?'

Jenny started to tell Jonny about the houses that she had seen and the grim lives that the people were leading.'

Jonny's face sobered.

'I can believe it. The house we lived in before we went into the workhouse was just like that. But what can you do? You have never owned houses before.'

'I can make them a lot better than they are now, and healthier.'

'But won't it cost a lot of money to improve them?'

'Yes, but I will have the satisfaction of knowing that I have helped these people.'

Jonny sighed. He thought it was rather an ambitious scheme, but knew better than to say so to this entrepreneurial wife of his. Besides, she would make a project of it and would succeed. She seemed to succeed in everything that she did.

'What was the sigh for?'

'Nothing dear. Just go on saving the world, if it keeps you happy.'

'But we can afford it, Jonny. I want to use my wealth to give people a better life.'

'I know. I just wish that we had had someone like you before we were sent into the workhouse.'

'Never mind, Jonny, we have the best of lives, now. It is just my way of giving back.'

'Yes, I know. And that is why I love you. Well, one of the reasons,' he grinned wickedly, as he gave her a hug.

Jenny extricated herself from the hug, knowing where it would lead.

'Come on, back to work. We have some houses to rebuild. We need some more money.'

'I am proud of you, Jenny. You're a credit to the town. Perhaps you should be Lord Mayor of Clitheroe.' They both laughed at the thought of a woman being allowed to be the Lord Mayor.

'Perhaps one day, perhaps our granddaughter may be the first woman Mayor.' They both laughed as they went into the main shop and back to their own duties.

Chapter 31

During the spring that year, Jenny, Jonny and the children enjoyed an early holiday at Blackpool. The children were ecstatic. They saw a different side to their busy parents. Although they both made time for the children, running two businesses did inevitably make inroads on the time that they had available.

They had lovely family photographs taken at the booths on the Promenade. The children were very reluctant to go home and Jenny had to promise them that they would return in the summer.

One evening in late spring, Jenny realised that Jonny hadn't come home. He had said that he only had a short delivery and would be home by five of the clock. It got to six of the clock and Jenny was ready for shutting the shop.

She started going to each department collecting their money and sales slips as she usually did when she could. She liked to do this herself, as she felt that it gave the staff time to see the boss if they wanted to. The workforce was so large now; she hardly knew some of the staff.

Suddenly there was a commotion downstairs. Jenny wondered who on earth it could be. Janet came running upstairs to find her.

'Mrs Marshall, there's been an accident. Come quickly.'

Jenny's heart lurched. Her poor precious children. Which one of them had had an accident?

'Where, when, how?' Jenny bombarded Janet with questions.

'I don't know. They just said to get you.'

Jenny followed Janet to Moor Lane. There, halfway down the hill, a crowd of people were gathered. Jenny pushed her way through.

'At least the bairn's saved,' said a man dressed in a mill workers clothes.

'Thank God,' thought Jenny, 'my child is saved.'

But the child that was being cuddled and checked over for bruises was not her child. Had there been a mistake? Did someone mistake this child for one of her own?

People were starting to push and shove.

'Make way, make way, let the doctor through,' shouted a woman.

It was then that Jenny turned and saw a man's body on the floor. He had a brown suit on, with cream trimmings. It was Jonny. She heard someone screaming, but didn't realise that it was herself. She threw herself down on to the ground and hugged him to her. He was pale and lifeless.

She cradled his head on her lap, and saw blood on her hands and skirt. The doctor lent over to her.

'Let me look, Madam. Is this your husband?'

'Yes, what is the matter? How long will he be ill? Can I take him home to nurse him myself?'

The doctor was looking grave. 'I will just finish my examination. Perhaps you could stand over there, Madam.'

'No, I will stay here. Hurry, do tell me what his injuries are.'

The doctor examined Jonny at length, and then turned to Jenny.

'I am sorry, my dear, there is nothing that I can do.'

'Nothing? What do you mean, nothing? He's bleeding. Can't you stitch his wounds up?'

'My dear, he is dead. There is nothing anyone can do.'

It was then that the screaming started again. She vaguely remembered someone taking Jonny away, after covering him with a blanket.

She tried to stop them, even fighting the doctor, but then Marian's Will came. He gently led her away and back to the shop. He handed her over to the women who got Jenny into bed in the children's nursery on the top floor.

Jenny curled up in a ball. She refused to talk to anyone, or eat anything. A funeral was held for Jonny three days later, but Jenny was inconsolable and refused to attend.

The days passed into weeks and still Jenny refused to come out of the children's nursery. She seemed to find comfort in the bed where she had given birth to her first two children. Sometimes Susy or Sarah brought the children to see her, but after a weak smile, she would curl back up into a ball and ignore them.

She rocked and rocked herself, alternately thanking God for giving her such happiness with Jonny, then berating Him angrily for taking Jonny away. 'Why me?' she frequently railed.

During the second week, she lost the baby. It was a boy. This made her withdraw even further into herself. 'That was all I had left of Jonny,' she screamed 'and now God has taken my baby boy away.'

Even the children failed to bring her out of herself. It was as if she had retreated into her own little world and she had to cry herself out.

'How can I go on living?' she kept repeating to herself. 'My whole reason for living has been taken away from me. I cannot go on without Jonny by my side. I loved him so much and life is pointless now.'

Mrs Marshall was able to get small amounts of broth into her, but little else. Jenny had never been plump, but she wasted away to nothing. The doctor was getting worried.

Suddenly, without warning, Jenny sat up one morning.

'I want Susy,' she said dully.

Susy came into the bedroom, amazed that Jenny had communicated at long last.

'Hello Jenny,' she said softly. 'How are you?'

'What happened?'

'What do you mean?'

'What happened to Jonny? How did he die?' she said slowly, hesitating over saying Jonny's name, and the word 'die'.

'He got run over by a horse.'

'How?'

'He ran into the road to rescue a child who had fallen and was going to be trampled by the horse. He saved her life,' Susy said proudly.

'And the child?'

'She is fit and well, although she was a little shaken by the episode.'

'I would like to see her.'

'Oh Jenny, do you think that is wise?'

'I need to see her.'

'I will try and get the mother to bring her in to you. Will that be alright?'

'Yes,' said Jenny and fell back down on to the bed, exhausted.

A few days later, a poor looking woman and child came into the shop, asking for Jenny.

They were taken into the 'jewellery room' and given a cup of tea and biscuits. It was obvious that the woman was very nervous and apprehensive.

Jenny entered the room slowly and looked at the child.

'Is this the child my husband saved?'

'Yes,' replied the woman nervously.

'Is she well, then?'

'Quite well, thank you Madam.'

'Good. That is good. I am a mother, too. I am glad that your child is well.' The little girl stood up, walked over to Jenny and gave her a posy of hedgerow flowers. Jenny cried.

'Thank you for the beautiful flowers. It was very kind of you to bring them. I am glad my husband saved you. He didn't die in vain. Thank you for coming. I would like to be alone now.' Jenny turned and walked out of the room, leaving a relieved Susy to escort the couple out of the shop.

Susy then went up to the nursery and found Jenny sat by the fire.

'Susy, I am sorry that I have been such a burden to you and your mother. I have been selfish. You are grieving too, but I have taken no account of your grief. I felt that I was the only one ever to feel grief. I will be all right now. I heard one of the children crying earlier. Are they all right? It was Ellen I think.'

'No, not really, the children are struggling without you. They are grieving too. We have all tried our best. The bottom has fallen out of their world as well and their only comfort will be from you. We have all tried to help them but they need you.' Jenny sighed.

'I have been a bad mother. How could I desert my children? It's not like me. I have just felt so overwhelmed with losing Jonny. I wasn't sure that I could carry on alone, or whether I even wanted to go on living.' She sat in silence for a moment. Susy also remained silent. Eventually Jenny spoke.

'Tonight, I will go home with my children,' said Jenny resolutely. 'They need their mother. I am all they have got now.'

Jenny turned sadly away and went to get her children from Mary Jane before going home, leaving Susy mightily relieved that Jenny seemed to have come round again.

Susy asked Mary Jane to go home with Jenny to make sure that she would be all right with the children. Susy didn't want to leave Jenny on her own just yet. It was perhaps as well, as Jenny was still acting automatically, and was not back to her normal self.

Very slowly, Jenny picked up the reigns of her life. She tried to be two parents to her small, fatherless children. At least she was in a financial position where she could support her children. Many other women like her would have had no option but to go into the workhouse. So really, she was fortunate after all.

The customers and townspeople all sent cards, flowers and letters, commiserating with her. It was hard reading all their good wishes and Jenny cried many times as she tried to answer all of the letters or write thank you notes.

A large bouquet of flowers came from the Dowager Lady Carroll, which Jenny thought was especially sweet. She had written on the card, 'Knowing how you feel at this moment.' Many people had said that to her, but she knew that Lady Carroll really did know how she felt. The others may have meant well, but had no real perception of what she was going through.

The house purchases and improvements had carried on during her sickness. Now Mr Briggs wanted to know if she wanted any kind of opening ceremony, as the improvements had been the talk of the town. There was now a waiting list to be one of Jenny's tenants.

Bathrooms had been installed in each house, with running water freely available. She had also reduced the rents, and made sure that there were far less tenants in each house. The ground floor of the end house had been turned into a small shop, which was run on the basis of the Rochdale co-operative, that she had set up in her own shop.

A small ceremony was arranged. The buildings were to be opened by the Mayor. Jenny smiled sadly at the irony of this. She remembered Jonny and herself laughing about her becoming the Mayor of Clitheroe.

The opening ceremony was blessed by good weather; Jenny named the buildings Marshall's Buildings in memory of Jonny.

Shortly after the ceremony, young Robert came to Jenny and asked if he could run the delivery businesses for her. Jenny looked at the tall young man that Robert had become. Jonny had had great faith in his capabilities.

'Of course, Robert, I would be delighted. If you like, you could start buying the business from me. Or you can wait until later. Whatever you think is best for you.'

'I would still like to work for you if you don't mind, Mrs Marshall. I don't have a mind to be my own boss, yet a while.'

'Well, the offer is there, when you are ready. And thank you Robert, for all that you have done.'

Looking embarrassed, Robert left the room. He left Jenny thinking about her life. She had been lucky.

She had three wonderful children. A wonderful man had loved her. She had a beautiful house. And she had three businesses; a large department store, a delivery business and some property.

She would survive. She would have to, for her children's sake.

And her husband hadn't died for nothing. He had died so that the little girl might live. There was no greater gift that anyone could do, than to give his life for another. She had heard that said before somewhere, but couldn't just remember where she had heard it, or in what context.

Why, she thought, remembering the lessons learnt in church, it was like Jesus himself, dying so that we might live. That was where she had heard the phrase, she remembered. At church.

Her husband had followed the example of Jesus. Somehow, that fact seemed to ease the pain a little. Yes, Jonny had died, but the little girl had lived. Something good could come out of her grief at last.

The shop had continued to run in her absence; Jenny was grateful to all her staff and decided to give them a treat. She would close the shop for a Saturday and take them all to Blackpool on the train. And all the children and families as well. She would probably need the whole train, she mused to herself with a grin.

That would give her something to start planning. Yes, that was what she needed. Something to start planning. Something to take her mind off what had happened.

But first, she would go up to the Parish church where she got married and look at Jonny's grave. Susy had told her where it was. They had put him near to a large willow tree in the back of the churchyard.

She wanted to say goodbye. All on her own. She wanted to say thank you to Jonny for giving her the best days of her life. And for giving her three lovely children.

She caught hold of her locket, the light catching on the engraving. Jenny decided that she would put two pictures of Jonny in there now.

She already had pictures of her children and young George on her piano. Anyway, the children were still with her, Jonny was not. He deserved this pride of place in her locket, her first gift from a grateful customer.

Jenny slipped the locket back under her clothes. She would alter it later, and spend a precious evening choosing which pictures to put in.

But first, she had to go to the graveyard and then back to the shop. Marian had just told her that there was a new booking for a wedding to plan. She had better get her thinking cap on and start the initial plans before the family came back for a consultation.

She sighed deeply to herself, and then pulled her cloak on. This first visit to the grave would be on her own. Next time she would take the children.

Jenny wasn't sure how she would explain things to the children about the grave, but she would have to try. They were still very tearful at bedtime, which exacerbated Jenny's grief.

But it was for the children that she must survive. She had to keep the business going so that she could provide for them when they were older, then they would have a business to run, when she was too old to understand.

And perhaps her grandchildren would be prepared to come into the business too. Perhaps a granddaughter may even be Mayor of Clitheroe one day, just like she and Jonny had laughed about.

Then Jenny laughed to herself. A female Mayor? That was too preposterous. They would never allow it. But then times were changing very rapidly.

And Jenny and her business would have to change with those times. She was ready for the challenge. She had a wedding waiting to be planned.

Yes, she would survive.

Enjoyed this book? Then follow Jenny's story in another two books. Book 2 is called 'Changes', and book 3 in the series is called 'New Century:Changed Lives'. And who knows, there might even be a book 4 before too long. Watch this space – or Amazon!